ASHLEY FARLEY

Sweet Tea
Tuesdays

ISBN-13: 978-0-9982741-3-3

BY ASHLEY FARLEY

Sweeney Sisters Series
Tangle of Strings
Boots and Bedlam
Lowcountry Stranger
Her Sister's Shoes

Adventures of Scottie
Breaking the Story
Merry Mary

Also by Ashley Farley
Saving Ben

For my besties,
I'm grateful to each and every one of you.

CHAPTER ONE
LULA

THE THERMOSTAT ON Lula's insides was dialed up to broil. Only this time it had nothing to do with hot flashes. Her air conditioner had been on the fritz for two days. The sultry summer air permeated the house through open windows, but the ceiling fans spinning at full blast did little to cool down the rooms. The walls sweated. The doors swelled. Every surface was covered in a sticky film. The heat index in the kitchen was higher by ten degrees than the rest of the house thanks to the pot of butterbeans simmering on the stove and the oven preheating to roast.

The thought of eating a heavy meal in this heat made the meager contents of Lula's stomach sour. Her ideal supper on a blazing hot day consisted of a spoonful of chicken salad and a cup of gazpacho made fresh from the summer's ripe tomatoes, topped off with a scoop of caramel praline crunch ice cream for dessert. Such meager fixings would not do for her husband. Phillip had grown to expect a three-course meal every night of the week. And she'd done everything in her power as a housewife to foster that growth. She prided herself on her skills as a homemaker—her culinary talents, green thumb, and special knack for making their abode cozy and inviting.

Lula seasoned her eye-of-round roast with salt and pepper and slid the pan into the oven, lowering the temperature to 475 degrees. "Woo wee, it's hot in here," she said as she straightened up, a hand pressed firmly on her aching lower back. She caught sight of her seven-year-old Lhasa Apso who lay panting on his bed in the corner as if he'd chased the neighbor's cat up a tree even though he hadn't left his bed since breakfast.

"Are you dying over there, Pooh?"

The dog thumped its tail once and snorted.

"I know, sweet boy. You'll be cool soon. They should be here any minute." She glanced at the clock hanging above the kitchen table. Fashioned out of an old piece of driftwood and seashells, the clock her father had helped her create when she was in the fourth grade was part of a Girl Scout project. The clock had marked the time for the last forty-five years of Lula's life. Just as it had marked the last five hours.

"We'll send a technician out today between ten and three," the bored-sounding woman had said when Lula called the repair service about her broken air conditioner. It was now three thirty. Which meant she would be late. And she hadn't missed her standing four o'clock social with her besties since... since never in all the twenty-six years of Tuesdays they'd been getting together for sweet tea and girl talk at Georgia's. Was she just going to let these repair people hold her hostage all afternoon in her own home?

"I suppose we have no choice." She looked down into Pooh's sad brown eyes. "We won't be able to sleep tonight if we don't get the air conditioner fixed."

She ripped a piece of paper towel off the roll mounted under the cabinet and mopped the sweat from her brow. She wadded it up, tossed it into the trash can, and tore off two more sheets. She lifted her cotton blouse, and stuffed the paper towel in the damp spots under both breasts. Eek! She really needed to do something about her soft doughy midsection that was getting softer and doughier by the day in spite of her active life. She served meals at homeless shelters and tutored at after school programs for underprivileged children. She tended her perennial garden, cleaned her house from top to bottom once a week, and spent hours on her feet in the kitchen cooking for her family and the sick folks who belonged to her church.

So many of her friends had gone gaga over physical fitness. Midge, her next-door neighbor to her left, pounded the pavement every morning running no fewer than three miles; and Georgia, her neighbor on the other side, attended yoga classes several times a week. The gals in her bridge and book clubs talked incessantly about the exercise classes they attended—spinning and core barre, hot yoga, Pilates, and total body conditioning. Wasn't boot camp for the Marines? Sixty is the new fifty, blah blah blah. In Lula's case fifty-five was the new sixty-five and she was darn proud of it. Walking Pooh to the stop sign at the end of the street and back three times a day offered ample exertion. Anything extra might cause her ticker to tock.

Lula heard her cell phone ringing in a distant part of the house. She froze, listening. She didn't want to miss the repairman calling to say he was on the way. She'd told the dispatch woman to have him ring her on the house line, but the woman had been too bored to pay attention. She followed the ringing sound through the back hallway to the new part of the house. Despite the cozy feel of the room—the leather-upholstered furniture, thick wool carpet, and stone fireplace—they referred to this space as the Florida room. The large windows allowed sunlight to beam in and provided a lovely view of her perennial garden, now in full bloom, in the tiny backyard.

Her oldest daughter had already hung up by the time Lula located the phone wedged between the sofa cushions. Brooke knew better than to call her on her cell phone. Lula despised modern technology. She preferred paperback copies over e-books. She wanted her mail delivered by the mailman. And she would rather read a road map than listen to an automated voice on a GPS instructing her where to go. One day all the electronic devices would explode at once and set the world on fire. She laughed out loud at the vision of throngs of tourists walking the downtown streets of Charleston with flaming cell phones pressed to their ears. She'd been having the strangest thoughts lately.

One Christmas several years ago, her family gave her a computer, one of the portable kind that you opened up in your lap. She'd taken it back to the Apple Store and gotten an iPad instead. The handheld gadget served its purpose. She was able to get the e-mails she couldn't avoid—correspondence relating to family business and confirmation notices of her online purchases. Lula loved to shop for china and crystal on eBay. She now had enough of her wedding and holiday patterns to feed twenty-four. One day her daughters would bring home their spouses and offspring for the holidays. She aimed to be prepared for Thanksgiving and Easter and every other occasion in between.

Lula took the phone back to the kitchen and collapsed in a chair at the table. She clicked on the missed call. She had to admit that being instantly connected to her loved ones without having to punch the numbers into her wall phone was convenient.

Brooke answered on the first ring. "Did you lose your phone again, Mom? Where was it this time, at the bottom of your bag?"

Lula brushed her damp auburn bangs off her sweaty forehead. "At the bottom of the sofa, actually."

"Since when do you sit on the sofa?"

Lula smiled to herself. She was not a TV watcher, other than on Sunday evenings when she and Phillip ate their supper while watching Sixty Minutes. She worked from the time her feet hit the hardwood floor in the morning until she fell into bed at night. Even then, she read a chapter in one of her romance novels before turning out the light. "Musta fallen out of my pocket while I was plumping up the sofa cushions. But that's neither here nor there. It's good to hear your voice. How are you, darling?"

"I'm fine." Brooke sounded chipper. "And how are things with you?"

"It's as hot as the blazing fires of hell. But other than that, everything is dandy."

"Listen, Mom, I'm at work, and I can't talk long. But I wanted to tell you I'm planning to come home for a visit."

Lula jerked her head up. Why now after three years? "That's wonderful, honey! When?"

"I'm not sure of the exact date yet. Sometime around the end of the month. I've been thinking a lot about all the summers spent out at the beach. The Fourth of July isn't the same in San Francisco. I miss the cookouts and the fireworks. I even miss the heat and humidity. It's chilly here in the summertime."

"You know, Brooke, it just occurred to me that it's been years since we've had our Fourth of July Party. Wouldn't it be fun to get all our friends together again?"

"Don't go to any trouble for me, Mom. I haven't kept up with many of my friends from home."

"Then it's time for you to reconnect with them." Excitement stirred in Lula's belly as the idea began to take root. Images from past parties flashed through her mind. Hot dogs and hamburgers sizzling on the grill. Children diving for live goldfish in the pool while their parents sipped vodka tonics. Men setting off fireworks after dark. "It won't be any trouble at all. We'll make it a welcome home party in your honor. Are you bringing anyone with you?" She held her breath. Wouldn't it be wonderful if Brooke brought home a beau?

"Oh, Mom, I've gotta go now. My boss is giving me the hairy eyeball. I'll text you when I know my travel plans." Her daughter ended the call before she could ask any more questions.

Lula stared at the calendar pinned to the wall beneath the phone that seldom rang. The Fourth of July was only a month away. So much to do and only four weeks' time to do it in. She wondered if the blue grass band they all loved so much was still available. She should give them a call. Where in the world was her address book? She hopped up out of her chair, took a step, and then leaned against the table when the room began to spin. Spots appeared before her eyes and her skin felt clammy despite the heat. She was groping for the chair to sit back down when everything suddenly went black.

CHAPTER TWO
GEORGIA

GEORGIA SENT MIDGE over to check on Lula when she failed to arrive promptly at four o'clock. Midge came running back less than a minute later. "Come quick!" she said, her electric-blue eyes huge and her arms flailing. "Lula's passed out on the kitchen floor. I pounded on the door but she won't wake up. Hurry. Get the spare key."

By the time Georgia located the key in her junk drawer and hurried down the sliver of lawn that separated their houses, Midge had shimmied up the side of the house and was clambering through the open window. Georgia unlocked the door and let herself in. Midge stood over Lula's still form, shaking her gently and saying her name in a soft voice as though trying to rouse a small child from sleep.

Georgia knelt down beside her. "You listen to me now, Lula Horne. It's time for you to get up!" When Lula didn't respond, she smacked her on the cheek. "Wake up, Lula! Now. If you don't get up, I'm going to have to call an ambulance."

Lula's green eyes popped open and rolled around in her head before closing again.

"Thatta girl, sweetheart." Georgia tapped her cheek again. "Once more, but this time try to keep them open."

Lula's freckles were more pronounced against her pale skin and her auburn hairline was speckled with gray. For years Lula had considered dying her hair to get rid of the gray. Maybe the time had finally come. Georgia's salt and pepper could definitely use more pepper, but her husband insisted she not change a thing about her appearance. Langdon claimed she looked dignified. Georgia thought she looked like an old lady. She would make an appointment at her salon next week, and she and Lula would go for their first dye job together.

Lula opened her eyes again and looked around the room. "Why am I lying on the kitchen floor?" she asked in a hoarse voice.

"That's what we want to know. It might have something to do with the heat." Georgia fanned herself. "It's hot as blazes in here. I can barely catch my breath."

"That's because my air conditioner's on the fritz," Lula said.

"What's that smell?" Georgia went to the stove, turned off the burner, and lifted the lid on the smoking pot. "Whatever this was is now charred."

Lula rolled her head to the side toward the stove. "Butterbeans. For Phillip's dinner."

"You'll never get this pot clean. You're better off throwing it away." Georgia felt heat emanating from the oven. "What on earth are you cooking in here?" She turned on the oven light. "You've got it set on 475 degrees."

"A roast," Lula said. "You can turn it off now."

Georgia pressed the off button. "Do you want me to take it out of the oven?"

Lula shook her head. "I'm using the high temperature method. It has to sit in the hot oven for a couple of hours."

"Whatever you say." Georgia was in no position to argue. She could manage the basics, but she was not a seasoned cook like Lula.

Lula held her hand out to Midge. "Help me up."

Gripping her hand, Midge helped her into a sitting position. "Take it slow. You don't want to overdo it."

Georgia removed a glass from the cabinet beside the sink and filled it with cold water from the dispenser on the refrigerator door. Returning to Lula's side, she handed her the glass. "Here. Drink this."

Lula guzzled down the water. "I must have fainted from all the excitement."

"What excitement?" Midge asked.

"I just received a call from—"

"Stop!" Georgia thrust her hand out like a traffic cop. "Save it for tea time. Let's go to my porch. It's easily twenty degrees cooler outside than it is in here."

Lula glanced up at the clock. "I can't leave. I'm waiting for the repairman. I won't be able to sleep in this house tonight because of the heat." She drained the rest of the water and handed the glass to Georgia. When she moved to get up, Midge and Georgia each took an arm and eased Lula into the nearest chair.

"We can watch for the repairman from my porch," Georgia said. "This house is not currently safe for habitation, even for a dog."

All eyes traveled to the corner where Pooh was watching

them from his bed. He lay perfectly still, aside from the rapid rise and fall of his tiny chest as he breathed. "We'll bring him with us." Georgia nudged Midge with her elbow. "Pick up the dog, will ya?"

Midge shot Georgia an evil look, but she did as she was told despite her fear of dogs. With the dog cradled in her outstretched arms and Lula and Georgia on her heels, the threesome paraded single file back down the narrow space between their houses. While Midge and Lula settled themselves on the porch, Georgia went to the kitchen for the tea tray, returning a second time for a bowl of water for Pooh. She opened the living room windows and lifted two box fans to the sill. Turned on high, the fan sucked the cool air out of the house and onto the porch.

The porch furniture had changed often over the years, from a conglomeration of wicker and rattan love seats and rockers to the now more contemporary metal lounge chairs arranged around a matching coffee table. From October to May, Georgia substituted the coffee table for a round gas fire pit that enabled them to enjoy the porch all year round.

Lula leaned her head back against the chair and closed her eyes. "Ahhh... that's so nice," she said, savoring the cool air on her face. "I'm not complaining, mind you, but doesn't your utility bill make Lang angry?"

"He doesn't know. I'm the one who pays the bills." She poured three glasses of tea from her pitcher. "I wouldn't care, even if he did get mad."

"Ouch!" Lula's eyes shot open. "Sounds like trouble in paradise."

"Honey, paradise is so far in my rearview mirror, I wouldn't know what it looked like if it smacked me in the face." Georgia sat back and crossed her legs. "I don't want to talk about Langdon today. But I do have news. It's not exciting enough to cause anyone to faint, but it involves a lifestyle change for me."

Midge took a sip of tea and set her glass on the table. "My news might make you faint. Although not from excitement."

Georgia cocked a meticulously plucked eyebrow. "Now you've got my curiosity up." She reached for the deck of cards she'd brought out on the tray. She shuffled the deck several times and set it facedown on the coffee table. They took turns choosing a card. Midge drew the highest card with a queen of hearts. Lula came in second with a ten of spades, and Georgia lost the round with a five of clubs. Back in the day, when their children were little and their husbands were working late, there'd been many times when the tea sipping had led to wine guzzling and they'd ordered four or five large pizzas for dinner for their rowdy little group. They'd spent so much time together in those years they knew everything there was to know about one another. But now that their lives were so busy and independent of one another, most Tuesdays they all had tidbits of news or gossip to share. Instead of trying to talk over each other at once, they adopted the card method as a fair means of taking turns.

"Looks like I get to go first." Midge straightened herself, holding her blonde head high and sticking out her perky breasts.

Midge had a physical advantage over most women their age. She'd never carried an eight-pound baby to term or nursed it for six months afterward. Even though Georgia aspired to have a toned figure like Midge's, she didn't envy her friend her inability to have children. Being infertile was the single biggest disappointment in Midge's life. The years of trying to conceive had taken its toll on her marriage and led her husband to seek comfort from another woman. Much to her credit, Midge had slammed the door shut on her unfaithful husband, taken up marathon running, and launched a new career as a real estate agent. Lacking the connections to break into the downtown market, she'd ventured out to the residential areas west of the Ashley River and made a name for herself there.

"Bennett asked me to marry him." Midge held out her left hand. Rays of afternoon sunlight reflected off the large diamond on her ring finger.

Georgia gaped at the ring. "Good gravy! Did that rotten rascal chisel that stone off the side of Mount Rushmore?"

Midge's body went rigid. "For your information, Georgia, the ring belonged to his grandmother."

Georgia stared her down. "Bennett has been married and divorced three times already. You mean to tell me he's just now getting around to using his grandmother's engagement ring?"

Midge lowered her hand to her lap. "You've been mean about him since we started dating, Georgia, and I'm tired of it. He's actually a very nice person. He's not perfect, but name someone who is."

She shook her head in disgust. "He's really done a snow job on you. You've only been dating him for two months. I've known him his entire life. Don't say I didn't warn you."

Georgia had grown up in the same neighborhood as Bennett Calhoun. His family lived on Legare Street, and hers two blocks over on Gibbes. Bennett ran around in the same crowd as her younger brother. She had enough firsthand knowledge of his unscrupulous behavior to legitimately call him a scoundrel. All the parents had loved him. "Such a nice boy. Such polite manners. Did you know he's a direct descendant of John C. Calhoun?" The neighborhood children had worshipped him as well. Bennett was the go-to guy when they'd needed a parent's signature on a bad report card. Or when they'd wanted to get high.

Lula grabbed Midge's hand, holding it far enough away so she could inspect the stone without needing her readers. "I think it's lovely. When's the big day?"

Midge flashed her a radiant smile. "Sometime next month. Or we may wait until August. Neither of us wants a big wedding. We're thinking of flying down to the Caribbean and having a private ceremony, just the two of us, at one of those destination wedding places."

Hard as she tried, Georgia couldn't keep her mouth shut. "What's the big rush? Why not take some time to get to know one another better?"

"I'm fifty years old this year," Midge said. "And Bennett is forty-nine. Why have a long courtship to prove we're perfect for one another? We both know what we want out of life. Why wait when we can be together now?"

"I see a lot of point in waiting," Georgia said. "It's only a matter of time before that rotten rascal shows his true colors. Then you'll wish you'd waited. Mark my words, Midge. Once a scoundrel, always a scoundrel."

"Georgia, stop!" Lula said. "You're spoiling her moment."

While Midge and Lula talked on about Caribbean wedding destinations, Georgia's mind wandered back to the first time she'd invited Midge and Lula over for tea on a sweltering day in late July of 1991. Lula's father had recently passed away, and her mother had wasted no time in moving to a chichi retirement community in Virginia. At her mother's insistence, Lula and Phillip had taken up permanent residence in her childhood home on Tradd Street to await the birth of their first child. Georgia, herself, was also pregnant at the time, six weeks away from delivering her second child.

She was reading on her front porch when she noticed Lula pulling weeds in the flower bed bordering her front walk. As native Charlestonians, their paths had crossed many times before, but they'd never considered themselves friends. She maneuvered her swollen body off the sofa and waddled over to the railing. "Considering your condition," she called to Lula, "maybe you should hire someone to do that for you."

Lula waved Georgia off with a dirty gloved hand. "My parents kept this garden immaculate for thirty years without any help from outsiders."

"Are you sure about that?" Georgia asked with raised eyebrows.

Lula sat back on her haunches. "Now that you mention it, no." She wiped the sweat off her forehead with the back of her hand, leaving behind a streak of dirt. She looked up at Georgia. "You were their neighbor. You should know. Did they hire someone to help with the yard?"

Georgia hunched her shoulders in a casual shrug. "I may have seen someone other than your father mowing the grass on Wednesday afternoons."

Lula slowly got to her feet. "This is hard work," she said, rubbing her belly. "Maybe I should hire someone. At least until after the baby comes."

"You'd be doing yourself and the baby a favor," Georgia said. "Would you like to come over for a glass of sweet tea?"

Lula nodded her head enthusiastically. "Iced tea sounds perfect right about now."

Georgia saw the new neighbor in the house on the other side of Lula walking toward them, carrying a pie in her outstretched hands. Georgia felt a pang of guilt. The young couple had been in the house since April, but she'd yet to welcome the woman to the neighborhood.

The woman was petite, no taller than five feet if Georgia had to guess, with shoulder-length blonde hair and attractive features. She stopped at Lula's gate and presented her a foil-wrapped pie plate. "I brought you a peach cobbler, to welcome you to the neighborhood."

"That's so nice of you." Lula lifted her hands to show the woman her dirty gloves. "Do you mind placing it on the table on the porch?"

"Not at all." The petite blonde walked the pie to the porch and returned to where Lula was standing. "I'm sorry for your loss. Your father was helping me identify some of the plants in my jungle when he had his heart attack. I'm Mary Margaret Wilkins, by the way. My friends call me Midge. Not because I'm short. Although, as you can see, I'm definitely below average in height. My parents meant for Madge to be my nickname, but my baby brother had a difficult time pronouncing it. Although I don't think Madge is that difficult to say. Any more so than Midge. Funny how nicknames get started. I'm sorry for babbling. I get nervous when I meet new people."

"No need to be nervous, honey. I promise I won't bite." Lula reached out to touch Midge's arm, but quickly withdrew her dirty glove. "My mother spoke of you, of your kindness toward her that day. Thank you for being there for her." She removed her gloves. "I was just getting ready to go next door for tea. Do you have room for one more?" she hollered over to Georgia who was still standing at the railing eavesdropping on their conversation.

"Of course! I'd love for you to join us." Georgia waved Midge on. "I have plenty of tea and some shortbread biscuits."

They'd sipped tea and talked for hours that day. And nearly every day for the next ten years. From Georgia's porch they observed the seasons change and watched the children grow from toddlers to adolescents to young adults. With no children of her own, Midge showered Georgia's and Lula's with affection. As the years went on and their separate lives drew them apart, so as not to lose touch completely, they reduced their meetings to once a week, on Tuesday afternoons at four.

Georgia was brought back to the present by the sound of ice clanking in Midge's empty glass. "So... Lula," she said as she refilled their glasses. "I'm dying to hear the news that made you faint."

Despite her earlier fainting spell, Lula positively glowed as she began to speak. "It's just the best news ever." She clasped her hands together. "Brooke is coming home for a visit!"

"How lovely." Forcing her lips into a thin smile, under her breath, Georgia added, "The Christ child returneth."

None of the mothers Georgia knew would ever admit to having a favorite child. But Lula's prejudice toward her oldest daughter was apparent. Georgia preferred the easy manner and thoughtfulness of Lula's younger daughter, Lizbet, to the aloof and competitive Brooke.

Shooting Georgia a warning glare, Midge said, "That's so exciting, Lula. How long has it been since she was last home?"

"Three years. Remember she was home for a month

the summer after she graduated from Stanford, before she accepted the job in San Francisco."

Lula had been so proud of Brooke when she'd gotten accepted to Stanford. Georgia had often marveled at how different the girls were that one would go so far away while the other had chosen to attend the College of Charleston to be closer to her parents. "When will she arrive?" Georgia asked.

"I'm not sure of the exact date yet, but she'll be here for the Fourth. Do you think it's too late for me to pull together a party?"

"Not if you hire a caterer. You should talk to Heidi Butler." A confused expression crossed Lula's face. "You know, Tasty Provisions, the new catering company your daughter is working for. Surely you've been in the shop to see Lizbet."

Lula chewed on her lower lip. "Not yet. I keep meaning to get in there. I just haven't had the time."

"You should make the time," Georgia said. "The store is one of a kind. I loved it so much, I've taken a job there myself. I start on Thursday."

Lula let out a bark of laughter. "What're you talking about? You've never worked a day in your life."

Georgia lifted her chin high. "I beg your pardon. I've served on every board in this city at least once. I've chaired dinners and organized auctions. I've hosted important dignitaries in my home and delivered speeches to rooms packed with people. If that isn't work, I don't know what is. At least with this new job I'll get paid."

"What happened to your renovation project?" Midge asked. "I thought you were planning to make an offer on that house on South Battery."

Georgia dismissed Midge with a flick of her wrist. "That

property was all wrong for us. We're still looking, though. In the meantime I've decided to try something new. There is a glitch, though. I'm afraid my work schedule may interfere with tea time."

Lula scowled at her. "I'm sorry, Georgia, but that simply won't do. You'll have to figure something else out. We've been meeting every Tuesday for as long as I can remember. We can't stop now because you decided to get a job. Why do you need a job anyway? Don't you have plenty to keep you busy at home?"

CHAPTER THREE
MIDGE

MIDGE WAS SURPRISED, and a little bit irritated, when she arrived home and found Bennett lounging on her sofa, his Gucci loafers propped up on her marble coffee table and her MacBook open in his lap. She snatched her laptop away from him and snapped it shut. "How'd you get in?"

"You gave me a key, remember?" He held up a single silver house key.

She looked closely at the key. "All my spares are attached to plastic yellow rings. And no, I don't remember giving that to you." That's not to say she hadn't given him the key. Her memory had begun to fail her in recent years, along with other parts of her body she was working hard to maintain. Did she mind him having a key to her house? To be honest, she wasn't sure. He was her fiancé, but she hadn't shared her living space with anyone since her ex moved out twenty years ago.

He folded his fingers around the key, and flashed her that naughty boy grin that reached his delicious dimples and melted her heart, sending jolts of electricity to remote parts of her body. She always defended Bennett to Georgia—despite the little things he did that made her question his motives—because she loved him and he made her feel alive again for the first time in twenty years. "Fine, you can keep the key for now. But don't abuse the privilege."

He stood to face her. ""Where have you been, anyway?" Burying his face in her neck, he breathed in her scent. "Phew, you're all sweaty."

She pushed him away. "I've been down the street having tea with Georgia and Lula on Georgia's porch. Of course I'm sweaty. It's summertime in the South."

"Why do you waste your time with those women?"

"Because they're my friends."

"They have nothing to offer you. If you stick with me, you'll have a whole new set of friends in six months' time. You won't miss those old bags one bit." He aimed his thumb at the stairs. "Now go get dressed. We have cocktails with the Lelands tonight."

Confusion crossed her face. "What're you talking about? And who are the Lelands?"

"I sent you an e-mail about it three days ago. They're having a party tonight to show off their recently renovated condo on the waterfront."

She paused to search her memory but came up empty. "I must have forgotten to add it to my calendar."

"Go!" He nudged her in the direction of the stairs. "And be quick about it. Wear that black dress I love. The one that shows off your fine ass." He gave her butt a little squeeze.

Midge tucked her laptop under her arm, retrieved the stack of mail from the table beside the sofa, and dashed up the stairs to her room. She placed the laptop and mail on her bed-side table and opened the double doors to her closet. Running a finger down the row of cocktail dresses, she skipped over the black dress that showed off her butt and stopped at a pink silk sheath that hung straight from her shoulders. Slipping the dress over her head, she eyed her queen-size bed as she struggled with the zipper. She longed to put on her nightgown and spread out on the pillow top memory-foam mattress with a carton of yogurt and a glass of white wine, and binge-watch a series on Netflix.

No, Midge! She turned her back on her bed. You need to enjoy tonight. You finally have a date to the ball. She went to the window and peeked through the blinds. Night after night for most of her adult life, she'd watched Georgia and Lula leave for social engagements. Georgia to her charity functions and dinners with her husband's doctor friends and their wives, and Lula to neighborhood gatherings that Midge was never invited to. The other wives stopped including her in their backyard barbecues and holiday cocktail parties after her divorce. She was the pariah, the woman no one wanted to associate with for fear their husbands might be tempted by the attractive young divorcée.

Midge knew Bennett wasn't perfect, but she did her best to ignore gossip about his failed marriages and shady business dealings. She and Bennett were meant to be together. They dreamed of opening a boutique real estate firm where she would handle the residential and he the commercial transactions. Their model would provide their wealthy clients with a one-stop shop for all their real estate needs. They planned to manage the firm for ten years before retiring and turning it over to a trusted employee to run while they traveled the world. Midge had worked hard in her career, and she had a considerable portfolio to prove it. They couldn't go wrong with his name and her business acumen.

Their relationship wasn't all about business. Bennett had a soft side to him that he seldom let show, and the glimpses she'd seen of his compassion and vulnerability had endeared him to her. She'd dated several men since her divorce. Too many to count, in fact. But few had asked her out a second time, while only one had ended in a relationship that lasted exactly one month. She'd never connected with anyone the way she connected with Bennett. The only other man she'd ever loved was her childhood sweetheart, and their love was based on friendship. Desperate to get away from her overbearing parents, she'd married Taylor right out of high school and supported him while he attended college. She trusted him with her heart and her future and he'd jumped ship when it became clear she would never be able to give birth to their child. He refused to consider adoption or surrogacy. After years of therapy, she finally realized he'd used her infertility as a convenient excuse to divorce a woman he had never really loved.

Midge had never considered going to college, but with no children to take care of nor a husband to support her, she found herself in need of a career. Selling houses didn't feel like work. Finding the right home for her buyer was a game, one she never gave up on until she won.

She smeared shimmering gloss across her lips, slipped on her low-heeled sandals, and grabbed her Tory Burch clutch. Midge loved to shop. In the absence of a husband or children to spoil, she rewarded herself for all her hard work by buying beautiful clothes.

"You look like you're wearing a shopping bag from

Victoria's Secret," Bennett said when he saw her in the pink sheath. "What happened to the black dress?"

She waved him off. "It's too hot for that cling wrap. Pink is more summery, don't you think?"

"Your summery is not the right kind of hot." He picked his keys up off the coffee table. "Don't blame me when none of the men look at you."

"This may come as a surprise, but I don't care if men look at me or not." She turned on her heel and headed out the front door. Men had been ogling Midge all her life. She didn't want them to look at her. She wanted them to see her, to open the cover and read her thoughts. While she had an innate sense for the real estate market, her success had not happened overnight. A shy girl from a small hick town with no more than a high school education, she lacked the social skills to charm her clients. To overcome her shortcomings, she educated herself by studying the habits of men and women she admired and reading everything she could get her hands on—from biographies of famous Southerners to accounts of historical events to local and national periodicals relating to news, fashion, decorating, food and wine. She became an expert on everything that had to do with Charleston and the Lowcountry. To her clients she appeared knowledgeable about local goings-on and engaged in lively political debates whenever the opportunity arose.

She slipped into the passenger side and settled into the leather seats of Bennett's sports car. "So... where is this waterfront condo?"

"On Concord, near the pineapple fountain in Waterfront Park." He put the car in gear and zoomed down the street, too fast for Midge's comfort. "Rumor has it, they hired a New

York designer for the redo. I understand a unit might be coming available soon. It would be perfect for us."

She gripped the handle on the roof. "What'd you mean, for us? I assumed you would move in with me." The tiny carriage house Bennett rented on Council Street had nice features, but it was way too small for two of them.

He flipped on his blinker and made a left turn onto East Bay. "Tradd Street is so pedestrian. We need to find something better suited to our lifestyle. Something swanky and sophisticated."

Midge wasn't sure she wanted swanky and sophisticated. She was content with cozy and predictable.

They found a parking place on the street and walked two blocks along the waterfront to the address. As they entered the small lobby, Midge felt butterflies in her belly. Her social skills, refined as they were, had yet to be proven in Bennett's world.

The elevator deposited them in the penthouse foyer, where Grace Leland greeted guests as they entered. The combination of her white sundress that hugged her slim figure along with her white-blonde hair pulled back at the nape of her neck presented an image of elegance as she gave warm smiles to new arrivals. But when she saw Midge and Bennett, her blue eyes turn cold. She all but cringed when Bennett kissed her cheek. "How nice of you to come," Grace said through tight lips. Midge offered her hand, but Grace ignored it, turning her attention to the couple behind them.

Midge found their hostess's behavior odd, borderline rude. She understood why a little while later when she overheard Grace whispering to a man Midge assumed was her husband. "What is Bennett Calhoun doing here?" the husband asked. "Did you invite him?"

Bennett had struck up a conversation over the buffet table with an elderly gentleman about fishing, and Midge had wandered off to explore the Lelands' sophisticated and swanky penthouse pad. When her self-guided tour ended, she stopped by the bar for a refill on her Chardonnay and planted herself near the fireplace. The elegant couple didn't realize she was standing behind them, in close enough proximity to overhear their conversation.

Grace's face registered surprise. "Why would I invite him? I barely even know him, Tyler. I thought you invited him."

"I've never spoken to the man in my life. That's what you get for sending the invitations by e-mail. His contact information must have somehow gotten mixed in with the others."

Grace placed her long fingers on her boney hip. "Why would I have his contact information? We went to preschool together. I've only seen him a few times since then." She touched her fingertips to her lips in feigned horror. "You don't think he's casing out our home, planning to rob us, do you?"

Tyler rolled his eyes. "He's a realtor, Gracie. I'm sure he just wanted to see what we've done with the place."

Midge inched away before Grace noticed her. She made a beeline to Bennett who was still conversing with the same elderly gentleman about the same blue marlin he'd caught in a fishing tournament in May. She tugged on his jacket sleeve. "Can we go, please? I don't feel well all of a sudden. It must be something I ate."

His face tightened. "Already? We just got here."

She flashed the elderly gentleman a smile. "It may seem that way, darling, because you've been talking this poor gentleman's ear off about your marlin. But we've actually been here for quite sometime. And I have an early meeting in the morning."

The gentleman's eyes twinkled as he clapped Bennett on the shoulder. "Why are you still standing here? You heard the pretty lady. She wants you to take her home."

Midge started toward the elevator. "Shouldn't we thank our hosts?" Bennett asked, and she responded in a clipped tone, "I already did."

Bennett talked all the way home about the Lelands as though they were his best friends. Midge didn't have the heart to tell him what she'd overheard. She convinced herself that Tyler was right about the mix-up with the invitation. Bennett would never go to a party uninvited.

When they reached her house and he begged to come inside, Midge said, "I'm sorry. I enjoyed the evening, but I have a full day tomorrow and need to get some sleep."

She went straight upstairs to her room. She washed her face, brushed her teeth, and changed into her nightgown. She then turned back the bedspread and crawled between the cool crisp sheets. After retrieving her computer and the stack of mail from the bedside table where she'd left them earlier, she thumbed through the mail and was surprised to see her statement from Wells Fargo Bank had been opened. That's odd. Opening her laptop, she was even more surprised to find her Internet browser still connected to her bank's website. Back off! she told the nagging feeling in her gut. I'm sure it's just a coincidence. Bennett banks with Wells Fargo as well.

Returning the computer and mail to the bedside table, she removed her bottle of sleeping pills from the top drawer. She usually only took half a pill, but tonight she swallowed one whole.

CHAPTER FOUR
LULA

LULA WAS WAITING on her front porch early on Wednesday afternoon when Lizbet's little red Honda came speeding down the street. She parked at an angle to the curb, hopped out of the car, and rushed up the sidewalk. "What's wrong, Mom? Are you okay? Did you fall? Are you hurt?"

"Of course not. I'm fine." With a flick of her wrist, Lula dismissed her daughter's concern. "But I have big news I wanted to share with you. Your sister is coming home for a visit. She'll be here over the Fourth. You and I have a party to plan."

Lizbet's pale gray eyes narrowed and her lips drew thin. "Wait a minute. You texted me to get over here as fast as I could to tell me Brooke is coming home for a visit?"

Her daughter's angry tone caused Lula to take a step back. "I thought you'd be excited to hear the news."

"I have a full-time job now, Mother. I can't come running over here every time you need me to help you with your iPad or to carry a basket of laundry upstairs when your back is bothering you."

Lula couldn't remember the last time Lizbet had called her Mother, if ever. "But we always plan the Fourth of July party together. There's so little time and so much to do. We need to send out invitations and hire a band. Would your boss consider catering the party? Nothing fancy, just burgers and dogs."

Lizbet leaned back against the porch column. "Heidi doesn't do burgers and dogs. I assume you're planning to have this party at the beach house. Why don't you get Home Team BBQ to cater it?"

Lula turned up her nose. "Barbecue is so common."

Lizbet rolled her eyes. "What do you call hamburgers and hot dogs?"

Lula folded her arms over her chest. "Then you tell me. What kind of food would Heidi suggest for a party like this?"

"I have no idea. I don't plan the menus. I help prepare the food and serve the guests. She would probably suggest you have a Southern summer supper—light fare like cold salads and deviled eggs."

Lula tapped her chin as she considered the idea. "I like the sound of that. The invitation could read A Southern Summer Supper to Celebrate the Fourth."

"I wouldn't get your hopes up. It's so last minute, I doubt Heidi can accommodate you. And don't count on me coming to the party. I'm sure I'll be working."

Lula blinked hard. "What do you mean? Of course, you're coming to your sister's welcome home party. You'll have to tell this Heidi person you have a family commitment."

"I hate to break it to you, Mom. But the real world doesn't work that way." A group of youngsters skateboarding down the center of the road caught Lizbet's attention and she watched them for a minute before turning back to her. "We haven't had our Fourth of July party in years. Is all this trouble for Brooke?"

"She'll be the honored guest, of course. I think it'd be nice for her to see some of her old friends."

"Whatever." Lizbet fanned herself. "God it's hot out here. I'm going to get a bottled water." She brushed past Lula and entered the house.

Lula followed her daughter to the kitchen. "I stopped buying bottled water. I got tired of throwing away the half-empties. We have a Brita dispenser now."

"I'm sure the environment thanks you." Lizbet filled a tumbler with ice and water from the Brita pitcher. "It's so out of the blue. Did Brooke say why she decided to come home?"

"She hasn't been to Charleston since she graduated from college. I think it's time, don't you?"

"I think it's past time," Lizbet said and took a gulp of water. "But I get it. She lives in California. She has a high-pressured job with very little time off. Is she bringing anyone with her? I wonder if she has a boyfriend."

"As far as I know she's coming alone," Lula said, dropping down to the nearest chair at the kitchen table. "I'm not privy to the details of her love life. Has she mentioned anything to you about a special someone?"

"I haven't talked to Brooke since Christmas. In the posts I see of her on Facebook and Instagram, she's always with her girlfriends." Lizbet sat down opposite her and studied her face. "You look pale, Mom. Are you feeling all right?"

Lula was glad her daughter had softened her tone. She found her hostility unbecoming. "It's the heat," she said, slumping back in her chair like a wilted flower. "For some reason it's getting to me more than usual this year."

"Spending a month at the beach will do you good. You can go for your morning walks on the beach and read away the afternoon. Why don't you move out to Sullivan's early? There's nothing keeping you here."

"Haven't you been listening to me, Lizbet? I have a party to plan. And since you won't help me, I'll have to do it all myself." Reaching for her pen and notepad, she flipped to a clean sheet and scrawled To Do on the top of the page. "I need to get the invitations in the mail yesterday. I wonder if that stationery place on Broad is still open."

"The Fourth is only a month away. You don't have enough time to have an invitation printed and mailed out. You should send an e-vite."

E-vite. Bug bite. All is not right in a world where the postman doesn't deliver party invitations. Lula shook her head as if to clear it. There was that strange voice again.

"You'll bury me at Magnolia Cemetery before I'll send an e-vite to a party I'm hosting," she said. "I wouldn't begin to know how to send one, anyway."

"E-mail invitations are acceptable, even expected, these days." Lizbet planted her palms on the table. "Tell you what. I have Sunday free until three o'clock. I can come over and help you in the morning."

Lula looked up from her list. "Oh, honey, would you do that for me? We can go to church together and then get right to work."

Lizbet tugged at her ponytail. "But—"

"Please, sweetheart. I'd be ever so grateful.

Her daughter's lips parted in a smile, revealing the pearly

white teeth Lula had paid the orthodontist thousands of dollars to make straight. "Can we have those omelets I love, the ones with the spinach, goat cheese, and mushrooms?" She snapped her fingers. "And mimosas. We've gotta have mimosas. It won't take long to create your e-vite. Be sure to have your list of names and e-mail addresses ready."

Lula pointed her pen at Lizbet. "I'll get to work on it right away." She watched her daughter tug her ponytail free of the elastic band and smooth out her hair before tying it back again. Brooke was the stunning beauty that turned all the heads in the room while Lizbet was more of a china doll with petite features, plump rosy lips, and wide-set gray eyes.

"I should probably get back to work," Lizbet said, pushing back from the table. "We're swamped at the store. I can hardly wait for Georgia to start tomorrow. We really need her help."

"Humph. I can't imagine what your lady boss hired Georgia to do. She's certainly not a gourmet cook. And she's too old to be serving food to people at parties."

"Mooom! That's mean." Lizbet snickered. "But I guess it's true. At least the part about her not being a good cook. But don't tell her I said so. She has plenty of other qualifications and impeccable taste. Heidi, my lady boss, has hired her to manage the showroom."

The more she thought about it, the more Lula liked the idea of being a shopkeeper at a specialty food boutique. "Do you think Heidi would give me a job? I could use a new challenge. I'm tired of sitting around here doing nothing. Fixing your father's dinner is the highlight of my day."

Lizbet laughed. "Right, like when was the last time you sat around doing nothing?" She shook her head. "You don't want to work, Mom. Be thankful you don't have to."

Lula tossed her pen onto the table. "You're just being nice. What you really mean to say is that I'm not qualified to work. I have zero job experience, volunteer or otherwise, and no skills to speak of. I've never been anything but a housewife and stay-at-home mom."

"Puh-lease. You would make a great salesperson. You could charm the customers into buying molded cheese and stale bread. Although I think conducting electronic transactions might frustrate you." Lizbet got up from the table and emptied her tumbler in the sink before placing it in the dishwasher. She crossed the room to the paned door and stared out at Lula's perennial garden. "Would you be interested in selling some of your flowers through the store? Heidi mentioned the other day that she'd like to have some small bouquets and arrangements on hand for our customers who are hosting impromptu dinner parties. Not the cookie-cutter kind you can buy in the grocery store, but fresh-from-the-garden flowers like yours."

Lula left the table and went to stand beside her daughter. "I've only done arrangements for my own enjoyment. Do you think others would like them?"

"I'm sure of it. Why not give it a try? Your garden is certainly bountiful. You could start with a couple of small bouquets." Lizbet opened the backdoor. "Get your clippers. I'll take some flowers to Heidi and see what she thinks." She held the door open for Pooh, and then followed him outside.

Lula went to her supply closet for a roll of lavender tissue paper and a spool of raffia. She slipped on her green rubber clogs, fastened her tool belt around her waist, and joined her daughter in the garden.

Lizbet was throwing Pooh's rubber ball for him to fetch.

When she stopped, the little dog raced around her feet begging for more. She scooped him up and tucked him under her arm, and then walked the length of Lula's perennial bed. "I never knew you had such a wide variety of flowers. They all look so healthy."

"I planted a new crop of perennials this spring. They are really doing nicely." Lula aimed her clippers at Georgia's live oak. "The Murdaughs' tree allows them to get just the right amount of filtered sunlight."

They noticed Georgia at her kitchen window and waved. Cupping her hands around her mouth, Lizbet hollered, "See you at work tomorrow." Georgia offered her a thumbs-up in return.

Lula clipped a few more stems. "While my garden is bountiful, my supply of blooms is not limitless. I'd hate to deplete my stock."

With her free hand, Lizbet fingered the petal of a purple coneflower. "Could you get some filler flowers or greenery from a wholesale florist to mix in?"

"That's a good idea. I don't know any wholesale florists off the top of my head, but I'll see what I can come up with."

Lula carried her bucket inside. Separating her stems into two bunches on the kitchen counter, she wrapped each bouquet in tissue paper and tied them off with a length of raffia. "Here you go." She scooped up the bouquets and placed them in her daughter's outstretched arms.

Lizbet sniffed the flowers. "They smell so sweet. Careful what you wish for, Mom. You may have found yourself a new part-time job."

CHAPTER FIVE
LIZBET

LIZBET WEAVED HER way over to the waterfront and parallel parked her car on East Bay Street. Eyeing the flowers on the passenger seat, she surmised that a few minutes in the heat wouldn't cause them to wilt. She needed to clear her head and gather her thoughts before she returned to work. She got out of the car and climbed the concrete steps to the promenade where she leaned against the railing and stared out across Charleston Harbor.

It bothered her that her mother would fake an emergency so as to drag her away from work. So what if her sister was coming home for a visit. Big deal. Wasn't planning a party in her honor a bit extreme? It's not like they were announcing Brooke's engagement to get married. Or were they? Her mother claimed to know nothing about Brooke's love life, but she wouldn't put it past Lula to keep a secret like that for the sake of a big surprise announcement at the party. Her mother was beyond herself with excitement over the impending visit. If she missed Brooke so terribly, why had she never flown out to California to visit her? Not even once in the entire seven years her sister had lived on the West Coast. Not on move-in day her freshman year at Stanford. Or for any of the parents' weekends during the four years she'd been enrolled there. Her parents had even invented a lame excuse not to attend Brooke's graduation. Lizbet had made every effort to persuade her parents to make a family vacation out of the trip. "We can see the wine country, spend some time in San Francisco, and drive down to Carmel." But her parents had refused to consider it.

"Brooke will be busy celebrating with her friends," Lula had said. "She won't even know we're there. Let's wait and go later, after she's settled in her new job."

But that later had never come.

The last family vacation they'd taken had been an educational trip to the Smithsonian in Washington DC for spring break her first year in high school. Growing up, they'd gone to Disney World, the Florida Keys, and to New York City to see the Statue of Liberty. And that summed up the extent of their family travels. Lizbet never complained, though. She was grateful for their summers spent on Sullivan's Island, which itself was a three-month vacation.

Lizbet walked farther down the promenade. She cupped her hand over her eyes to shield them from the glare of the sun on the water as she watched a daysailer dance across the harbor.

She remembered, as if it were yesterday, coming home from high school one late September afternoon three weeks after Brooke had left for Stanford. The sight of her mother in bed with a damp washcloth on her forehead and the drapes drawn tight surprised her. She'd never known her mother to have a headache, let alone the flu or anything else. Lula had more energy than a six-year-old child, bouncing from one project to the next from sunrise to sunset.

Lizbet had tiptoed into the room. "Mama, are you okay? Are you sick?"

"I'm fine, honey. I just needed a rest." Lula lifted back the covers. "I have to start dinner soon, but crawl in with me for a minute and tell me about your day."

Finding the warmth of her mother's body comforting, Lizbet had settled in and told Lula all about the experiment she and her lab partner had bombed, quite literally, in chemistry. "I'm not kidding, Mom. Smoke was everywhere. The fire alarm went off and everything."

Lula's lips formed an O. "Did the fire department come?"

She giggled. "I don't think so."

Lizbet still remembered the satisfying feeling of having her mother all to herself for the very first time. She'd rushed home from school the next day and every day for the rest of that week to find her mother in her darkened bedroom with a washcloth over her forehead. She snuggled up to Lula and told her all the funny and the not-so-funny things that had happened that day. She thought her mother had come down with the flu, but Lula admitted on Friday that she was suffering from empty-nest syndrome. "I miss Brooke more than I ever thought I would."

Lizbet's heart had sunk to the bottom of the Charleston Harbor.

Lula continued to lavish her attention on Lizbet, and two months later, when she'd begged Lizbet not to ever leave her, Lizbet vowed to always stay close to home. She'd finally gotten her mother's attention. And she had no intention of giving that up.

As a child, Lizbet had worshipped her mother and her older sister. They were the center of her universe—the sun and the moon. Her father was a star, serving little purpose except to brighten her nights when he came home from work. Lula, Brooke, and Lizbet went everywhere together. They learned to swim, play tennis, and sail. Weather permitting, they packed picnic lunches and explored surrounding beaches and the grounds of local plantations. Lula often said, "We belong to our very own sorority, the Tri Hornes."

Lula and Brooke were the sorority sisters, but Lizbet was their pledge. She trotted along after them, forcing them to wait for her to catch up. She always got the smallest slice of pizza, the third choice in whatever they were choosing, and the last say in whatever they were deciding—which movie to see or which restaurant to go to for lunch. Her sister took full advantage of having the upper hand. When Brooke left the water running and the bathtub overflowed, she blamed it on Lizbet. She blamed it on Lizbet when she broke their grandmother's oriental vase and when she hid their mother's car keys so they'd be late to the dentist. The final straw, the one that made Lizbet drop out of the sorority, happened on Saturday, the twenty-second of October, during the early hours of the morning following her thirteenth birthday.

Lizbet had been sound asleep for hours when she heard someone tapping on her bedroom window. She rolled out of bed and crept across the room. Peeking through the blinds, she saw Brooke clinging to the tree outside her window. She threw open the window. "Are you crazy? Get in here before you fall." She gripped her sister by the arm and yanked her inside.

Brooke stumbled and knocked a lamp off Lizbet's chest of drawers. "Shhh!" She pressed her finger to her lips, more to the side of her mouth than to her lips. "You'll wake up Mom and Dad."

"What's wrong with you?" Lizbet noticed her sister's bloodshot eyes and smeared mascara. "Are you drunk?"

"I might have a teensy weensy buzz," she said and let out a hiccup.

The door swung open and light from the hallway filled the room. "What's going on in here?" Lula demanded as she entered the room.

Brooke straightened, suddenly sober. "I was helping Lizbet. She got locked out of the house."

"Really." Lula narrowed her eyes at Lizbet. "How did you get locked out of the house? I checked on you just before eleven and you were sound asleep."

"Don't be too hard on her, Mom," Brooke said, rubbing their mother's back as if consoling her. "It's Lizzy's thirteenth birthday. She wanted to celebrate with friends. Good thing I heard her knocking at the window. She might have fallen from the tree."

Her face flushed with anger, Lula moved closer to Lizbet. "Have you been drinking?" she asked sniffing Lizbet's breath.

Lizbet shook her head, too dumbfounded to speak. She couldn't believe her mother was buying her sister's lies. Why wasn't Lula sniffing Brooke's breath? She was the older sister by four years. It stood to reason that Brooke would be the one sneaking out of the house. Never mind that Brooke was fully clothed while Lizbet was wearing her pajamas. She experienced an anger like she'd never felt before, but she kept her lips zipped. She didn't stand a chance arguing against the two of them.

"Get in that bed and go to sleep." Lula went to the window, checking to make certain it was locked. "We'll talk about this in the morning."

But when morning came, her mother was even angrier at Lizbet, more convinced than ever that she was the one who'd snuck out of the house. She grounded Lizbet for two weeks. "No TV or sleepovers. Come straight home from school and do your homework."

Lizbet accepted her punishment and served her time stoically. Brooke never uttered a word of apology. The shy glances she cast toward Lizbet during dinner were as close to an admission of guilt as she would get.

One good thing had come from her punishment. On Monday of the second week, Lula sent Lizbet next door to borrow a cup of sugar. Georgia invited her in and offered her a glass of lemonade. Lizbet readily accepted, eager to escape her mother's watchful eye. Georgia, recognizing her gloom, asked, "Is everything okay, sweetheart? You seem kinda down."

Lizbet burst into tears and told Georgia the whole story. "I don't understand. Brooke was clearly drunk. She was wearing jeans and a sweater, she even had on her coat, and I was standing there in my pajamas with dried drool all over my face. The truth was staring Mom in the face. She just didn't want to see it."

Georgia held her tight while she cried. "Even though I don't think it's fair, your willingness to take the punishment for your sister says a lot about your character."

They'd always shared a special bond, but Georgia and Lizbet grew even closer that day. Georgia was the one she bragged to when she received a good grade and the one who took her shopping when she got invited to the prom. Unlike her mother, Georgia never criticized and she never judged. Georgia was as different from her mother as two women could be. Lula was a headstrong woman with traditional values while Georgia was stylish and elegant, a trendsetter. Georgia could be demanding at times too, but her need to control was about getting things done. Lula's need to control was about getting her way. In her mind, her way was the only way.

In recent years, Lizbet had sensed a sad loneliness in Georgia. Her sons lived in Boston and Dr. Dog—a nickname bestowed upon him by Brooke when she struggled to say Murdaugh as a child—worked long hours at the hospital. Lizbet's heart went out to the woman she considered her mentor. She, too, understood how that kind of loneliness felt.

Not one to hold grudges, Lizbet had eventually forgiven her sister, but nothing was ever the same between them. Lizbet wasn't jealous of Brooke. She loved her, even though she didn't understand her. But how can you have a relationship with someone who lives on the other side of the country and see only once every three years? Maybe now that they were both out of college and on their own, they could find some common ground and start anew.

CHAPTER SIX
GEORGIA

STANDING AT HER kitchen window, Georgia watched Lula and her precious daughter poke around in the garden. Her own sons rarely came home for a visit. She had to travel to Boston in order to see them. During her last trip over Thanksgiving, they had bounced her back and forth like a basketball. Both had followed in their father's footsteps. Richard was a cardiologist and Martin a resident at Mass General. Neither had time for her and made it apparent her presence was a hindrance.

Georgia glanced at the clock on the stove. Four o'clock seemed awfully early for a drink, but she desperately needed something to calm her nerves. She filled a stemless goblet with pinot noir, and took the glass and the bottle into her library. She closed the plantation shutters and turned on the gas logs in the fireplace. She kept the thermostat set on sixty-eight degrees. Damn hot flashes. She should've been done with them years ago. Her obstetrician warned her that some women never got over them. The heat and humidity of the summer months only made matters worse. For an hour, maybe two, she would pretend like it was a brisk fall afternoon. She curled up on the leather sofa and spread a cashmere throw across her bare legs. She loved this room with its wood-paneled walls and oriental rug. She loved her whole house, truth be told.

Tradd Street was never meant to be their permanent home, but a stepping stone to a larger house on a more prestigious street. For years Georgia had dreamed of buying a fixer-upper. She'd dragged Langdon through countless properties, but none of them had been the right fit. At least not in his mind. She'd gotten her hopes up several times, only to be disappointed by his disinterest. He didn't care where they lived. He was never home anyway.

He stayed late at the hospital most nights and was up at dawn every morning—running three miles, showering, dressing, and dashing out the door before Georgia ever opened her eyes. He was as fit as the day they married. Every bit as handsome as well. Langdon didn't care much about food, except the nutritional value it offered his body. He ate his meals without tasting them. His time was too valuable to squander on luxuries like going out to dinner. At least not with her. But he never said no to a colleague. Or to one of his guy pals. He said no to Georgia every time she suggested they try one of the area's trendy restaurants or attend an art exhibit. When he wasn't busy removing cancer from people's brains, he spent his free time playing one of the many games he played with his friends.

She no longer dreamed about owning a larger home on the Battery. A bigger house meant more rooms for her to get lost in. One day she would consider downsizing. For now she was content living on Tradd Street with Lula and Midge as neighbors.

Georgia finished her wine and poured another glass. Why was she so anxious about starting this new job? She had a knack for entertaining. The idea of mingling with customers, of helping them pick out just the right food items and tableware for their dinner parties, excited her. Heidi had provided few details of her job description during her interview. She would be responsible for making sales transactions. Would she also be in charge of the bank deposits and stock inventory? She wanted so much to succeed. But what if she failed?

She picked up the most recent issue of Garden and Gun from the coffee table and settled back on the sofa. As she thumbed through the pages, her eyelids grew heavy and she dozed off to sleep. Langdon shook her awake sometime later.

"Georgia, why on earth are you drinking so early in the day?" He gestured at the empty glass and half-full bottle of wine on the coffee table. "Is this what you do all day when I'm at work? Please tell me you haven't become one of those pathetic women who starts drinking at breakfast and continues until bedtime. And what's with the fire? It's close to a hundred degrees outside."

Georgia sat up straight. "I was feeling anxious about starting my new job tomorrow and needed something to take the edge off." She ignored his comment about the fire.

"What job? Please tell me you didn't get suckered into running another charity benefit."

"This is a paying job, thank you very much, at Tasty Provisions, the new gourmet shop on East Bay. They hired me to work in their storefront. I told you about it. But you weren't listening as usual."

She stood to face him. He had a nice tan for someone who spent so many hours in the operating room. His department had recently hired a young doctor who'd just completed his residency at the Mayo Clinic. Langdon was fifty-eight, only two years away from mandatory retirement. Perhaps this new addition to the team was edging him out. Or maybe the head of his department wanted to get rid of him early. Wouldn't that be a blow to his ego?

She ran her finger down his stubbly cheek. "You're sporting quite the healthy glow these days. I'm glad to know one of us is enjoying the boat," she said in reference to their day-sailer, which they kept at Charleston City Marina. When the boys were little, they spent most Saturdays during the summer sailing out to the area beaches. It had been years since he'd invited Georgia to go sailing with him.

"Don't try to change the subject." He stared at her, his hazel eyes bewildered behind his wire-rimmed specs. "Why do you need to earn money? I thought I made enough for both of us."

She lifted her hair off her neck, feeling a hot flash coming on despite the cold air blowing through the vents. "It's not about the money, Langdon. I need to feel useful. The boys are gone, and you're hardly ever here."

"I can't tell you not to take the job, but I will advise you against neglecting your duties at home."

Her jaw went slack. "What duties? We have a service to take care of the yard. Clara comes in once a week to clean up what little mess we make. I rarely have any laundry to do, since you send everything to the cleaners except your boxers and undershirts. You seldom eat dinner here, so I've stopped buying groceries. Paying the bills takes very little time. So you tell me. What's left to do?" She crossed her arms, waiting for him to respond.

"The exterminator. You need to be here when the exterminator comes." He turned his back on her and crossed the room toward the door. "Speaking of eating, will you make me a sandwich? I need to get back to the hospital."

"I'm sure you do, after sailing away the afternoon." She hated the nagging tone in her voice, but she was powerless to control it. She followed him out of the room. "I don't buy bread anymore. And since I didn't expect you to be here for dinner, a chicken Caesar salad is the only thing I have to offer."

"Whatever is fine," he said as he started up the stairs. "I'm going to take a quick shower. I'll be down in a minute."

She removed the plastic salad container she'd purchased for her own dinner from the refrigerator, and transferred the contents to a plate. She added parmesan cheese, tossed in a few croutons, and drizzled dressing over the top. She was pouring two glasses of sweet tea when he returned, attired in linen slacks, golf shirt, and driving loafers.

"You're going to the hospital dressed like that?" she asked.

He avoided her gaze by turning his attention to the salad. "I'm meeting the guys for poker after I check on my patients."

She leaned back against the counter, sipping her tea. "You're spending an awful lot of time with the guys these days." She tried to sound casual and flirty. "Why don't you make it up to me by taking me out on the water on Sunday? We can pack a picnic and sail over to Folly Beach."

He looked up from his salad. "I thought you were starting a new job tomorrow."

"We're closed on Sundays."

He jabbed his fork in a chunk of chicken. "Gosh Georgie. I wish you'd asked me sooner. I've already made plans to play golf on Sunday."

"With the same guys you're playing poker with tonight?" What had gotten into her? She seldom questioned him about his extracurricular activities. He worked hard. He deserved some time off. But she was his wife. She deserved to have him spend some time with her as well.

"Your tone implies I've been neglecting you."

"I'm not implying anything. I'm simply suggesting we go sailing on Sunday. Do you remember the last time we spent any quality time together? Because I don't."

He stood up and walked his plate to the sink, scraping his half-eaten salad into the disposal. "I need to get to the hospital. I have a patient in critical condition. I'll see you tonight when I get home."

"I'm sure I'll be asleep," she said, ducking her head when he tried to kiss her forehead. She'd stopped waiting up for him when the boys were babies.

She waited for him to leave before slipping on her running shoes to go out. Despite the sultry air and the heat radiating off the pavement, she walked up and down, in and around the neighboring street. She inhaled the aromas from folks cooking on the grill and waved to those gathered on their porches with cocktails in hand. She envied them their time together with family and friends when all she had to look forward to during the evening hours was loneliness.

Was her husband really playing poker with his friends, or was he out with one of his nurses or some damsel in distress he'd encountered on the job? She'd had these same doubts for years. She should hire a private investigator to follow him. Problem was, she wasn't ready to face the truth.

CHAPTER SEVEN
MIDGE

AFTER A DISHEARTENING day on Tuesday—when Georgia had made such hateful remarks about Bennett at tea, and Bennett, in turn, had set off to prove Georgia right by snooping through Midge's bank account and taking her to a party where they weren't invited—Midge buried herself in her work as she often did when she needed a distraction. She spent the next three days working with a young couple who were relocating to Charleston from Nebraska. As first-time buyers, they insisted on seeing every house on the market despite the financing the bank had preapproved. Living on the water was not an option, but it took some convincing for the couple to realize that. They finally settled on a small new-construction home on a cul-de-sac in a neighborhood flooded with young families.

Late on Friday afternoon, Midge drove them back to the hotel out by the airport in North Charleston where they were staying. At a table in the corner of the lobby, the couple sipped on coffee while Midge crafted the electronic contract.

After submitting the contract, she walked her clients to the elevator and promised to contact them as soon as she heard back from the seller's agent. As the elevator doors closed on her clients, whisking them away to the fourth floor, the doors on the elevator to her right parted to reveal a middle-aged man and a much younger woman locked in a passionate embrace, mouths pressed together and arms groping at one another. As though sensing an audience, the couple separated and stepped out of the elevator. Midge recognized the man as Lang Murdaugh, but the woman was definitely not his wife.

"Lang!" Midge exclaimed and took a step back. "What're you doing here?" She eyed the woman up and down. Were her enormous breasts and curvy hips the reason he had chosen this mousey-looking creature over a classic beauty like Georgia?

Lang's tanned face took on a burgundy hue. "I could ask you the same thing."

Midge felt her anger rise. "I'm working with out-of-town clients who are staying here. Looks to me like you're here on business as well. Funny business."

"Huh? Oh, that," he said, as though getting caught making out with a strange woman in a hotel elevator was no big deal. "You misunderstood. Mrs. Jones's husband is a patient of mine." His fingers grazed the woman's elbow. "He's in critical condition. I was offering her consolation."

Midge arched an eyebrow. Jones? How original. "Your consolation gives new meaning to bedside manner. I don't know many doctors who make house calls to the Embassy Suites on Friday afternoons." She stepped out of their way. "By all means, don't let me keep you. I wish your husband a speedy recovery," she said to the woman, before turning on her heel and hurrying out of the lobby to her car.

She drove home on autopilot, barely aware of the afternoon traffic crawling along the interstate. Bile rose in her throat when she imagined what she'd say to Georgia. "By the way, I saw your husband making out with another woman in an elevator at the Embassy Suites out by the airport. She was half your age, but not nearly as pretty as you. You have nothing to worry about, though. Lang assured me he was there to consult with her about her husband's medical condition."

Would Georgia even believe Midge? Would she lash out at her and call her a liar? Georgia worshipped her husband. This would break her heart.

Two years ago, Georgia had thrown an elaborate dinner party to celebrate their thirtieth wedding anniversary. Midge considered their marriage rock solid. They had everything—power, prestige, and money. If Georgia and Lang couldn't make their marriage work after thirty-two years, Midge didn't stand a chance with Bennett, a man she'd known for only two months.

Midge exited the interstate toward downtown. She was stopped at the traffic light at Meeting and East Bay Streets when she spotted Bennett helping an attractive redhead out of a car in front of the Market Pavilion Hotel. He took the woman's hand and pulled her to him, embracing her and kissing her cheek in a manner that suggested they were more than friends. Her heart pounded against her rib cage and heat flushed through her body. Midge blew her horn and waved at him. She wanted Bennett to know she'd seen him, so he'd feel guilty if he did, in fact, have something to feel guilty about. Bennett lifted his pointer finger in response before placing his hand on the small of the woman's back and escorting her inside the hotel.

She sped home as quickly as she could navigate the downtown traffic. She changed into her running clothes, and took off down the street. When she hit Rutledge Avenue, she forced all thoughts of Lang and Bennett from her mind and concentrated on her breathing as she sprinted around Colonial Lake. When her chest and legs began to burn, she lowered her pace and walked the short distance home.

Stupid, naive Midge. She had only herself to blame if Bennett really was sleeping with the redhead. Aside from her ex-husband, she'd known only one other man sexually. Her lack of experience had made her shy in the bedroom. Bennett had tried to get her to experiment, but so far she'd been unable to lose her inhibitions. Had her self-consciousness driven her fiancé into the arms of another woman? Good riddance if he wasn't more patient and understanding than that. Maybe he was a dirty rotten rascal after all. Thank goodness she discovered the truth about him before they got married. It made her skin crawl to think how close she'd come to being his fourth ex-wife. She'd believed him when he told her she was different than his first three wives, that their relationship was special and he'd never loved the others as much as he loved her.

She straightened her shoulders and held her head high. If she could survive twenty years of being single, she would survive breaking up with Bennett. But Georgia was a different story. Georgia would have to face life alone after thirty-two years of marriage. She wondered if Lang had rushed home to confess his affair to his wife after his encounter with Midge. Would he offer Georgia the same lame explanation about his presence at a seedy out-of-the-way hotel on a Friday afternoon? Who did he think he was kidding?

On the upside, if Lang pled guilty to his wife, Midge would be off the hook from having to break the news herself.

Bennett was waiting for her when she returned home. This time, instead of snooping around on her laptop, he was rummaging through her refrigerator.

She held her hand out to him. "Give me the key, Bennett."

"Ouch! Hostile!" He rubbed his arm as though he'd been scalded. "What're you so angry about?"

"Seriously? You have to ask? I just saw you going into a hotel with a gorgeous redhead."

"Come on, babe." He stepped toward her, but she backed away. "You know me better than that. She's a business associate."

"Right, and I'm the Queen of England. I'm not stupid, Bennett. Or blind. I saw the way you greeted her. You really should be more careful, kissing and hugging like that on the sidewalk on East Bay Street for all of Charleston to see. No wonder you couldn't make your three marriages work, if you can't cheat on your wives better than that."

"You've got it all wrong, Midge. I've been working with that woman on a deal for a couple of years. I've gotten to know her pretty well, and I consider her my friend, but I promise you we're just business acquaintances."

"Oh really?" Midge cocked her head to the side. "What deal?"

"I can't talk about it just yet. But soon. And you'll be the first person I tell." He flashed an innocent little-boy smile, while the overhead lights in the kitchen made his blue eyes twinkle like the sun reflecting off the ocean. For a weak moment she was tempted to believe him, but then her voice of reason reminded her of his reputation.

"I don't believe you." She held her hand out again. "Give me the key. Now. Regardless of who that woman is, I'm not comfortable with you having a key to my house. You can't just come and go as you please. We're not married. At this rate, we never will be."

Lines creased his forehead as he pressed the house key into her palm. "I thought our relationship was stronger than this."

She slipped the key inside her sports bra and went to the refrigerator for a bottle of water. "I don't know anymore, Bennett. I think maybe I'm better off being alone. I suck at relationships. I've managed fine for all these years without a man in my life."

His wounded expression deepened. "Why would you say that when we're so good together?"

She shrugged. "Who knows? Maybe my trust issues are left over from the breakup of my marriage. Or maybe your reputation for being a scoundrel and a playboy makes me second-guess everything you do."

"Scoundrel? That hurts," he said, slumping his shoulders. "I guess I deserve being labeled a playboy after getting married and divorced three times. But, contrary to what you think, I never slept around."

"Give me a break!" She slammed the bottle of water down on the kitchen counter. "You and Lang Murdaugh are cut from the same cloth."

"What's that supposed to mean? What does Georgia's husband have to do with us?"

"Remember I told you about my out-of-town clients?"

she asked and he nodded. "I saw Lang with another woman at the hotel where they're staying today."

He dropped down on the nearest bar stool. "So the brilliant Dr. Murdaugh has a girlfriend. Can't say I blame him, being married to that old cow."

Midge realized her mistake. She should never have mentioned seeing Lang. There was no love lost between Georgia and Bennett. He would delight in seeing her hurt. "Forget I said anything. It's none of my business anyway."

"Consider it forgotten." Bennett pulled Midge down on his lap. "I snagged a late reservation for dinner at Husk. Why don't we grab some drinks beforehand, someplace with a view of the sunset?"

"Sorry." Midge pushed herself off his lap. "But I'm spending the weekend with my brother and his family on the Isle of Palms."

He narrowed his eyes. "But we have the Ravenel wedding tomorrow night."

"Sorry," she said, lifting her shoulder in a shrug. "I didn't know about it until this morning. Keith left me a message. At the last minute his boss offered him his beach house for the weekend. You know me. I never pass up a chance to bask in the sun and sip margaritas."

Bennett appeared wounded. "What about me? Am I not invited?"

"He included you, but I told him you already had plans. I knew you wouldn't want to miss the wedding."

Midge had been too busy with her out-of-town clients to return her brother's phone call. She'd planned to turn down his invitation, but she suddenly found the idea of spending the weekend away from Bennett appealing. She picked her phone up and shot off a quick text to her brother letting him know she would be there in time for dinner. Alone.

She glanced at her watch. "I need to get going if I want to beat the traffic. If you don't mind." She motioned him toward the door.

"Fine." He jumped to his feet, knocking the bar stool over. "Go ahead to the beach without me. I'll find someone else to spend my weekend with."

"I'm sure you will. You can take the redhead to the wedding with you." Her voice quavered as she choked back the tears.

Bennett's expression changed from anger to sorrow. "I'm so sorry, baby. I didn't mean it. You know I'm not going to spend my weekend with anyone else but you. Please, don't go. Stay here with me. We can talk about whatever it is that's troubling you."

"I need some space, Bennett. I have a lot of things I need to think about."

He threw his head back in frustration. "Whatever, Midge."

She walked him to the door. He leaned down to kiss her, but she turned her cheek. "Don't forget we have dinner with my family on Tuesday. I trust you'll be back from the beach by then."

She hesitated before answering him. She'd been looking forward to meeting his parents. "I'll go, but that's the only promise I'm making for now."

CHAPTER EIGHT
LULA

LULA WAS PUTTING the finishing touches on her flower arrangements when Phillip came downstairs for breakfast.

"What's all this?" he asked about the mess spread out on the kitchen counter.

"I'm making these for Lizbet to sell at the store where she works. What do you think?"

He examined the arrangements from several angles. "I think they're very nice. But you won't have any flowers left in your garden if you're not careful."

"That's exactly what I told our daughter." She straightened his tie and thumbed off a smudge of shaving cream near his ear. "Sit down and I'll get your breakfast."

She ladled two scoops of oatmeal into a bowl, tossed in a handful of blueberries, and sprinkled brown sugar on top. She set the bowl, a glass of orange juice, and a cup of coffee in front of him. Her husband ate the same thing for breakfast every morning, and Lula packed the same turkey and swiss on wheat sandwich for his lunch every day. He seldom deviated from his work attire—crisp white shirts, striped ties, and dark-gray suits—even though his accounting firm had long since adopted a more casual dress code. He celebrated his success modestly and took life's hardships in stride. He was as happy staying home on a Friday night curled up in his favorite leather chair with a good book as he was having drinks with the neighbors or going out to dinner with friends. His steady demeanor balanced out Lula's high-strung temperament. Although his methodical way of thinking often irritated her, most of the time she was grateful for his calming presence.

Pooh came over and sniffed Phillip's shoes. Lula lifted the little dog into her arms and sat down at the table across from her husband. "I'm meeting with Heidi, the caterer, about the menu for the party. Do you think we should have froufrou food or keep it simple?"

"I'll leave that to you, Lula. Just make sure you have enough of whatever you decide."

"We're calling the party a summer supper," Lula said. "I think the name suggests more than burgers and dogs."

He dragged his spoon around his bowl mixing the berries and sugar with the oatmeal. "Don't get yourself worked into a tizzy over this party. We haven't seen Brooke in a very long time. Spending quality time with her is more important than entertaining a bunch of folks we hardly ever see."

"That's why I'm hiring a caterer."

"That doesn't mean anything," he said, slurping on his coffee. "Not having to worry about the food will free you to fuss over the rest of the details."

"Now that you mention it, if we have Heidi supply the alcohol and bring in a couple of bartenders, we won't have to worry about anything but making the house and yard look nice." A mischievous smirk played on her thin lips as she waited for his response.

He pointed a boney finger at her. "You set me up for that one."

Lula waved Pooh's paw at him. "Let's just say you fell into my trap." Phillip seldom denied her anything. Then again, she rarely asked for much. She wasn't high maintenance like many of her middle-aged friends. She didn't buy expensive shoes and clothing or visit the plastic surgeon for monthly injections.

"I'm looking forward to seeing Brooke. I've missed her more than I realized." He removed his horn-rimmed glasses and dabbed at his eyes with his napkin. The simplest things caused him to tear up. Lula teased him about being sentimental. Although she'd never admitted it to him, she found his tenderheartedness endearing.

Lula set Pooh down on the floor and returned to her flowers, talking on about the party while Phillip finished his breakfast. He placed his plate in the dishwasher, and poured his coffee in a to-go cup.

"Do you mind helping me to the car with this on your way out?" She gestured at the large metal tray she was using to transport her arrangements.

"Of course," he said, and handed her his coffee. "You hold this while I get the tray."

She held the backdoor open for him and then followed him out to her minivan. He stored the tray of flowers in the back, slammed the rear door, and kissed her cheek like he did every time they parted, whether he was leaving the room or leaving for work.

Lula locked up the house and drove the few blocks to

Tasty Provisions. Lizbet had recommended she park in the small lot behind the building, but Lula was fortunate to find a parking space directly in front of the store. She tried the door but found it locked, and then noticed the sign in the window that indicated a ten 'clock opening time. Cupping her hand over her eyes, she peered inside and saw Georgia rearranging a display of stemware near the back. She pounded on the door. Georgia looked up and waved.

Georgia opened the door and stepped aside so Lula could enter. "Good morning. Welcome to Tasty Provisions."

Lula entered the showroom and wandered around, examining the gourmet cookies and assortment of fresh baked breads. "So this is where one comes to shop when they don't like to cook. It's right up your alley, Georgia."

Georgia's smile fell into a thin line. "We're not all blessed with your talents, Lula."

Lizbet emerged from the back. "Hi, Mom. I thought that might be you. Heidi called a minute ago. She wanted me to tell you she's running a little late."

"I hope she won't be long. I have a busy day ahead of me." Lizbet and Georgia exchanged a look that made Lula's stomach harden, just as it did whenever she saw her daughter and her friend drinking icy glasses of lemonade and nibbling ginger snap cookies on Georgia's front porch. She'd never understood what they found to talk about for hours. Or why her daughter felt more comfortable talking to Georgia than her own mother. She often wondered if they were talking about her.

"While we're waiting…" She handed Lizbet her car keys. "I have a tray of flower arrangements in the car. Will you be a good girl and run get them for me before they wilt?"

"Sure." Lizbet hurried out the front door and returned a minute later, struggling under the weight of the heavy tray.

Georgia rushed to help her with the door. "Lord in Heaven, Lula. Did you leave any flowers in the garden?"

Lizbet set the tray down on the counter. "Seriously, Mom? Why did you make so many arrangements? You have enough flowers here to supply a wedding. I'm pretty sure Heidi had in mind for us to try a few at a time."

Lula replaced a stem that had fallen loose from one of the arrangements. "I may have gotten a little carried away experimenting. I took your advice, Lizbet, and contacted a wholesale florist. He sold me these cute little glass cubes and three bunches of filler material. If I want to buy from him in the future, I will need a tax ID number, whatever that is."

"That's no problem," Georgia said. "We have one you can use."

"I made mock-ups of several different styles of arrangements," Lula said. "I'm curious to see which ones Heidi fancies."

"Did someone mention my name?" A striking woman Lula guessed to be in her mid to late thirties teetered into the showroom from the kitchen on heels too high for a woman of any age to wear. Lula knew her type well, the girl all the boys chased in high school who became the woman all the men ogled at cocktail parties, a lifelong blonde with the size breasts that fit into everything and long shapely legs that looked splendid in short skirts. "Ooh." She bent down to sniff the flowers. "Did these come from your garden?"

Lula felt herself blush under the gaze of Heidi's emerald eyes. "Only the showy blooms. I bought the filler material from the wholesale florist. I got a little carried away and made too many arrangements. I'll drop whatever you can't use off at my church."

Heidi's face lit up. "Actually, I just received a call from the client whose event I'm catering tonight. She forgot to order flowers. If you can repurpose some of the smaller ones into a larger arrangement, we might be able to use all of them."

Lula took a step back so as to envision the flowers in a larger arrangement. "The stems aren't very long, but I'm sure I can come up with something, maybe a shallow bowl on a tall pedestal. Does she have a particular container she'd like to use?"

"Let me give her a call. She sounded desperate earlier. I imagine she'd be thrilled with anything." Heidi pulled out a cell phone from her apron pocket and clicked on a number. She stepped away from the counter, holding up a finger to indicate she'd be only a minute.

"It might be easier for you to rework the flowers here instead of taking them home again. I can clear off a spot for you in the kitchen," Lizbet said, gesturing toward the back of the building.

The idea of working in someone else's kitchen appealed to Lula as much as the thought of having to wrestle the flowers home again. "I don't have my supplies with me, but I can run home and get what I need. I could use a few more stems from the garden anyway." She cut her eyes at Georgia. "I have the whole day free, since I'm not meeting my best friends for tea for the first time in twenty-six years."

Lizbet squished her eyebrows together. "Didn't you just say you had a busy day ahead of you?"

"Nothing I can't postpone," Lula said.

Georgia gave Lula a half hug. "Believe it or not, I'm as

disappointed as you are about our tea time. I've given some thought to our scheduling problem—"

"Our scheduling problem?" Lula elbowed Georgia away. "This is your scheduling problem. You're the one responsible for ruining our tea time."

"I realize that," Georgia said. "But I'm trying to tell you I may have a solution. What do you think about moving our tea time to Sunday?"

Lula shook her head. "That won't work. Sunday is family day."

"Maybe it was when the children were young. But your girls are grown." Georgia turned to Lizbet. "When's the last time you spent any time on a Sunday with your parents?"

"This past Sunday, actually. I was helping Mom with the invitations for the Fourth of July party." Lizbet paused as she thought about it. "But you're right. Before that, I can't remember spending a Sunday at home since I graduated from high school."

Lula pressed her lips into a tight line. "I refuse to have my Sunday afternoons disrupted because you decided to get a job. Phillip would not approve anyway. Just because Lang is never home doesn't mean other women don't like to keep their weekends free for their husbands."

Georgia squeezed her arm. "Don't be so difficult, Lu. Surely you can spare an hour out of your weekend for your friends. You might even find you like it. We can meet earlier in the afternoon if it suits you, maybe around three. Why don't we at least ask Midge how she feels about Sundays?"

"You do what you want, but leave me out of it. I'm going home to get my supplies." Lula marched across the store to the door, but instead of opening it, she turned back around to face them. "I know what you're trying to do, Georgia. This is some kind of conspiracy to get rid of me. Well, consider me gone." She raised her hand in the air above her head and flicked her fingers. "Poof! No more Lula for tea time."

She felt their eyes on her back as she exited the building. What on earth had made her say that?

CHAPTER NINE

GEORGIA

GEORGIA AND LIZBET stood together at the window watching Lula get in her car and drive away.

"What was that all about?" Lizbet asked, a bewildered expression on her face.

"Your mama's gotten herself all worked up over your sister's visit and this Fourth of July party, and she's taking her stress out on me. Don't worry. I'm used to it."

"You're not the only one she's taking it out on," Lizbet grumbled.

"You know how she is. When she gets a bee in her bonnet, she expects everyone around her to make honey. Best just to do what she asks and stay out of her way."

"You're probably right." Lizbet left the door and walked over to the checkout counter. "What I don't understand is why Brooke has suddenly decided to come home."

Georgia joined her at the counter. "She's been away from her family for a long time. She's probably homesick and longing for the lazy summers of her youth."

"Ha. Brooke doesn't have fond memories about anything relating to home. Not Charleston or our family. If she missed us, she would have come home long ago. I've never understood how, as sisters, we can be so different. We share the same parents and the same DNA. We grew up in the same house, attended the same high school and, for the most part, participated in the same activities. Yet she couldn't wait to get as far away from South Carolina as possible and I never wanted to leave. Until recently, that is." Lizbet slumped back against the counter. "Brooke has an agenda, a purpose for making this trip. She'll arrive with drama folded neatly in her suitcase waiting to escape."

"Maybe she'll surprise you," Georgia said, although she suspected Lizbet was right. Brooke did have a tendency toward the melodramatic. "I didn't know you were considering leaving Charleston. Where would you go?"

"To New York with Annie. I want to apply to culinary school, but I need to save the money for tuition first. I can't ask Mom and Dad to help me, not after they just paid four years' tuition at the College of Charleston."

Georgia was crazy about Heidi's daughter, Annie—a honey-haired beauty who was every bit as gifted and resourceful as her mother—and she knew Lizbet felt the same. "As talented as you are in the kitchen, I imagine culinary school would be a good fit for you. Have you considered attending the culinary school here in town?"

"That's my second choice. I really feel like I need to get away. At least for a while. Please don't say anything to Mom. I haven't mentioned it to her yet."

Georgia ran an imaginary zipper across her lips. "Mum's the word."

Heidi came out of the kitchen, her face flustered and her cell phone gripped in her hand. "Where'd your mother go?" she asked Lizbet.

"Home, to get her supplies and cut some more flowers."

"Okay, great," Georgia said. "Now that the flower problem is solved, I need to locate a bartender. I just got off the phone with Justin. He has the stomach flu. Do either of you know anyone who might be free at the last minute?"

Georgia raised her hand without hesitation. "I'll do it. I'm an expert at pouring wine. And I can mix a killer martini."

Heidi studied Georgia's face as she considered the idea. "I have no doubt but what you can handle it. Bartending at this type event is different than at a nightclub. Drink requests are usually straightforward like wine, beer, and vodka tonics. But I want you to think about it carefully before you agree to do it. You might have to serve your own friends. That could get awkward."

"I hadn't thought of that." Georgia pursed her lips in thought. "Who's hosting the party?"

"Dean and Marta Underwood. They live on the waterfront in Mount Pleasant."

"Never heard of them. Which means it's highly unlikely I know any of their friends." Working the party was preferable to spending another evening at home alone. Anything, in fact, was preferable to spending another evening home alone. "I'm fine with it really, Heidi. I think it'd be fun to work the party."

Heidi clapped her hands together. "In that case, you're hired. And don't worry. You won't be alone. Jessie will be the head bartender. You'll be her helper." She eyed Georgia's clothing. "You'll need to wear black pants, a white blouse of some sort—nothing nice in case you have spills—and comfortable shoes."

Georgia envisioned the contents of her closet. "That shouldn't be a problem. I'll run home and get them during my lunch break."

*

Lula returned to the store an hour later with a small canvas tool bag slung over her shoulder and an armful of flowers. Georgia suspected the blue hydrangea blooms came from her yard, since Lula's hydrangeas bushes were all pink. But she held her tongue. She was used to Lula helping herself to her flowers.

The rest of the day passed in a flurry of activity, tourists moseying about shopping for trinkets and locals rushing in and out picking up salads for lunch, casseroles for dinner, and odds and ends for their social functions. Five days in and Georgia had settled into her new job with ease. She enjoyed the customers and the opportunity to meet interesting new people every day. She was pleased that Heidi planned not only to take her to market on the next trip to Atlanta but also to eventually turn the responsibility of merchandising and staffing the retail side of the business over to her. She was even already thinking about how she would decorate the showroom for the upcoming holiday season—Halloween, followed by Thanksgiving and Christmas. With a dedicated, energetic woman like Heidi at the helm and Annie following in her footsteps, Tasty Provisions had a long and prosperous future ahead. Which would mean job security for Georgia and perhaps a promotion if she worked hard enough.

Georgia locked the door at six o'clock sharp and quickly changed into her server attire in the employee bathroom off the kitchen. As she crossed the Cooper River Bridge to Mount Pleasant, she was relieved to find that the afternoon commuter traffic had dwindled, but her stomach turned a somersault the moment she entered the house through the backdoor. "This was a bad idea, Georgie," she muttered to herself when she saw the catering staff bustling about in the kitchen. If she ran into someone she knew here tonight, word would travel back to Langdon in the seconds it took for that someone to type a text message and click send. And her husband would be furious.

Gripping her handbag to her chest, Georgia was contemplating a dash for the door when Heidi spotted her from across the kitchen and waved her over. "Put your bag in here," Heidi said as she opened a pantry door and pointed inside. "Jessie is waiting for you at the bar in the living room at the front of the house, down the center hall, second door on the right."

Georgia avoided eye contact with the guests as she worked her way through the already crowded house, a restored early twentieth-century Georgian with plush fabrics and carpets and lovely antiques. People were already lined up three deep, one behind the other, waiting for a drink. She took her place beside Jessie behind the bar, and began filling orders. For the next two-plus hours, Georgia poured wine and mixed vodka with tonic and scotch with soda. She recognized no one and no one recognized her. She was invisible to the men and women who presented their empty glasses for refills. She was a nobody, put on the planet to perform a service for them.

As the night wore on and the alcohol began to dull their

senses, they began to speak freely in front of her as if she wasn't there at all. Men and women in small groups of two and three lingered in front of the bar as they drained the last drops of liquid from their glasses. The men complained of problems at work and diminishing golf handicaps, while the women made snarky remarks and shared petty gossip. The pretty women made fun of the ones who hadn't aged so well. Those women, in turn, criticized the pretty women for their revealing clothing and flawless skin made possible by frequent visits to the plastic surgeon. She heard rumors of extramarital affairs and couples forced into bankruptcy from the poor economy. The women bragged about their children's accomplishments and boasted about their husbands' promotions. By eleven o'clock, when the hostess finally bid goodnight to the last guests, Georgia was more than ready to return to the solitude of her own home. She felt utterly depleted.

As best she could remember, Georgia had never witnessed such cattiness at any of the cocktail parties she and Langdon attended over the years. Was this how people behaved at social gatherings these days? Come to think of it, when was the last time they went to a cocktail party? How had she failed to notice that the number of invitations they received had dwindled to none? Once upon a time, and not that long ago, they'd gone out several times a week. Some events were strictly personal while others were related to the hospital or her volunteer work. She no longer served on nonprofit boards, but surely Langdon's business associates still had their functions. Did he attend these gatherings alone? And what about their friends? Had their peers stopped entertaining altogether or were the Murdaughs considered personae non gratae? Tears blurred Georgia's vision as she drove back across the bridge toward home. She was no longer sure of where she belonged. Her old life, the one centering around her family and volunteer work, felt like a dress that had grown out of style. But the life she was currently living, with her new job and friends at Tasty Provisions, felt like a pair of new boots she'd yet to break in.

For the first time ever, she was relieved to discover her husband had not yet come home. She peeled off her clothes, slipped beneath the covers, and fell into a deep sleep.

CHAPTER TEN
MIDGE

AS THE MINUTES ticked slowly off the clock on Tuesday, Midge was all too aware of the void in her afternoon schedule. For the first time in twenty-six years, the standing four o'clock tea time with Georgia and Lula no longer stood. On the flip side, not meeting for tea meant she could delay telling Georgia about her encounter with Lang and Mrs. Jones at the seedy airport hotel on Friday.

Spending the weekend with her brother and his wife had helped Midge realign her perspective on a lot of things. They were sitting on the beach late in the day on Saturday, their heads buzzing from too many margaritas, when she mentioned seeing her fiancé with another woman. "He claims she's a business associate, and that they are putting together some kind of secret deal. He's not at liberty to talk about it yet."

"Sounds like you don't believe him," Kara, her sister-in-law, said.

Midge dug her toes in the sand. "I want to believe him, but something's holding me back. I don't know if it's my past or his past or a little bit of both." She wished she could travel back two months to when they'd first started seeing one another. She was so in love with him, she'd believed everything he'd told her. Had there been any warning signs? Or had she ignored them? Could she have fallen out of love that quickly? Midge didn't think so.

"You haven't opened yourself up to anyone in a long time," Keith said. "It's normal for you to feel vulnerable. Listen closely to your heart and your gut. If both are telling you the same thing, you have your answer. But if your emotions are at odds, you need to continue searching for your answer."

Midge sipped her margarita as she thought about her brother's advice. Her heart loved Bennett, but her gut warned her to be wary of him. She would proceed with caution until one of her emotions prevailed.

"Since you have all the answers, little brother, explain to me what makes a man cheat on his wife." She told Keith and Kara about running into Georgia's husband at a hotel with another woman.

Keith gave a solemn shake of his head. "I can't answer that, Midge. I like to look at other women as much as the next guy, but I've never been tempted to cheat on my wife. Kara and I respect one another, and we treat each other with kindness. Ours is a give/give relationship. Most importantly, we take our commitment to our family seriously."

"Georgia has devoted her life to her family and look where it's gotten her," Midge said. "I wouldn't be surprised if she doesn't already suspect something. She hasn't been herself lately. I can't explain it except to say that some of her sparkle has faded. Her voice no longer softens when she talks about Lang. And they rarely attend social functions together anymore. Most evenings, I see him speeding off alone in his convertible Audi. And he isn't always dressed for the hospital. Maybe I should let her figure it out on her own."

"You can't do that," Kara said. "You have to tell her. Wouldn't you want Georgia to tell you if Bennett was sleeping with another woman?"

She sank farther down in her beach chair. "I guess you're right."

*

Midge was due to meet Bennett's family for the first time that night. She had no idea what to expect—burgers on the grill or a seven-course seated dinner in the formal dining room—and she was too embarrassed to ask. His family played in a totally different league than hers. They represented money and power. With the exception of Bennett, the Calhoun men had been providing legal counsel for Charlestonians since his great grandfather established the family firm, Calhoun and Sons, in the early 1920s. Bennett had broken the mold by going into commercial real estate. The town gossipers claimed he'd failed the LSAT, that he wasn't smart enough to attend law school, but Midge thought him better suited to building things than tearing them apart.

After changing outfits four or five times, she decided on her best pair of white jeans, a pale-blue silk tunic, and strappy pewter-colored sandals. She teased her hair to give it some volume and gave it a heavy coat of spray to keep it in place. She was waiting on her front porch when Bennett swung by to pick her up a few minutes before six.

Midge hadn't communicated with him all weekend, and as

they drove three blocks south to his parents' stunning four-story home on Legare Street, she made no mention of his redheaded business associate or of their argument on Friday. She would take her brother's advice and keep an open mind and heart while she searched for her answers.

Bennett's sisters-in-law, Virginia and Sara, could have passed for his sisters they looked so much like his mother, Lucille. All three women had blonde hair and blue eyes and wore casual dresses that accented their boyish figures. Recognizing the styles, Midge assumed the labels were the real deal—Herrera, Ortiz, Oscar de la Renta. The women greeted Midge like an old friend with warm hugs and kind smiles while Bennett's brothers—dressed in khaki slacks and knit shirts—offered token kisses on the cheek. Bennett's father, every bit as handsome as his sons, gave her shoulder a pat and handed her a glass of rosé. Eager to see the inside of the house, Midge was disappointed when they led her to a side porch instead. Bee, a black woman in a maid's uniform, with a crop of gray hair and folds of fat around her neck, appeared with a tray of canapés.

For the next hour, they discussed the leisure-time summer activities of the wealthy—golfing, boating, and extended trips to Maine and Martha's Vineyard. Midge listened intently, but had little to add to the discussion. The conversation continued over a four-course dinner—white gazpacho, mixed green salad, blackened Mahi, Key lime pie, and a different wine to go with each dish. Dinner was served at a farm table—set with casual linens, china, and glassware—at the other end of the porch. After dessert the men excused themselves to smoke cigars in Bennett's father's study and the women gathered at one end of the table to linger over coffee.

"Disgusting habit, if you ask me," Virginia said about the cigars.

Lucille smiled at her daughter-in-law. "Good luck getting them to quit. Believe me, I've tried."

"Speaking of cancer," Sara said, even though no one had mentioned cancer, "did you hear about poor Betty Washington? Stage four pancreatic cancer. They've given her two weeks to live."

Midge didn't know Betty Washington, so she remained silent while the others talked about how lost Betty's husband and their two sons would be once she was gone. When they finally exhausted the subject of Betty Washington, Lucille rose from the table. "I'm going to say goodnight. I have an early day tomorrow," she said and then floated through the french doors with the grace of a ballerina.

"Now that it's just us girls," Virginia said, and both sisters-in-law scooted their chairs closer to Midge, sandwiching her in.

"You seem like a nice person. We'd hate to see you get hurt." Sara's tone sounded sincere, but her stony expression suggested otherwise. Midge understood she'd been set up, and wondered whether Lucille was aware of the conspiracy.

Virginia folded her hands in her lap. "You do know that Bennett's been married before."

"Three times in fact," Sara added. "He cheated on the first. Grew tired of number two pleading for children he didn't want. And stole money from number three's father."

"He stole money from her father?" Midge repeated to confirm she'd heard Sara correctly.

Virginia cut her eyes at her sister-in-law. "That's not entirely accurate. Number three's father caught Bennett breaking into his safe, the one on the wall of his study behind the portrait of his beloved daughter where he keeps stacks of hundred-dollar bills. Bennett never actually got away with the money."

Sara tossed her hands in the air. "A technicality. But you get the point."

"I'm aware of Bennett's somewhat colorful past. But none of that has anything to do with our relationship. He's older now, more mature," said Midge.

"I wouldn't count on it," Virginia muttered under her breath.

"Bennett and I have talked about his failed marriages," Midge continued, "and I'm convinced he's learned from those experiences. Otherwise we wouldn't be together. That's not to say I have no concerns. But he's agreed to wait as long as it takes for me to be comfortable with the situation."

Sara leaned across the table toward Midge. "Then why are you wearing his ring if you're not comfortable with the situation? That ring belonged to their grandmother. You'll have to give it back if... when... you become uncomfortable with the situation."

Midge twisted the ring on her finger so the stone was facing inward. "What I'm uncomfortable with is this conversation. You are out of line sticking your nose into our business. I'm a grown woman, not some debutante you can bully into running off with her tail between her legs. Of course, I'll give the ring back if I decide not to marry him. Until then, I'll wear it as a symbol of our commitment to one another. And we are committed to one another."

Sara shot Virginia a look that Midge didn't miss. They were tag-teaming her, and now it was Virginia's turn.

"Calm down, Midge, honey," Virginia said, stroking her arm. "Sara didn't mean to upset you. It's just...well..." She lowered her voice. "Can I be frank with you? I need to trust that this conversation won't leave the table."

Gritting her teeth, Midge nodded her head. She had no intention of telling Bennett about this conversation. To do so would make her appear weak, as though she couldn't handle these women, as though she believed anything they'd said.

"The truth is, Sara and I are worried sick about Lucille. She's not as strong as she looks. She falls apart every time Bennett has one of his crises. And I don't just mean the divorces. I'm talking about the other scandals. I trust you know about the other scandals."

Midge knew of no other scandals nor was she in the mood to handle anymore bad news tonight. "Bennett and I don't keep secrets from one another," she blurted even though she suspected it was a lie.

"Good!" Sara said. "Then you won't have a problem signing a prenuptial agreement."

Midge held her gaze. "I have no problem with it. In fact, I insist on it. Bennett and I both plan to sign prenuptial agreements." They'd never discussed it, but after this conversation, Midge would protect her assets at all costs. "This might come as a surprise to you, but I have just as much to lose as Bennett."

Virginia's eyes lit up. "That's great news! I'm glad to know you'll be able to put food on the table. Because Bennett's broke. I assume you already know this, though, since you don't keep secrets from one another. He does, however, stand to inherit a lot of money. Old money that needs to be protected."

It sounded to Midge like that old money needed protection

from Bennett, not from her. She didn't want his money. She wanted the Bennett who had courted her with flowers and romantic dinners out. She wanted the Bennett who loved to run marathons and window-shop on King Street and go to Saturday afternoon matinees. She wanted their dreams of owning a boutique agency to come true. She wanted to forget all that had happened in recent days—Bennett opening her mail and showing up at the Lelands' cocktail party uninvited, Bennett's lovely redheaded business associate. She wanted to forget about this conversation, this night, these tacky women and their condescending attitudes.

An hour later, when he parked the car alongside the curb in front of her house and killed the engine as though preparing to go inside with her, she slipped the engagement ring off her finger and held it out to him. "I have some serious concerns about our relationship, Bennett. You better hold on to this until I've sorted out my issues."

He stared at the ring, but he didn't appear surprised. "Please don't do this."

She pressed the ring in the palm of his hand and wrapped his fingers around it. "Just give me some time."

He hung his head. "I understand. With my track record, I don't blame you for not trusting me. Take all the time you need. I want you to be comfortable with your decision to marry me. But you're not going to get rid of me that easily."

CHAPTER ELEVEN
MIDGE

MIDGE FELL INTO a depression like she hadn't experienced since the days of trying, and failing, to conceive a baby twenty-some years ago. For the most part Bennett respected her need for space, but he still called and texted her with requests to join him for drinks and dinner. She hoped that by taking a step back from their relationship she could rediscover the qualities that had attracted her to him in the first place. She declined all his invitations except the one for the Fourth of July. They made plans to spend the day on the water with his parents in their new Hinckley picnic boat, and then drive out to Sullivan's Island for Lula's party. Midge had no clue what a picnic boat was, only that Bennett was as excited as a boy with a new toy over the recent addition to the family's fleet. As far as she knew, his evil sisters-in-law had other plans for the holiday.

Midge had lost five pounds in the two weeks since she'd had dinner with Bennett's family. Which was a considerable amount for a woman of her small stature. Her time-out from

Bennett wasn't the only source of her angst. Harboring the knowledge of her best friend's husband's extramarital affair was eating away at her like Betty Washington's cancer cells were eating away at her pancreas. With no appetite, she'd all but stopped eating. Running was the only thing that relieved the tension in her body and the constant queasy feeling in her gut. She spent her free time spying on Georgia from her bedroom window, watching for signs of unrest in the Murdaugh household.

Reluctant to get involved, she hoped Lang would confess his infidelity or Georgia would discover it on her own. In the ten days Midge had been on surveillance, Georgia seldom deviated from her schedule. Morning walk at seven. Departure for work at nine. Return home around six thirty with a grocery bag from Harris Teeter tucked beneath each arm. Glass of wine on the porch while she opened her mail. Inside by eight. Bedroom light on at nine. Bedroom light out at ten. Lang's schedule was nearly as predictable. Morning run at five. Departure for work by six thirty. Home around five, dressed in tennis attire on four of the ten days. Out of the house again by five thirty wearing khaki slacks and a knit shirt. Midge had no idea what time he came home at night. She was never awake.

Georgia had sent five separate group texts inviting Midge and Lula for tea on different days at different times. For each one, Midge waited for Lula to respond first, and when Lula declined the invitation, Midge texted: "I can make anything work." The most recent invitation had arrived that very morning, a Tuesday three weeks after their last tea date. Georgia had arranged to have the afternoon off in the hopes they could get together before the busy holiday week. Lula once again texted she couldn't make it for tea because she was too busy getting ready for Brooke's visit. Even though Midge's afternoon was free, she followed with a text that read: "Sorry. Busy day. Maybe next time."

Midge knew she was behaving like a coward. What was she so afraid of now after all their years of friendship? True, Georgia had intimidated her when they first met, for Midge, an uneducated girl from McClellanville, had nothing in common with a Charlestonian socialite. But Georgia had spoken freely with her and treated her as an equal, thus putting her at ease and helping her come out of her shell. She knew that although Georgia had recently given her a hard time about Bennett, calling him a rotten rascal, she had done it only because she didn't want to see Midge hurt.

Anymore than Midge wanted to see Georgia hurt.

Stop being ridiculous, Midge! You've waited long enough. March yourself on over to Georgia's house and tell her about your encounter with Lang at the Embassy Suites. You know Georgia would do the same for you if the situation was reversed.

Midge sucked in a deep breath. She would break the news, and then offer Georgia a shoulder to cry on. She expected Georgia to get angry. She might even take her anger out on Midge. But Georgia was a reasonable person, and when she calmed down, she'd realize that Midge was merely the messenger. Midge wasn't the one breaking Georgia's heart. That was all Lang's doing.

She waited until Georgia emerged from her house, dressed for work in a colorful print skirt and white cotton blouse, before bolting down the stairs and out the front door like she'd done a dozen times in the past few days. As had happened in those previous dozen times, she made it to the end of the short sidewalk before she lost her nerve. She picked up her newspaper and waved to Georgia. "I miss seeing you," she called. "I'm sorry we couldn't make tea work today. We really need to figure out a time to get together."

Georgia gave her a thumbs-up and hollered back. "I'm working on it."

As Midge started back toward the porch, the burden of Lang's affair weighed her down, making every step akin to plodding through marsh mud. She stopped in her tracks. She lacked the guts to break the news to Georgia, but there was nothing preventing her from confiding in someone else. Lula would know how to handle the situation. She tossed the newspaper on her porch and strode across the yard.

She found Lula on her hands and knees weeding in her garden. "Morning," Midge said. "Do you have time for a cup of coffee? I have something I need to talk to you about."

"Can we talk while I work?" Lula said without looking up. "Brooke is flying in tomorrow and there's still so much to do."

"I would prefer to see your face when we talk, Lula, not your fanny. This is important. It's about Georgia."

Lula sat back on her haunches and adjusted her sun hat. "Is it so urgent it can't wait?"

Midge was horrified when her lip began to quiver. "I can't keep it to myself anymore. I should have told you two weeks ago."

"Aw, honey. It can't be all that bad." Lula held out her hand and Midge helped her to her feet. "Let's go inside, and I'll put on a fresh pot of coffee."

They walked arm in arm to the house and made small talk about Brooke's visit while the coffee brewed. But once they were sitting across from one another at the table, Midge described her encounter with Lang at the seedy hotel on the north side of town, explaining she'd been there to work up a contract with her out-of-town clients.

"And you're sure this man was Lang?" Lula asked when Midge had finished talking.

"Yes, of course, Lula. We've been neighbors for twenty-six years. I'm sure it was Lang. We even acknowledged one another. He introduced the woman to me as Mrs. Jones."

Lula tilted her head to the side, her eyebrows merging with her hairline. "Mrs. Jones?"

"Original, right? For a brilliant surgeon, the man is slow to think on his feet."

"I can't say I'm surprised." Lula set down her mug. "Langdon Murdaugh is too handsome for his own good. I suspected he was a womanizer. I've felt his eyes on my backside a time or two."

"Really?" Midge doubted if this was true. Lula was a lot of things, but a sex object wasn't one of them. "He's never been anything but a gentleman to me."

"He's no gentleman. He's a snake in the grass. I'm surprised he hasn't called you or shown up on your doorstep begging you not to tell Georgia that you caught him red-handed with his lover. Men are not to be trusted. With the exception of Phillip, of course."

There was something to be said for trust and security, but Midge questioned how much excitement existed in a marriage to a do-gooder like Phillip.

Lula's eyes dropped to Midge's hand. "Why aren't you wearing your engagement ring?"

Midge placed her right hand over her left to cover her

bare ring finger. "We're taking a break. Marriage is a big step. I want to get it right this time around."

Lula leaned across the table toward Midge. "Listen to me, honey. Marriage is a journey filled with peaks and valleys and tidal waves. If you're having problems now, tying the knot will only make them worse down the road."

"I've been married before, Lula. I understand all too well how vile men can be."

"That was so long ago it hardly counts," Lula said, dismissing her five-year marriage.

All Midge's nerve endings stood on end. "Like hell it doesn't. Taylor was my childhood sweetheart. I planned to grow old with him, but he abandoned me at the first sign of trouble."

"Please! Lower your voice. I have a headache." Lula lifted her hand to her forehead, her face pinched in pain.

Midge studied her friend. Lula's skin was one shade lighter than the gray roots sprouting along her part. And it wasn't just her physical appearance. She seemed off in other ways as well. "Are you okay?"

"I keep getting these stabbing pains. Nothing a little aspirin won't cure." She grabbed the bottle of Bayer on the table in front of her and shook out two pills into her hand. "This party is causing me too much stress. I don't know what I was thinking about when I decided to have it. In my younger days, I could throw a party together at the drop of a hat."

"You should call it off if it's too much for you. Everyone would understand."

"Nah… I'll be fine." She popped the aspirin into her mouth and swallowed them down with a sip of coffee. "Now." She screwed the lid back on the Bayer bottle. "What were we talking about? Right. Georgia. Tell me again why you haven't told her about Lang's affair."

Tell me again? Midge had never told her the first time. "Because I don't want to be the one who ruins her life."

"So you're just going to sit by while he makes a fool of her instead?"

Midge gestured at the phone on the wall behind Lula. "Go ahead and call her if you think it's so easy."

"Fine." Lula rose from her chair and lifted the receiver. She punched in four numbers and then paused for thirty seconds before hanging up. She sat back down.

"I've been carrying this information around with me for two weeks. I can't sleep. I can't eat. I've neglected my job. I know I have to tell her. But I don't know how."

"So you decided to drag me into it. You can't come in here and dump this in my lap when I'm already losing sleep over this party. My daughter is arriving tomorrow. I haven't seen her in ages. I'd like to enjoy her company without having to concern myself with Georgia's love life."

Midge jumped to her feet. "Georgia's love life? This is not middle school, Lula. Our best friend's marriage is in trouble. What is wrong with you? I'm not dumping this in your lap. I came to you for advice on how to handle the situation. But never mind. I'll figure it out myself."

She moved for the door, but Lula stood to block her path. "I'm sorry, honey. You're right. I was out of line. I haven't been myself lately. Will you forgive me?"

Midge's angry expression softened into a smile. Lula infuriated her at times, but she could never stay mad at her for long. She meant well despite her brusque delivery. "I forgive you. It was insensitive of me to drag you into this with all you have going on. Don't worry. I'll think of something to tell Georgia."

"Now that you've dragged me into it, I might as well help you figure it out." She pointed at Midge's empty chair. "Sit. I'll get us some more coffee." She topped off their coffee and sat down across from her. "Now that I think about it, maybe we shouldn't be in such a rush to tell her."

"But—"

Lula gripped Midge's wrist. "Hear me out before you argue. I ran into Georgia yesterday when I was dropping some flowers off at Tasty. Her face lit up like a firecracker when she told me she was hopeful that Lang would come to the party with her. He's gotta be sweating it out waiting for you to drop your bomb. What if he's reconsidering his extramarital activities? What if this close encounter with divorce has made him realize he still loves Georgia?"

"I wouldn't hold my breath. Not after what I witnessed at that hotel."

"Perhaps not," Lula said. "But you've waited this long. Why not wait a few more days, until after the holiday?"

"What if they do get back together? Are we just supposed to forget about his fling with Mrs. Jones?" As much as she dreaded telling Georgia about her husband's affair, carrying the knowledge of Lang's infidelity to her grave sounded even less appealing. "I'd be willing to bet there have been other women. Don't you think Georgia deserves to know the truth?" Midge buried her face in her hands. "This is an impossible situation. I don't think I can bear another week of this agony."

CHAPTER TWELVE
GEORGIA

GEORGIA WAS UNPACKING groceries when she caught a glimpse of Lula through her window, clipping away at the wide assortment of colorful blooms in her garden. The more she cut, the more her flowers seemed to grow. Her bouquets were a big hit at Tasty. They now had a waiting list of customers requesting arrangements for certain dates.

She hadn't lied to Lula when she told her she hoped Langdon would accompany her to the party on the Fourth. She just hadn't gotten the nerve up to ask him yet. But she had the afternoon free and she planned to butter him up by cooking his favorite dinner. She had it all figured out. The aroma of fresh marinara, made from summer tomatoes and basil, wafting through the house would grab his attention when he came through the door around five. He would go upstairs to change out of his scrubs or sweaty tennis clothes and shower. She would have a scotch on the rocks waiting for him when he came back downstairs. One drink would lead to another, which would lead to a candlelit dinner followed by romance. She felt a stirring in her nether regions. It had been too long.

While the marinara simmered, she straightened the house, set the table on the patio, and put on white linen slacks and her favorite silk blouse, the color of slate that made her eyes look more blue than gray. She heard the creak of the front door a few minutes past five. Right on schedule. She listened intently for the moans of delight once he got a whiff of his favorite dinner, but all she heard was the squeak of his tennis shoes on the hardwood floors.

Langdon entered the kitchen, set his wallet and phone down on the island, and went to the sink for a glass of water. "What smells so good?"

"You don't recognize the aroma? Has it been that long since I made your favorite dinner?"

He peeked in the oven. "Right, chicken parmesan. It's been awhile." He gulped down half the glass of water and wiped his lips with the back of his hand. "I hope you didn't go to any trouble for me. I don't have time for dinner. I'm headed back to the hospital to check on a patient."

"Seriously?" Georgia asked, unable to hide her disappointment. "I was hoping we could spend some time together. I can't remember the last time we had a real conversation."

"I remember it well. It was before you went out and found yourself a job."

Georgia planted her fists on her hips. "You're being absurd if you're suggesting my job is the reason we never spend time together anymore. We haven't spent any quality time with one another in years. Years, Langdon. Not just the weeks since I started working at Tasty. You're never here. You can't deny that."

"You're right. I can't deny that." He drained the rest of his water and refilled his glass. "I'm sorry about dinner, Georgie. But you should've asked. You know how busy I am."

"Busy? I know you're busy doing a lot of extracurricular activities outside of the hospital that don't include me." Turning away from him to hide her tears, she went to the oven and removed the casserole dish. "I can keep dinner warm, if you want to go check on your patients and come back."

He set the glass down in the sink. "You better go ahead and eat without me. I'll probably be awhile." He glanced at the Rolex Submariner she'd given him for their twenty-fifth wedding anniversary. She'd scrimped on her household expenses for a year to be able to afford it. "In fact, I'd better get going." He exited the room, leaving behind a trail of green granules.

"Take off those shoes," she called after him. "You're tracking your tennis court all over my house."

That went well, she thought to herself as she turned off the oven and sank down to the nearest stool at the island. She should've texted him about dinner. He led a busy life. His job didn't end when he left the operating room. He was responsible for his patients' recovery as well. They counted on him to adjust their meds, order any necessary tests, and release them from the hospital when they were well enough to go home. She shouldn't expect him to drop everything because she wanted to have a discussion about their plans for the Fourth of July.

Langdon's phone vibrated on the counter. Georgia glanced at the screen and saw that the text was from a Tina Olson. She couldn't recall ever having met a Tina Olson. She picked up the phone and read the text: "What's taking you so long? I rented our normal room." She clicked on the text bubble, but the phone prevented her from reading the rest of the message without Langdon's password. This Tina Olson person was waiting for him in their normal room. A hotel room, obviously. Normal implying they rented it on a routine basis. Her body broke out in a cold sweat and she suddenly found it difficult to breathe. Her husband was having an affair. Bastard.

As she held the phone in her hand, an image of a woman with sharp pointy features popped onto the screen signaling an incoming call. Tina's red-painted lips were pursed in a seductive kiss meant for the photographer. Langford.

Georgia picked up the call, saying "Georgia Murdaugh, here. Who may I tell my husband is calling?"

She heard a click and the line went dead. She held the phone in a death grip, imagining her fingers wrapped around her husband's neck instead of the phone. The sound of the shower running overhead jolted her out of her trance. Wonder what other secrets he's been keeping. She took the phone across the hall to the library and sat down in the leather chair behind the desk they shared. Hers were the drawers on the right, and his the ones on the left. She paid all the household bills, including the credit cards. She always studied the monthly statements to make certain all the charges were legitimate. To her best recollection, she'd never come across anything suspicious.

She opened his bottom drawer and thumbed through the hanging files until she came to one that wasn't labeled. She removed the file and flipped through past statements from an American Express account with a number she didn't recognize. The statements went back four years and consisted of charges from hotels, restaurants, and a host of online lingerie sites.

Her husband had played her like a fool. Langdon was so certain of her love for him, he hadn't bothered to lock the drawer that contained the evidence of his affair. Four years was a long time. Had there been more than one mistress?

She heard the pounding of feet on the stairs followed a minute later by her husband calling her name.

"I'm in here," she called back.

He appeared in the doorway. "Have you seen my phone?"

"You mean this?" She tossed the phone across the room to him. "Tee-na texted while you were in the shower. She's waiting for you in your 'normal' room." She used air quotes for emphasis. "I take it she isn't one of your nurses. Maybe she is one of your nurses. It's just that you've always been so critical of doctors who get involved with their nurses. Silly me for blabbering on without giving you a chance to explain. I'm not sure how I'm supposed to behave or what I should say. Discovering my husband is having an affair is a new experience for me. Is she one of your nurses, Langdon?"

He hung his head. "She doesn't work for me. She works for another doctor in a different department."

"Oh. I see. That makes it okay, then." Georgia pushed back from the desk and went to the minibar in the corner. She removed two lowball glasses from the shelf, poured a finger of scotch in each, and handed one of the glasses to Langdon. "I gather Tee-na is married; otherwise, you'd be meeting for sex at her home instead of a hotel."

He downed the scotch in one gulp. "She's married."

"Her husband and I have something in common, then. I'd like to meet Mr. Olson some time. We can talk about what naive fools we've been for trusting our spouses to be faithful to our marriages." She took a sip of the scotch, and then drained the glass.

"Calm down, Georgie. If you'll give me a chance to explain."

"You don't have time for lengthy explanations. You're already late for your hotel rendezvous with Tee-na, the other doctor's nurse."

Langdon hung his head. "I'm sorry, sweetheart. I never meant to hurt you. This has nothing to do with you, with us, or our marriage. This is all on me. I'm having a midlife crisis, however cliché that may sound."

She gestured at the file lying open on the desk. "Your credit card statements go back four years. That's some midlife crisis. Or was it a bunch of mini midlife crises strung together? Tell me, Langdon. How many nurses have you slept with in the past four years, since you opened your own American Express account to hide your secret charges—your hotel rooms, romantic dinners, and sexy lingerie?"

He went to the bar and refilled his glass with ice and scotch. He turned back around to face her. "That's the thing, Georgie. None of these women meant anything to me. Not like you mean to me. But somewhere along the road, I lost you. To the boys. To your volunteer commitments. I desperately needed you and you weren't here for me."

"Are you saying it's my fault you cheated on me?"

He lifted one shoulder in a nonchalant shrug. "I guess maybe I am."

"That is so unfair." She slammed her empty glass down on the desk. "I've always put your needs first. Look at me. I'm the dutiful doctor's wife who has fulfilled her husband's every wish and command for the past three decades." When he refused to meet her eyes, she screamed, "Look at me, damn it! I'm your wife. I've been right here all along, cooking and cleaning and raising your children while you've been off having sex with other women." She pointed at the door. "I want you to leave."

He had the gall to look surprised. "You don't mean that."

"Like hell I don't." Turning her back on him, she moved to the window.

She felt his footsteps on the carpet, and then his presence behind her. He wrapped his arms around her and pressed his lips against her neck. "I'm not leaving, Georgie. I won't give up on our marriage. I love you too much. Those other women aren't important. It was all about the sex. I've tried to stop, but I can't. I think maybe I should see a therapist. Please don't abandon me now. Not when I need you the most."

Her chin quivered and tears welled in her eyes. When racking sobs overtook her body, she gave into them and leaned back against him for support. Marriage was a journey with lots of ups and downs. After more than three decades, theirs seemed more like a voyage over calm oceans and stormy seas. How could she turn her back on him if he truly had a problem? Addiction came in many forms, not just alcohol and drugs. They would need counseling, individually for his addiction and together for the problems in their marriage. And he would have to prove his commitment to her and to their future. She hoped their marriage had a strong enough foundation to get them through this. She owed it to him and to their children to at least try.

CHAPTER THIRTEEN

LULA

L ULA PLOPPED DOWN in the nearest vacant seat in the arrival lounge at the Charleston International Airport and fell fast asleep sitting up. The loud speaker announcing the arrival of her daughter's American Airlines flight from San Francisco via Charlotte startled her awake a few minutes later. She shook her head to clear the fuzzy feeling that had inhabited her brain the past few weeks. She hadn't felt like herself in the three weeks since Brooke had called to say she was coming for a visit and Lula had made the foolhardy decision to throw a party. She was too old to plan parties on a whim. She was too old for a lot of things, or so it seemed her body was warning her. In her younger days, she'd been able to multitask like nobody's business. Now, on the Wednesday before the Fourth, with only six days to go until the party, she wished she could cancel the whole thing and spend a quiet holiday with just her family. So many details whirling around in her mind like a funnel cloud gave her one great big headache. To rent a tent or not was the source of her angst today.

"I recommend all my clients rent tents for outdoor events this time of year," Heidi had said to her on the phone that morning.

"Have you seen the weather forecast? There's only a twenty percent chance of afternoon thunderstorms," Lula had argued.

"I haven't see your house, Lula. Can you fit a hundred people inside if it rains?"

"Let me worry about the weather. I'm confident it's not going to rain."

Heidi sighed. "I think you're making a big mistake. At least look into it."

Lula had taken her advice and called Melissa, the event-planning specialist she'd been working with at the rental company. As she suspected, the cost of renting a tent the size she needed was way over her budget. The weather forecast was now added to her list of obsessions.

Everything else for the party was falling into place. She'd spent several days at the beach cottage during the past week, changing linens and stocking the pantry and refreshing the annuals in the planters stationed around the property. Her family—minus Lizbet who had a hectic work schedule—would head to the beach on Friday, which would give Lula several days before the party to tie up loose ends. Her plan was to stay at the beach until the following Sunday when Brooke returned to California. The rentals—tables, cloths, and chairs—were scheduled for delivery on Monday, the day before the party. Heidi's crew of bartenders and servers would arrive no later than three on Tuesday. Which, for Lula, cut, a little too close to the five o'clock start time, but Heidi assured her they would have ample time to set everything up. She'd confirmed and reconfirmed with the band and the man she'd hired for the fireworks display. Nothing could possibly go wrong.

Locating the nearest women's restroom, Lula splashed water on her face and dabbed on some lipstick. For some reason, the pinkish coral color she'd worn for years suddenly seemed all wrong, and she wiped it off with a paper towel. She returned to the arrival lounge, and waited for her daughter to emerge from the B Concourse. When a stream of travelers approached, she searched the crowd for Brooke. A stunning young woman with wide-set hazel eyes and a boyish hairdo stopped in front of her. On closer inspection she realized this exotic creature was her daughter.

"Mom! I've missed you so much." She threw herself into Lula's arms.

"Brooke? What on earth happened to your hair?" She held her daughter at arm's length. "Oh god! Please tell me you don't have cancer."

"Of course I don't have cancer, Mom. Geez." Brooke ran her hand over her bleached blonde crop of hair. "I take it you don't like it?"

Lula studied her daughter closely. Missing were the eyeliner, blush, and lipstick Brooke had worn every waking hour of every day since Lula had agreed to let her try makeup on her fourteenth birthday. Missing were the long, sandy, wavy locks that Brooke, as a child, had insisted Lula brush one hundred times every night at bedtime. The girl who, as a teenager, fussed for hours with her hair, finding the right ribbon for her ponytail or ironing it straight as a board with a flatiron— that girl had transformed into a young woman Lula barely recognized. Something told her this change had everything to do with her daughter's personal growth and little to do with her makeup and hairstyle.

Lula cupped her daughter's chin, turning her head one way and then another. "It's gonna take some getting used to, but I like it. It's sassy, like you." She kissed her fingertips and touched them to Brooke's cheek. "Welcome home, darling. Shall we go claim your luggage."

"I already have my bags. I carried them on the plane with me."

Lula eyed her daughter's rolling suitcase. "You packed for ten days in that?"

"I have this bag as well." She tugged at the strap of the small duffel slung over her shoulder. "I'm trying to save money. I didn't want to pay to check my bags."

"Since when do the airlines charge for checked luggage?"

Brooke laughed. "You really should get out more, Mom."

"I can't argue with that." They walked toward the exit. "Are you hungry? I made a tub of your favorite pimento cheese."

Brooke licked her lips. "Yummy. I've been craving your pimento cheese."

She hooked her arm through Brooke's. "I'm glad to hear your taste buds haven't changed."

"Oh they have. I don't eat beef anymore. Only chicken and seafood." Brooke flashed Lula a smile she remembered, one that hinted at mischief but was loving just the same. "And cheese. I'll never give up cheese."

Lula cast frequent glances at her daughter on the twenty-minute drive home, trying but failing to get used to her new look. She longed for the little girl with the braided pigtails, the child whose angelic face lit up when Lula entered the room.

But that child was gone, and in her place was a stranger. She'd been harboring hope that Brooke would one day move back to Charleston or somewhere on the East Coast. Seeing this confident creature beside her, she realized that wasn't likely to happen. Brooke had set out into the world and made a life for herself on the other side of the country. A life that didn't include Lula. Her baby girl was lost to her forever.

*

Brooke excused herself after lunch and went upstairs to unpack and rest. She didn't come back down until nearly five o'clock. Lula kept herself busy at the kitchen table, going over her to-do list and counting and recounting the RSVPs for the party. When Lizbet had come over to help with the invitations, she'd cautioned Lula against inviting so many people. "You're throwing the party on such short notice, I'm sure most of these people already have plans."

"I don't expect them to come," Lula had said. "But I'll get brownie points for including them."

Lizbet had rolled her eyes. "And you won't have to pay the caterer for their share."

As it turned out, she received way more acceptances than regrets, and was glad about it. She hadn't seen some of these friends in years. The party couldn't help but be a success with old friends, delicious food, live entertainment, and free-flowing alcoholic beverages. Only rain could put a damper on their good time. Maybe she should rent that tent after all. She went to the wall phone, punched in the now-familiar number for the party rental place, and asked to speak to Melissa.

"May I say who's calling?" the receptionist asked.

"Lula Horne."

She watched the clock tick off five minutes while she waited. Melissa sounded exasperated when she finally came on the line. "How can I help you, Mrs. Horne?"

"I'm calling back about the tent," Lula said. "How much would it cost if I rented two smaller ones instead of that giant circus thing?"

Melissa released an audible sigh. "Let me check our availability and work up the pricing. I'll call you back in a few minutes."

She waited all afternoon, but Melissa never called. Lula took that as a sign from above that a tent was unnecessary.

Brooke had just come downstairs from her nap when Phillip arrived home around five thirty. He embraced his daughter in a bear hug and then held her at arm's length. "You changed your hair. It looks nice."

Humph. Her husband wasn't one to criticize or praise. Nice was the only adjective in his vocabulary. She could be wearing a cow patty on her head and he would say it looked nice. He didn't mention Brooke's attire. She'd changed into a sheer sundress that barely covered her breasts. Did he think the black bikini top she wore underneath it instead of a bra looked nice too?

"I made a fresh pitcher of tea." Lula gestured at the tray on the counter that held a pitcher of sweet tea and three tall glasses. "Why don't we go sit a bit on the porch?"

They had just gotten settled when Lizbet's Honda pulled up to the curve. She hopped out of the car, removed two shopping bags from the trunk, and started up the sidewalk. "Heidi sent dinner," she called to them, holding up the bags.

"Chicken enchiladas, a fruit salad, and blonde brownies for dessert."

"That was kind of her. Never mind that I spent the morning making Brooke's favorite." Lula patted her daughter's knee beneath the flimsy fabric of her dress. "Although I guess lasagna is no longer your favorite since you gave up red meat."

Lizbet smiled at her sister. "Hi, you. Let me put these inside," she said, struggling to open the door with her hands full. "I'll be right back."

Lula followed Lizbet to the kitchen. "You knew about her hair, didn't you? Why didn't you tell me?"

Lizbet set the bags on the counter. "How did you not know about it?"

"I haven't seen her in years, remember? How would I have known about it? She certainly didn't call me up and tell me she'd cut off all her hair."

"Social media, maybe? Facebook. Instagram. Snapchat."

"You know I don't do social media." Lula ran her hand down Lizbet's mahogany mane. "Her hair was so pretty, lighter in color than yours but with the same thick waves."

Lizbet brushed Lula's hand away. "I think her hairstyle fits her artsy personality." She rolled an elastic band off her wrist and gathered her hair into a messy ponytail. "I don't know why you're making a big deal about it, anyway. She got her hair cut, not a sex change."

The creases in her forehead deepened. "Artsy? Since when did Brooke become artsy?"

Lizbet narrowed her eyes at Lula. "She's a graphics designer. Of course she's artsy. Where have you been?"

"I never thought of it that way." Lula removed the containers from the shopping bags and lifted the casserole's lid. "This looks delicious. I hope you're planning to stay for dinner."

"Sorry, but I can't. Not tonight."

"But you promised." She fastened the lid back onto the disposable casserole dish. "I wanted us to have a family dinner to properly welcome your sister home."

"I'm pretty sure I never promised I'd eat dinner with you tonight. I can only stay for a minute. I need to get organized before the weekend." Lizbet left the room putting an end to the discussion.

Lula trailed her down the hall and onto the porch.

Lizbet nudged Brooke over and sat down next to her on the bench swing. "You look good. California agrees with you. How's work?"

Brooke smiled. "Going well! I just got a promotion."

Lula gasped. "That's great! Why didn't you tell me?"

"Because it wasn't a done deal until yesterday," Brooke said.

"I'm proud of you, kiddo," Phillip said. "Your hard work is paying off."

"How about you?" Brooke elbowed her sister. "I hear you really like your new job."

Lizbet shrugged. "It's fine for now. We're crazy busy, which is good for me. I really need the money. But it also means I have to work straight through the Fourth."

Lula assumed Lizbet would have the day off to spend with her family, but she never thought to ask. "You mean to tell me, Heidi's making you work your own party?"

Lizbet stiffened. "It's not my party, Mom. It's yours. And Heidi isn't making me work. She's paying me to work. She's counting on me to serve dinner. After everything is cleaned up, I'll join the party for fireworks."

"I was counting on you to spend the night," Lula said.

Lizbet hesitated. "Let me look at the schedule. I might actually be able to spend two nights if we don't have any events planned for the fifth."

Brooke lay her head on Lizbet's shoulder. "Oh, please! Will you try? A friend of mine might be coming in from out of town. We can hang out."

Lula's hand flew to her chest. Her daughter had a boyfriend after all. "That's so exciting, honey. Does your friend have a name?" With any luck, her boyfriend would ask Phillip for her hand in marriage. The timing was perfect. They would announce her engagement at the party.

"Sawyer Glover," Brooke said.

"Sawyer Glover. That's a lovely name." Lula beamed. "When are you expecting Sawyer Glover to arrive?"

"I'm not sure yet," Brooke said. "I'll let you know when we figure out our plans."

Lula wanted to press her for more details—birthplace, job title, annual salary, family net worth—but sensing Brooke would say no more, she decided it best to keep her mouth shut. At least for now.

CHAPTER FOURTEEN
LIZBET

LIZBET NAVIGATED THE busy narrow streets to her apartment. She considered going for groceries, but she didn't want to waste valuable time crossing town to the Harris Teeter. She'd been neglecting her chores. She was down to her last pair of underwear, and her apartment was a wreck, since neither of her roommates helped out with the housework. To save money she'd lived at home during her first two years at the College of Charleston. The summer before her junior year, her father sat her down for a talk. "It's time you move out of the house. You're not getting the full college experience by living at home with your mother and me. I'm not suggesting you live in a dorm. Get an apartment with some of your friends." He'd insisted on paying the bills, but she'd gotten a job anyway to earn her spending money.

Two years later she still lived with her same roommates from college in the same second-floor apartment of a run-down old home on Society Street. She rarely saw her room-mates anymore, but she heard them most nights making loud sexual noises with their boyfriends in their bedrooms. The thought of moving into her own apartment appealed to her, but she'd never be able to afford living alone in downtown Charleston on her salary. She was beginning to realize she'd never be able to afford much of anything on her salary, aside from the basics. Brooke had worked several years before getting her first promotion. Lizbet had only just graduated from college. She'd learned a lot about managing her money in the six weeks since her father had stopped her allowance. Combined, the rent, electrical, cell phone, and car insurance all added up to zero money in her bank account. Lucky for her, her father had agreed to keep her on his health insurance plan. "At least until you find a more permanent job that offers benefits."

There were no promotions on the horizon for Lizbet. There were no positions at Tasty Provisions to be promoted to. She'd been so enamored with Heidi, she hadn't bothered to apply for jobs within her field of study—hospitality and tourism management. But, thanks to Heidi, she'd begun a love affair with food. She couldn't imagine working in any other industry. Instead of being deterred by the demands of a restaurant career, she thrived in her work with a team committed to a common goal—pleasing clients with unique and flavorful food. She enjoyed experimenting with new recipes, and was developing a talent for presentation. She had no choice but to make the best of the situation until she could save enough money for culinary school.

Lizbet gathered up her dirty clothes, stuffed them in her hamper, and carried it down the hall to the laundry room. She started a load of whites, retrieved her bucket of cleaning supplies, and set off to work.

She contemplated her future while cleaning her bedroom and all the common areas, including the bathroom, she shared with her roommates. She considered moving back in with her parents to save money on rent, but dismissed the idea right away. How could she live with her mother when she could barely stand to be in the same room with her for longer than a few minutes? A lump developed in the back of her throat. She didn't want to feel such... such what? Irritation and frustration? Did these emotions stem from anger? Deep down, she loved her mother. Lula hadn't always been so demanding. It was only in the past couple of years she'd grown more set in her ways. Unyielding in her opinions. Refusing to listen to anyone else's advice. Never mind that she was wrong more often than not.

When Lizbet finished cleaning, she returned the bucket to the laundry closet, moved her whites to the dryer, and started a load of darks. She went to the kitchen and poured herself a glass of Pinot Grigio and a bowl of Frosted Flakes. She imagined her family gathered around the kitchen table, chatting and laughing and devouring Heidi's delicious chicken enchilada casserole while she ate her cereal alone in her empty apartment. What was wrong with her? She'd once been so easy to please, a happy-go-lucky child who got along with everyone. Now she found fault with her mother, once the center of her universe, and her roommates who she'd once thought of as her best friends.

She finished her cereal, slurped the milk from the bowl, and placed it inside the dishwasher. Pouring the rest of the wine into her glass, she took it out onto the porch. Despite the thick humid air, the streets below teemed with students milling about, coming and going from their evening summer school classes or going out for a quick bite to eat before hitting the library. She spotted a couple, holding hands, walking toward her. She didn't recognize either of the girls, but something about the one on the left seemed oddly familiar. She waved down at them as they passed the house.

Holy cow! Lizbet fell back against the porch railing. The girl on the left with the super-short haircut and ankle-length skirt looked familiar because she reminded her of Brooke. Could her sister possibly be gay? Her mind reeled as the puzzle pieces fell into place in rapid succession. Brooke, traveling across country to attend college. Her long periods of absence. Her cropped hair and funky clothing. The social media posts with Brooke and her friends. All of them girls. Kissing each other's cheeks, hugging one another tight. So close, too familiar. Why had she never noticed it before? Everything suddenly made perfect sense. Brooke had chosen a college on the opposite side of the country because she had no other choice. In order to live her life the way she wanted to, the way she needed to, she had to get as far away as possible from Lula.

A friend of mine might be coming in from out of town. We can hang out. Lizbet had assumed the friend Brooke was talking about was her boyfriend. She didn't know anyone with the name Sawyer, boy or girl. She'd thought it sounded masculine, but plenty of parents gave their daughters a boy's name.

Lizbet set her wine glass on the railing and hurried inside for her phone. Accessing her Facebook app, she searched for Sawyer Glover. Facebook listed four matches, three of them female. When she clicked on the top listing, the profile for a stunning young brunette filled her screen. In her profile photo, Brooke was standing beside the brunette with her arm wrapped possessively around Sawyer.

Lizbet had heard the wedding chimes playing in her mother's head when Brooke mentioned a friend coming to visit. Lula was going to birth a baby calf when she found out that Sawyer, her future son-in-law and father of her grandchildren, wasn't a son and would never be a father, that Sawyer was actually her daughter's girlfriend—that her beloved daughter, her princess, was a lesbian.

CHAPTER FIFTEEN
LULA

LULA SPENT A quiet weekend with Brooke and Phillip at the cottage on Sullivan's Island. They ate seafood for every meal and slept long hours at night, but mostly they talked, making up for the years they'd been apart. They discussed world affairs, current events, and politics. Lula and Phillip discovered that the girl who'd left for college seven years ago, with Dave Matthews and Widespread Panic on her playlists and her dream of saving the world intact, had grown into an intelligent young woman. Brooke had developed an appreciation for classical music and a somewhat cynical view of the world. Lula agreed with her on most counts. It was hard to have faith in the future of a country with a broken political system.

Theirs was a rustic cottage with wraparound porches, spacious rooms, and few modern conveniences. On Saturday and Sunday, while Phillip dozed in the hammock on the porch, mother and daughter spent much of the day soaking up the sun on the beach—splashing in the waves, reading their summer romance novels, and sharing their lives with one another.

It was lunchtime on Sunday and they were eating ham and cheese sandwiches and sipping lemonade when Lula disclosed that she was considering starting her own flower business. "I've been supplying flowers to Tasty Provisions, the gourmet market where Lizbet works. I'm proud to say my bouquets have become a hot commodity."

"That's exciting, Mom. Your business will do well. You obviously have a green thumb. Your garden is certainly thriving."

While they finished their picnic, Brooke spoke of her friends in San Francisco and the apartment she rented in the Marina District. When she failed to mention her boyfriend, Lula pressed her. "Can you tell me a little more about Sawyer?"

Brooke stared for a long time at the waves as they crashed against the surf, her silence giving Lula the impression her daughter was preparing to open up about her love life. When she finally spoke, she said, "I'd rather wait and let you form your own opinion of Sawyer. But I need to borrow the car Tuesday morning to go to the airport. If that's okay with you."

Lula, though disappointed in Brooke's response to her question, didn't hesitate. "Of course you can use the car." She was prepared to drive to the airport herself if it meant she'd meet Sawyer sooner. "But why wait until Tuesday? Why doesn't Sawyer come tomorrow? That way we can all get acquainted before the party."

"Tuesday's soon enough." Brooke hauled herself out of her beach chair and stalked off across the sand down to the water.

Brooke's unwillingness to talk about her boyfriend struck

Lula as strange. Maybe they'd had a lover's spat. Or maybe they weren't in love after all.

Brooke kept to herself for the rest of the day, retreating to her bedroom right after dinner—and didn't emerge until Monday morning after Lula and Phillip had gone outside to work in the yard.

Lula cast frequent glances toward the porch where her daughter was rocking in the rocking chairs and fiddling with her phone. How could a rectangular device small enough to fit in the palm of one's hand hold someone's attention for so long? The three of them were gathered around the picnic table for lunch when it dawned on Lula that it wasn't a video game or social media that held her daughter's attention. It was the person on the other end of the phone. She watched Brooke nibbling at her salad, a fork gripped in her right hand while texting with her left. The signs were clear. The warm glow on her daughter's face and the gentle smile on her lips. The way she cocked her head back and laughed at the inside joke shared with the person on the phone. Her daughter was in love.

Lula's mind drifted off and she imagined the scene at her Fourth of July party. Her daughter and future son-in-law walking hand in hand up the boardwalk after the fireworks display on the beach, a diamond sparkling from the ring finger on her left hand. Phillip stepping up to the band's microphone to announce their daughter's engagement to their friends. Heidi's servers offering champagne to the guest.

First came love. Then came marriage. Then came Brooke pushing Lula's grandchildren in a baby carriage. Lula shook her head. Where were these strange thoughts coming from these days?

*

Lula panicked when the chance of afternoon thunderstorms on the Fourth of July increased to seventy percent, but when Tuesday dawned bright and beautiful, she laughed at herself for even considering a tent. As the day wore on, the temperatures soared and the air grew thick with humidity, making it difficult to breathe. Brooke left for the airport around eleven. With her party preparations complete and hours to go before the caterer arrived, feeling weak in the knees from the heat and yesterday's yard work, Lula retired to her room for a nap. She slipped off her clothes and stretched out in her underwear on the bed, letting the cool air from the window unit blow across her body. She dozed off and was awakened sometime later to the sound of gravel crunching in the driveway outside her window. Rolling out of bed, she tugged on her clothes and patted her hair into place before hurrying outside to meet her new son-in-law.

Careful, Lula, she cautioned herself. He hasn't proposed yet. A thought suddenly occurred to her. What if she didn't like him? What if he had terrible table manners and used bad grammar? What if he was a foreigner or a hog farmer? But the he who emerged from the passenger side of Lula's minivan was a she, a striking brunette wearing a gauzy sundress and dainty sandals.

Lula had never met a female named Sawyer. Then again, she'd never met anyone named Sawyer. With the force of a two-by-four smacking her in the head, Lula realized they'd never used pronouns when discussing Brooke's out-of-town guest.

The tall lovely came around the van and greeted Lula

with a warm embrace. "Thank you so much for having me, Mrs. Horne. I'm glad to finally meet you. I've heard so much about you."

"I wish I could say the same about you," Lula mumbled.

To avoid her gaze, Brooke busied herself with retrieving Sawyer's bag from the back of the minivan. When Brooke wheeled the suitcase past Lula, she grabbed her daughter by the arm. "Excuse us a moment," she said to Sawyer and pulled Brooke aside. "Did I miss something? I was under the impression you were picking your boyfriend up from the airport."

"I don't have a boyfriend, Mom. Sawyer is my girlfriend. We've been together for two years."

Lula felt the ground sway beneath her feet. "I don't understand." She slumped against the van. "Are you telling me you're gay?"

Sawyer couldn't help but overhear Lula's raised voice. "Are you kidding me, Brooke? Your parents don't know you're gay?"

"They do now," Brooke said, and snatched her arm away from Lula. She dragged Sawyer's suitcase through the gravel driveway to the sidewalk and up onto the porch. Sawyer followed her with Lula right behind them, staying close enough to eavesdrop on their heated exchange.

"I can't believe you ambushed me like that," Sawyer said. "That's seriously the most insensitive coming-out ever. They're your parents, Brooke. You should consider their feelings."

"They had to find out somehow." Brooke held the porch door open for Sawyer. "And I didn't know how else to tell them. They're not as understanding as your parents." Brooke and Sawyer crossed the sitting room to Brooke's bedroom and disappeared inside.

Lula was still staring at the closed bedroom door when Phillip came up from the beach a few minutes later. "Do you fancy a swim before the party? The ocean is calm today." He stopped in his tracks when he saw her serious face. "Is something wrong?"

She spun around, turning her back on her daughter's bedroom door. "Yes, Phillip. Something is very wrong. In a few hours, ninety people will arrive here for a party given in your daughter's honor. And she picks now to tell us she's gay."

His brow furrowed in confusion. "I don't understand."

"Turns out that Sawyer, the boyfriend Brooke went to pick up from the airport, is actually her girlfriend." Lula went into her bedroom and slammed the door.

Phillip entered the room behind her. "There must be some mistake. Maybe she's just going through a phase."

Lula sank down to the bed and fell back flat against the pillows. "Adolescents go through phases. Our daughter is a twenty-six-year-old woman who knows her own mind. It makes perfect sense when you think about it. Why she wanted to go to college in California, and why she never calls or comes home for a visit. She's been hiding this secret life from us. We've gotta do something, Phillip. We can't just let her go on living in sin." She sat bolt upright. "We'll stop paying her bills! That's what we'll do. That'll show her who's boss."

Phillip lowered himself to the edge of the bed beside her. "We're not Brooke's boss anymore, sweetheart. We haven't paid her bills since she graduated from college."

Lula stared at her husband, her face contorted in confusion. "Oh. Right." She lay back down again. "Get me a cold cloth and some Advil, will ya? I feel a migraine coming on."

He disappeared into the adjoining bathroom. When he

returned, he handed her two Advil and a three-ounce dispos-able cup of water. "We need to think long and hard about how we handle this situation," he said, positioning the cloth on her forehead. "If we make a wrong move, we could end up losing our daughter for good."

"I'm sorry, Phillip. But I refuse to accept that my daugh-ter is gay." She shooed her husband away from the bed. "Please leave. I need to pull myself together before the cater-ers arrive."

*

Lula never fell asleep, but she stayed in bed until she heard Phillip turn on the shower a few minutes before three. She popped three more Advil and stuffed her limbs into a pair of white slacks and a blue gingham blouse before going out to greet the Tasty Provisions van that had just pulled into the driveway. The burden of Brooke's revelation weighed on her like a ten-ton boulder. How would she ever face ninety guests?

She found Heidi on the lawn surveying the surround-ings, marveling at the large expanse of lawn leading down to white sandy dunes and the ocean beyond. "This is lovely, Lula. Where's the tent?"

"I decided not to rent a tent, Lula said. "It's a good thing too, since it's such a lovely day."

Heidi turned to face her. "The sun may be shining now, but it won't be for long. Have you seen the forecast?"

Lula tilted her head back and inspected the sky. "Why, there's not a cloud in sight. You can't trust the forecast. Those weather people get it wrong all the time."

"Not in this case." Heidi removed her phone from her

back pocket and jabbed a finger at the screen. "You can see the line of thunderstorms heading this way on the radar." She held the phone up for Lula to inspect the clusters of green, yellow, and red moving across the screen. "According to the hour by hour, the first storm will hit around five. What's your latest head count? We need to prepare for the worst and hope for the best."

"Ninety, give or take a few."

Heidi climbed the stairs to the porch. "You can count on a percentage of those not showing up due to the threat of bad weather." She walked around the side of the house, disappeared inside, and came out the backdoor. She clapped her hands at her crew standing idle beside their van. "Okay, listen up. We're gonna have to make do in the absence of a tent. We'll set up the food table along here,"—she waved a hand at the cedar shake back wall of the house—"close to the kitchen, and put the bar in the corner of the porch and the band around on the side. We'll scatter the tables on the lawn. It won't hurt anything if they get wet. If it rains, the guests can eat on the porch and inside. There's plenty of room. The house has great flow. Let's get busy."

Lula searched the group of workers for Lizbet. "Where's my daughter? Isn't she working the party?"

"She's cleaning up from our last event. She should be here within the hour." Heidi held the door open while her workers paraded into the house with trays of food. "We'll get your tables and chairs set up for you. I assume you want the arrangements in the center of the tables." She gestured at the small arrangements of blue hydrangeas lined up on the kitchen counter. "They're perfect for the occasion, by the way." Lula had cut the blooms early that morning, while

Phillip and Brooke were still asleep, before Brooke left to pick up her girlfriend from the airport.

"Thanks."

"If you'll show me the plates, cups, and napkins, we can get started."

"What're you talking about?" Lula asked with a dazed expression on her face. "I don't know anything about any plates, cups, and napkins."

"We talked about this at length, Lula. You insisted on purchasing the paper goods for the party. You were even going to pick out the plastic utensils. You said you wanted a patriotic theme, but you wanted to make sure they were the right shades of red and blue. Remember?"

Unshed tears stung Lula's eyes. "I must have forgotten. I can't seem to remember my own name these days. I'll run over to the grocery store in Mount Pleasant." She patted her pockets. "Where on earth did I put my keys?"

"Calm down, honey." Heidi squeezed Lula's arm. "There's no need for you to go anywhere. I'll get Lizbet to stop by the shop on her way here. We have plenty of supplies there."

Lula nodded, biting down on her quivering lip.

"You look like you could use something cold to drink. Why don't you have a seat in one of these rockers and I'll bring you some tea."

A tall glass of sweet tea was exactly what she needed. What she needed even more was the friendship that went along with it. A month had passed since she'd last gotten together with Georgia and Midge for tea. How would she ever be able to break the news to them that her daughter was a lesbian? She would keep it to herself for now. Until she came to terms with it. If she ever came to terms with it. Brooke will never get married or have children, she thought, and then realized in an instant that her daughter could, and probably would, do both. Same-sex marriages were legal in every state in the country. And a sperm donor was all a woman needed to have a baby. Lula rested her head against the back of the chair and closed her eyes. She didn't understand the world, didn't belong in this century. Lula Horne had been born a hundred years too late.

She was still sitting in the rocker with her eyes closed and her head rested against the back when Lizbet nudged her sometime later. Blinking her eyes open, she saw that the tables and chairs had been set up on the lawn, the band was tuning their instruments on the side porch, the fireworks man was sorting through his rockets near the path to the beach, and dark clouds were rolling in from the west. Through the screen door behind her, she spotted Phillip in the kitchen with Heidi and caught a glimpse of Brooke's closed bedroom door.

She rose to face Lizbet. "You knew, didn't you?"

"Knew what, Mom? Heidi said you were acting kinda strange. What on earth is going on?"

Lula watched her daughter's face carefully. Lizbet did a poor job of feigning her nonchalance. She already knew her sister was gay.

"Your sister came out of the closet today. And I don't mean the closet where she hangs her clothes."

CHAPTER SIXTEEN
MIDGE

DESPITE HER RESERVATIONS about going, Midge enjoyed a lovely outing with Bennett's parents on their boat. The evil sisters-in-law and their husbands were either not included or chose not to come along—Midge wasn't sure and didn't really care. Bennett appeared adept at handling the boat, and his father seemed eager to let him take the helm. And his mother appeared more relaxed than she'd been at dinner with the rest of her family in attendance.

Midge sat with Lucille at the stern chatting over the roar of the engine while Bennetts Senior and Junior navigated the sleek picnic boat across the harbor. Of the three Calhoun sons, Bennett most resembled their father, who was every bit as handsome and charming as Bennett. Both men shared the same amused expression, permanently etched in their faces, as though the world was their playground.

As she watched father and son, Midge finally gathered the nerve to ask a question she'd often wondered about. "If you don't mind me asking, I'm curious why you waited until your third son to name him after your husband."

"You can ask me anything you'd like, dear. My life is an open book." Lucille crossed her lean tanned legs and settled back against the bench seat. "We never considered naming our older two sons after their father, actually. The name didn't feel like the right fit until Bennett was born. He's our baby by five years. We've always felt closer to him than the older two." Lucille playfully wagged her finger at Midge. "But don't you dare tell anyone I admitted that, most especially my older two boys or their wives."

Midge smiled. "My lips are sealed."

As the morning wore on, Midge noticed that Bennett, like his mother, was more relaxed than normal. They ate an early lunch of shrimp salad and gourmet deviled eggs accompanied by an assortment of cheeses, fruits, and a bubbling glass of Prosecco.

When they finished eating and were heading out toward Folly Beach, Lucille confessed that she and her son didn't keep many secrets from one another. "Maybe because we're so much alike, we understand one another. I hope you don't mind, but he mentioned your relationship has hit a rough patch."

Midge tried to hide her surprise. She didn't know too many grown men who talked to their mothers about their girl-friends. "To be honest I learned some things about his previous marriages that concern me."

"I assume you learned these things from Virginia and Sara," Lucille said in a questioning tone. When Midge didn't respond, she continued, "My daughters-in-law don't mean any harm. They think of Bennett as their baby brother, and therefore feel the need to protect him against women who might not have his best interests at heart. And there have been a few, believe me."

This remark tempted Midge to mention the prenuptial agreement, but then thought better of it. Her concerns about marrying him had nothing to do with money. If she decided to go through with the wedding, she would insist they both signed prenuptial agreements.

"You shouldn't believe everything you hear about Bennett. His lifestyle makes him an easy target for the rumors. He's always trying to impress others. Because he chose not to practice law like his Calhoun ancestors, he feels the need to prove he's worthy of the family name. Truth be told, the law profession would have been a terrible choice for him. His attention deficit disorder prevented him from being a good student. He would never have survived law school. He has too much energy to sit still for long periods of time. I'm sure you've noticed."

Bennett had never admitted to having ADD, but when she thought about how restless he always seemed, it made sense. "Now that you mention it, I have noticed that about him."

"He's a good boy at heart." Lucille laughed when Midge raised an eyebrow. "I'm well aware of his age, but in many ways, he's still a little boy. A naughty one at times. I won't argue that. But sweet and attentive and loving at others. Did you know we share the same birthday—June fourteenth, Flag Day? I was blowing out my candles, thirty-two of them to be exact, when I felt the first labor pains."

Midge did the mental math. Lucille Calhoun looked damn good for eighty-one in her navy linen slacks and white cotton tee with her blonde hair pulled back at the nape of her neck.

She watched Bennett standing next to his father at the steering wheel, his face as bright as a kid's at Christmas as he played with all the gadgets on the boat's instrument panel. "His childlike nature is one of the things I like the most about him."

"I hope you can work through your differences," Lucille said. "Because my son really cares for you. More than he's cared for another woman in a long time. Perhaps ever."

Midge wondered if that was true, although she didn't see what reason Bennett's mother would have to lie with her son's happiness at stake. "I'm past my childbearing years, Lucille, not that I was able to bear children during my prime. I'm sure you'd rather see your son marry someone younger, someone who can give you a grandchild."

"You're a dear to worry about such a thing, but Bennett is too set in his ways to be a father. I already have eight grandchildren. I can hardly keep up with their birthdays as it is."

They sat in silence.

When the boat bounced through a series of waves, Lucille and Midge ducked their heads to avoid getting wet, but they got sprayed with salt water anyway. Laughing it off, Lucille disappeared inside the cabin and returned with a stack of towels.

After they'd dried themselves off, Lucille said, "The way I hear it, you and Bennett have big plans for the future. You'll give birth to your boutique agency, nurture it, and watch it grow. Your business will be the glue that holds your marriage together."

"I hadn't thought about it like that, but you're right. We'll have our business to focus on just as we would a child." Midge liked this woman's way of thinking. Bennett couldn't be all bad with a mother like Lucille. She'd explained away many of

Midge's concerns. Except one. "Virginia and Sara mentioned additional scandals involving Bennett, but they didn't elaborate. Are these incidents anything I need to worry about?"

"There are no other scandals that I'm aware of. I think Virginia and Sara were trying to scare you off. I hope they haven't succeeded."

"They gave me plenty to think about, for sure. Next time I won't listen to them. But you've alleviated all my fears. Thank you for being so candid. You've really helped me see Bennett in a different light."

"Anytime, my dear. I want what's best for my son. And you're the best thing that's come his way in a long time."

*

Midge and Lucille rode in silence for the next thirty minutes, enjoying the passing scenery and the wind whipping through their hair. They set anchor at the tip of Morris Island. Bennett stripped off his T-shirt and dove off the stern. Giggling, Midge slipped out of her cover-up and jumped in after him. They paddled and floated and splashed one another while his parents sipped Prosecco with their faces tilted toward the sun.

Midge never remembered a more pleasant Fourth of July. And she still had Lula's party to look forward to that night. Back at the dock, after Bennett and Midge had helped his parents spray down the boat and carry the picnic baskets to the car, Midge offered Lucille a parting hug and kiss on the cheek. Lucille whispered in her ear, "Don't be a stranger. I realize my son is complicated. Call or come see me anytime with your concerns."

With the party starting in less than an hour, to save on

time, Midge volunteered to share her shower with Bennett, a first for the shy woman who refused to make love with the light on. By the time they dressed—her in a white maxi dress cut way down in the back, and him in seersucker slacks and a white Vineyard Vines polo—and drove out to Sullivan's Island, the party was already in full swing.

Bennett circled the block two times in his BMW before he found a place to park in front of a neighbor's house down the street. They joined the other attendees on the lawn behind Lula's house. With the bluegrass band playing in the background, they sipped vodka martinis and chatted with old friends while casting frequent nervous glances at the darkening sky. When the caterer rang the bell for dinner a few minutes before six, they made their way up to the porch to stand in line for the buffet.

Bennett leaned down and whispered in her ear. "It's getting ready to storm like a son of a bitch. Where will all these people go?"

Midge reached behind her and hugged his neck. "Don't worry. There's plenty of room inside. I'm sure Lula has a rain plan." She searched the crowd. "And speaking of our hostess, I haven't seen her yet."

"I'm sure she's here somewhere. It's hard to find anyone in this mob scene. How many people did you say she invited?"

"I didn't say. I have no clue." As she continued to search for Lula, she spotted Georgia at the end of the line behind them. Lang, the cheating bastard, was standing next to her. He didn't deserve someone as wonderful as Georgia. Midge should have told Georgia the very afternoon she encountered Lang and Mrs. Jones at the airport hotel. Instead she'd let her fears and insecurities cloud her judgment. She'd been a coward. Not just in the situation with Georgia and Lang but also in her relationship with Bennett. But all that was going to change.

Lucille's confidence in her had restored her faith in herself. She would tell Georgia about Lang. Not tonight. She wouldn't ruin the party for everyone. But after they finished eating, she would find Georgia and invite her over for tea for tomorrow.

CHAPTER SEVENTEEN
GEORGIA

GEORGIA DESPERATELY WANTED to forgive her husband. Lang had broken it off with Tee-na the very same night she discovered his affair, and spent every free moment of the next six days showering her with attention. He brought her flowers and chocolates home from work. He took her out for romantic candlelit dinners. He even bought her the diamond tennis bracelet she'd fancied for so long. Most nights, with the air conditioning turned down low, they sat in front of the fire in the study sipping red wine until the wee hours of the morning, reminiscing about years past and searching for answers of where things went wrong in their marriage.

"Somewhere along the way, home became a chaotic and confusing place for me," Langdon had told Georgia that first night. "That's normal, of course, for a household with two active teenage boys. Richard and Martin were either racing off to their next event or their friends were camped out in our family room. They had a different crisis every day—a college application was due or the coach wasn't giving them enough playing time or some girl broke one of their hearts. You were always right there in the middle of the turmoil, feeding them and counseling them and letting them cry on your shoulder. I felt like an intruder. I got to the point where I didn't want to come home anymore. I needed somewhere to decompress after a long day in the operating room, so I turned to a nurse, young and unmarried, who was willing to share her quiet apartment with me."

Active teenage boys? Georgia was taken so off guard, she didn't know how to respond. Her boys were now in their late twenties, which meant her husband had been having extramarital affairs for more than ten years. Had she been too busy raising her sons to notice? She wondered about the who and the where and the how many, but deep down she didn't really want to know. Knowing her husband had slept with even one pretty young nurse with a tight body and unlined face crushed her self-esteem. She couldn't bear to think about there being more of them, perhaps even dozens. He claimed to be a sex addict. Did that mean he picked up women in bars for one-night stands? The threat that he may have contracted a sexually transmitted disease was something to think about before she jumped back in the sack with him. Fortunately, their sex life had been almost nonexistent for months.

Langdon readily agreed to accompany Georgia to Lula's Fourth of July party. He even seemed pleased with the prospect of seeing Phillip again after so long. "I always enjoy his dry sense of humor," Langdon said, despite the many times he'd called Lula's husband a complete bore.

They were among the first to arrive at the party. Georgia was surprised, and more than a little worried, not to find either

Lula or Phillip out on the lawn greeting their guests. "I hope nothing's wrong," she said to her husband.

"I'm sure they're busy taking care of last-minute details." Langdon surveyed the scene, his face lighting up when he caught sight of the bar set up on the porch. "Why don't I grab us some cocktails. I think the holiday calls for gin and tonics."

Georgia watched her husband stride across the lawn to the porch. He stepped in line behind a gorgeous blonde, placing his hand gently on her shoulder. Who did he think he was kidding? He wasn't interested in a gin and tonic. The attraction at the bar was Sharon Parker, who tilted back her coiffed head and presented a smooth cheek for him to kiss. Sharon had spent some time with the plastic surgeon—that much was obvious—and the results were stunning. She smiled at something Langdon said, but when his hand slid down her cobalt-blue silk sheath to her rear end, her expression turned to stone and she stepped away. She took her glass of white wine from the bartender and left the porch. Sharon scanned the crowd until she spotted Georgia and hurried over.

"I take it you saw that," she said.

Georgia cleared her throat. "I saw it." Dressed in white jeans and a red tunic, Georgia felt frumpy standing next to Sharon. Her body was every bit as toned as Sharon's, the result of untold hours spent in the yoga studio. She should show more of it off by wearing low necklines and tight-fitting clothing. She made a mental note to go shopping on her next day off.

"Don't take it personally, Georgia. Men assume they can hit on me because I'm divorced."

Georgia had always envied Sharon's direct personality. She envied a lot of things about her, actually. Sharon was an artist whose contemporary works had grown in popularity in recent years. She'd recently opened a gallery downtown that showcased not only her paintings but works from other local artists as well. She was doing a lot of things right if her radiant glow was any indication.

"What's it like being divorced?" Georgia responded, the words slipping out before she could stop herself. "I don't mean to pry, but you look so happy. You seem so put together. Do you ever get lonely?"

Sharon let out a loud laugh that attracted the attention of several people around them. She covered her mouth with her hand. "Sorry. The irony struck me as funny. The truth is, I'm not nearly as lonely now as I was when I was married. Sure, I crave companionship sometimes, but now I'm free to call up whoever I want to go for drinks or dinner or a movie. I don't have to worry about anyone else but myself.

"Some divorcées can't handle the freedom after raising their families and being at someone else's beck and call for so many years. They don't know what to do with themselves. But I found divorce liberating. Having a career has saved me. It helps to have a commitment that provides a challenge, occupies your time, and forces you to leave the house. Speaking of which, I heard you're working at Tasty Provisions. I saw Heidi in the kitchen on my way in. She's a character."

"She is that." Georgia glanced around, wondering why she hadn't seen Heidi. "I'm managing her showroom, nothing nearly as impressive as being an artist, but it offers all those things you mentioned. Don't you ever worry about growing old alone?"

"Sometimes. But I have no control over that. What's with all the questions? Are you thinking about divorcing Lang? I can't say I blame you, after what just happened up there."

Sharon dipped her head in the direction of the bar, where Langdon was chatting up yet another pretty woman. "Who's he talking to by the way? I don't think I know her."

"I have no idea, but she's not his type. He prefers them right out of college."

Sharon touched her arm. "I'm sorry, honey. Divorce is never easy."

The old Georgia, the Georgia of a week ago, would never have betrayed her husband by talking about their problems at home. But the new Georgia was beginning to understand she didn't owe anything to anyone but herself. "Was it hard on your children when you got divorced?"

"Ha. My boys were both in college at the time. They were so self-absorbed they hardly noticed we weren't together anymore." She tilted her head to the side. "Okay… so maybe it bothered them a little bit, especially around the holidays. They're all grown now with children and careers of their own. We all get along fine."

Georgia saw Langdon headed their way, a gin and tonic in each hand. "Thanks, Sharon, for talking to me. I don't even know you that well."

"I sometimes find it easier to talk to people who've been through similar situations as me, regardless of whether I'm close to them or not. They know just the right thing to say, because they've already walked in those shoes." Sharon leaned in and pressed her cheek to Georgia's. "Feel free to call me anytime."

*

Georgia was taking her first sip of the gin and tonic when Lizbet appeared in front of her and greeted Langford with a smile. Georgia knew that Lizbet and Brooke secretly referred to her husband as Dr. Dog. How ironic given the circumstances.

Lizbet pulled Georgia aside. "I hate to ask you, but is there any way you can help us in the kitchen for a minute?" Strands of hair had fallen loose from her ponytail and were plastered to her sweaty forehead. Her eyes darted back and forth between the crowd and the black clouds. "Heidi wants to serve dinner before the storm hits, which could be any minute based on the way the sky looks. We just need help preparing the trays and getting them on the table."

"I'd be happy to help but you need to take a deep breath." She squeezed Lizbet's arm. "Everything's gonna be just fine. The best parties I've attended have been interrupted by thunderstorms. You run along back inside and I'll be right there."

Once Lizbet was gone, Georgia turned back to Langford. "If you'll excuse me for a minute, I'm needed inside."

His expression grew dark. "What'd you mean you're needed inside? Is Lula having some sort of crisis?"

"I haven't even seen Lula. But Heidi needs me. I won't be long." She started off but he grabbed her by the elbow, dragging her back.

"You're a guest at this party, not the hired help," he whispered loudly in her ear.

"Here. You finish this." She thrust the gin and tonic at him, spilling a little of the liquid on his hot-pink polo shirt. "I'm sure you can find someone to talk to. There are lots of pretty women around, although they may all be too old for you." She felt his eyes follow her as she paraded across the grass with her head held high, her chest stuck out, and her hips swaying.

Heidi's crew had taken over the kitchen with every individual engaged in a different task. But Lula was nowhere in sight. Georgia donned an apron and jumped into the assembly line of workers transferring food items from plastic containers to serving dishes. She noticed Phillip in the corner of the main room talking to Brooke and an exquisite young woman she didn't recognize. *I hope Langdon doesn't set his sights on that pretty young thing.* The minute the thought entered her head, Georgia knew with absolute certainty her marriage was over.

Two servers circled the crowd with trays of ham biscuits and bite-size pimento cheese sandwiches. The three remaining workers managed to get the food onto the tables in record time. Heidi rang her dinner bell and Phillip offered grace. After a brief blessing, he swept his hand at the dark sky. "I've spent the last twenty-three summers on Sullivan's Island, and I'm here to tell you we're about to have a humdinger of a storm. I encourage everyone to get a plate and come on inside. There's plenty of room. You're welcome to try your luck on the porch, but if the winds start to blow like I think it's gonna blow, you'll probably get drenched."

The crowd gravitated toward the porch, lining up single file for their turn at the food table. Georgia took off her apron and joined her husband at the back of the line. He leaned down and whispered, "Why don't we get out of here? I'd rather fix an omelet at home than deal with this mob scene."

"Go home if you want, but I'm not leaving. I see Midge and Bennett over there. I can get a ride home with them."

He hung his head. "No, I'll stay," he said in a tone that sounded irritated for the first time in six days.

Georgia and Langford followed Phillip's suggestion and

took their plates inside. They made their way through the crowded room to where Midge and Bennett stood against the far wall. Juggling their plates, they greeted one another with kisses and handshakes. When the two men launched into a conversation about boating, Midge turned to Georgia. "I've missed seeing you." She leaned in so Georgia could hear her over the noise of the crowd. "Any chance you're free tomorrow for tea? I have something important I need to talk to you about."

"I have to work until six, if that's not too late. We can substitute the tea for wine."

"Wine at six it is." Midge offered her a warm smile with a hint of something Georgia interpreted to be pity. Did Midge know something about her husband's philandering? Was that the something important she needed to talk to her about? Georgia dismissed the idea. Her best friend would have told her if she'd heard something about her cheating husband.

"I haven't seen Lula all night, have you?" Midge asked.

Georgia shook her head. "I've been looking for her too. I noticed her bedroom door is closed. I hope she's not sick."

"I have a feeling it has something to do with them."

Georgia followed Midge's gaze to the corner of the room where Brooke stood with the same exquisite creature she'd seen her with earlier. Something about the way they looked at one another, the way their bodies were pressed close together against the wall, gave Georgia the impression they were more than just friends. "Surely you don't think…"

"That Brooke is gay? That's exactly what I think. I'd be willing to bet that Brooke dropped this little bombshell on her family as recently as today. Considering Lula's absence,

Brooke's puffy red eyes, and Lizbet sulking around like she lost her puppy dog."

Georgia paused as she contemplated Midge's theory. "Phillip seems fine. Then again, Phillip's range of emotions is restricted to fine." She slumped against the wall. "Poor Lula. She's not likely to handle this development well."

"Why sugarcoat it? This news will destroy her. Lula doesn't understand our generation, let alone their generation. Hell, I don't understand that generation and I consider myself a forward-thinking woman."

For the next few minutes, while they picked at their food and the men talked on about boats, Midge and Georgia watched the two young women in the corner. They rarely touched, aside from an occasional brush of a hand against a shoulder, but their body language gave them away.

"At least she has good taste in women," Georgia said at last.

"Here, let me take that for you." Eager to leave, Langdon gathered their plates before they'd finished eating and set off to find the trash can.

Bennett nudged Georgia. "I'm glad to see the two of you are working things out. I'm surprised you let him come with you tonight after what happened."

Georgia froze. "What do you mean?"

Bennett gawked at Midge. "You didn't tell her?"

"Tell me what?" Georgia asked looking back and forth between them.

Midge shut him up with a death stare. "I was planning to tell you tomorrow. That's why I asked you to tea."

Georgia's face flushed crimson. "Whatever it is, I want to know now."

Midge's eyes traveled the room. "I'm not sure this is the right time or place. How about we go for coffee first thing in the morning."

"I don't want to wait until morning," Georgia said through gritted teeth. "Tell me now, Midge."

Midge sighed. "Okay, but you better brace yourself. This won't be easy to hear." She lowered her voice and pressed her body close to Georgia's. "I was picking up a contract from an out-of-town client at a hotel on the north side of town when I ran into Lang with another woman."

Georgia willed her voice to remain even. "When did this happen?"

"A few weeks ago, on a Friday afternoon."

Anger pulsed through Georgia's veins. "You've known about this for a few weeks and you're just now getting around to telling me."

Midge responded with a sheepish nod. "Lula and I decided it best to wait until after the holiday to tell you."

"So Lula knows too." Georgia's voice grew shrill, and heads turned to stare, but she didn't care who overheard. "And neither of you could find the time to tell me my husband is cheating on me with another woman. Obviously, our friendship means nothing to you."

Georgia forced her way through the crowd and fled the party through the back door, out into the stormy evening.

CHAPTER EIGHTEEN
MIDGE

"YOU'VE DONE SOME asinine things, Bennett, but that one really takes the cake," Midge said as they were leaving Sullivan's Island headed back toward Mount Pleasant.

Bennett struggled to see the road through the rain pounding the windshield. "How was I supposed to know you hadn't told her? Why haven't you told her? I'm still not clear on that. You saw Lang with this other woman weeks ago?"

"I've been summoning my courage. It's not easy breaking someone's heart. You heard what I said to Georgia. I was planning to tell her tomorrow. She worships Lang, however misguided those emotions may be."

"I don't understand you women. You were worried about hurting Georgia's feelings when what you should've been worried about was sparing her the humiliation of having the whole world find out her husband cheated on her."

"Shut up, Bennett." She punched him hard in the arm and he winced.

"Ouch! That hurt." He rested one hand on the steering wheel and rubbed his bruised arm with the other.

"You're so infuriating." She looked away from him and stared at the rain coming down in sheets. "We've had such a pleasant day and you had to go and ruin it. I was starting to reconnect with the Bennett I fell in love with, but now I'm wondering if that man is just an illusion. It's like you have a split personality or something. I don't understand how you can be so considerate and attentive one minute and such a jackass the next. Why did you do that to Georgia? Was it worth destroying her marriage just so you can be the center of attention?"

"I didn't destroy her marriage. Lang took care of that himself. And no, I don't always have to be the center of attention."

"You do when we're in public," Midge said. "Your mother even said so."

He tightened his grip on the steering wheel. "You talked to my mother about me?"

"No. She talked to me about you. Boy, you sure have her fooled."

He shot her a warning look. "Don't talk about my mother."

Midge folded her arms over her chest. "How about if we don't talk at all?"

They crossed the Cooper River bridge and drove through downtown in silence. The deep water on certain streets forced them to drive slow. When they finally arrived at her house, he parked his BMW behind her car on the curb and turned off the engine. "I didn't bring my umbrella. We'll have to make a run for it."

"Who says you're invited in?" she asked, her face set in defiance.

"Come on, baby. Don't be like that." He tried to kiss her, but she pushed him away.

"I'm serious, Bennett. This relationship is not working for me. Georgia's never going to speak to me again because of you."

He rolled his eyes. "Don't be ridiculous. Of course she will once she calms down."

"That's not the issue anyway. The issue is you and your crass attitude about everything. You can't just say whatever pops into your mind. You hurt people's feelings and ruin relationships. I'm sorry, Bennett, but I can't see you anymore." Slipping off her sandals and stuffing them into her bag, she opened the car door and sprinted up the flooded sidewalk to the house.

She went straight upstairs to her room where she towel-dried her hair and put on her flannel pajamas. Ignoring the pounding on her front door, she crawled under the comforter and read the first three chapters in Dot Frank's new summer release. When she went down to the kitchen for a cup of chamomile tea a few minutes before ten, she was surprised to see Bennett's car still parked on the street. She opened her front door and found him curled up in a ball, sound asleep, on her stoop.

She knelt down beside him and shook him awake. "Bennett, get up."

He cracked an eyelid. "Where am I?"

"On my front door stoop. You can't possibly be comfortable in that position."

He opened his eyes and rubbed them with his balled fists. "I must have fallen asleep."

"Well, you can't sleep here." Midge tugged on his arm. "Come on, get up. You need to go home."

"Please, Midge baby. I can't leave, not until we've had a chance to talk. I love you so much. I don't want our relationship to end like this."

His sad little-boy face melted some of her anger. "All right. You can come inside, but only for a few minutes. I have to work tomorrow. And somehow figure out a way to get Georgia to forgive me." He got up and followed her inside to the kitchen. "Would you like some tea?"

"Bourbon please," he said, taking a seat at the island.

"I'm not offering bourbon." She removed a mug from the cabinet. "It's tea or nothing."

"Nothing is fine. Thank you."

She smiled to herself as she set the chamomile K-Cup in her Keurig. He was so incorrigible. She wanted to ring his neck one minute and throw her arms around him the next. When the tea finished brewing, she added a drop of milk and sat down on the bar stool opposite him.

"You have every right to be mad at me," he said. "I was insensitive toward Georgia tonight and I'm sorry. Did my mom tell you about my impulse disorder?"

She stared at him, her face scrunched up in confusion. "She mentioned something about you having an attention deficit disorder."

He shrugged. "Same thing. My inability to focus causes me to sometimes act on impulse."

She stared up at the ceiling as she considered this. She didn't know much about ADD, but she could see where being unable to focus would make one restless. "I can understand how that might happen." She took a tentative sip of tea.

"Anyway, I'm as much to blame as you for tonight. I admit I mishandled the Georgia situation. Your impulse disorder aside, other things have happened that worry me, and I think we need to talk about them."

"Please tell me this isn't about the redhead. Because I told you we're business associates."

She placed her hands on the counter and intertwined her fingers. "Okay then. Tell me the redhead's name."

He shook his head. "I can't do that. Not until the papers are signed."

She wagged her finger at him. "You can't do that because you're afraid I'll Google her and find out she's a high-priced call girl."

"Don't be absurd. We're days away from finalizing the details. You're going to feel like an idiot when I tell you about this deal. I'm a lot of things, Midge, but I'm not a cheater."

"Are you a thief? You opened my mail and signed into my online bank account."

Pink spots appeared on his tanned cheeks. "Impulse disorder?" he asked, an eyebrow raised in question.

"Be serious, Bennett."

He tossed his hands in the air. "Guilty as charged. I don't know what made me do it, honestly. I was waiting for you, and nervous about being late to the Lelands' party. I picked your mail up off the floor beside the mail slot, and absentmindedly shuffled through it. I saw your bank statement and opened it without thinking about what I was doing. It was wrong of me. I make no excuses. But I don't know where you got the idea that I signed onto your bank account. I wouldn't do that."

"Are you sure? Because the Internet was still opened to the Wells Fargo website that night."

He placed his hand across his chest. "Honest to god, Midge. I bank at Wells Fargo too. I was probably checking my balance."

Studying him closely, she decided he was telling the truth.

"Was it curiosity that made you break into your father-in-law's safe? What marriage was that, number two?"

He pushed his bar stool back from the island. "Hold on a minute. Who told you that?" When she didn't answer, he said, "Right. Virginia and Sara. I should have known. Those two are always stirring up drama. That's simply not true. You can ask my mother."

"Maybe I will. She told me to call her anytime I had concerns." She jabbed the granite countertop with her finger. "Let's go back to the night of the Lelands' party for a minute. I overheard Grace telling her husband that she hadn't invited you to the party. What was that all about?"

The pink splotches returned to his cheeks. "I may have fudged that invitation. I overheard some of the guys in the locker room at the club talking about the party. They made is sound like everyone in town was invited. I really wanted to see that apartment, and I didn't think we'd be noticed." His hand shot up. "Don't say it. I know. I'm the guy who gives realtors a bad rap. Now that I think about it, that was a pretty lousy move."

"Yes it was. And you made me look like a fool."

Bennett got up and dragged his stool around to her side of the island. He sat down close to her, nudging her and then laying his head on her shoulder. "I never said I was perfect, Midge. I'm far from it, actually. My issues with impulse control are legit. I never intend to do stupid stuff. I get caught up in the moment, and I can't help myself." He lifted his head off her shoulder and ran a finger down her cheek. "I love you so much, more than I've ever loved any of my other wives."

She cut her eyes at him. "If that's supposed to make me feel better, it doesn't."

"I'm being serious. I'm crazy about you. You bring out the best in me. You make me want to be a better person. If you'll give me another chance, I know we can make our relationship work. I'll even see a therapist about my impulse control. I realize my track record for marriage sucks, but the last thing I want is another divorce. I want us to grow old together. You and me working our boutique agency by day and making love by night." He stood to go. "Think about what I've said. You can talk to me about whatever you want, whenever you want—or anytime you have concerns. I don't want us to keep secrets from one another." He kissed the top of her head and let himself out the front door.

Her heart ached to believe him, but her stomach churned sour against it.

CHAPTER NINETEEN
LIZBET

LIZBET FELT HERSELF being spread thinner and thinner as the party wore on. In addition to her catering responsibilities, she found herself playing hostess to friends of her parents she hadn't seen in years. They asked questions about her mother's health and whereabouts, neither of which she knew how to answer. She wanted to tell them her mother's heart was sick over the discovery that her oldest child was gay. No doubt they suspected something amiss with Brooke crying in the far corner of the room and the beautiful girl, whom no one seemed to know, comforting her. Her father did his best to maintain his composure, but his dull eyes and thin smile gave him away.

The crowd had dwindled and Lizbet was in the kitchen wrapping up leftovers when Heidi approached her. "I spoke with your mother when we first got here, but I haven't seen her since. I'm worried about her. Has she fallen ill?"

"No ma'am. She and my sister had an argument before we got here."

Heidi's eyes sought out her own daughter who was gathering dirty plates from around the room. "Oh goodness. I know how that is. Lord knows Annie and I have had our troubles. Should we fix her a plate?"

"That's not necessary. When Mom gets in one of these moods, it's best to leave her alone." She stacked several containers of leftovers and stored them in the refrigerator. "There's plenty of food in here if she gets hungry later."

Lizbet made certain her father paid the balance owed to the musicians and tipped the catering crew. Once they all had gone, as her father said goodnight to the last departing guests, she took a deep breath before approaching her sister who was still huddled in the same corner with Sawyer.

"I don't get it, Brooke. You've been here since last Wednesday. You had Mom and Dad to yourself all weekend. What made you decide to wait until right before the party to tell them you're…"

Brooke stiffened. "Come on, Lizzy, you can say it. I'm gay."

She cast her eyes on the young woman standing next to Brooke who could have passed for Georgia's daughter with her dark classic good looks. "You must be Sawyer. I'm Brooke's sister, Lizbet."

Sawyer held out her hand. "I'm sorry to be meeting you under such stressful circumstances." Her lips spread into a genuine smile. "Drama has a way of following Brooke around. As her sister, you no doubt already know this."

Lizbet sensed Sawyer's attempt to make light of the situation for everyone's sake, but she was in no mood for pleasantries. "I take it my sister failed to warn you about her sneak attack."

Sawyer lifted a boney shoulder. "I understand why she handled it the way she did."

"Really? Because I don't." Lizbet turned back to her sister. "Tell me, Brooke. Why did you decide to ambush us?"

Fresh tears welled up in her sister's eyes. "I wouldn't expect you to understand."

Lizbet crossed her arms. "Try me. We have the same parents. I would be the most likely to understand."

"They were going to freak out no matter how I told them," Brooke said. "Mom is so set in her ways with her old-fashioned values. She's never going to accept that I'm gay."

"She'll eventually come around," Lizbet said. "You can count on Dad to support you. He just needs a little time to adjust."

"I wouldn't count on it." Brooke swiped at the tears streaming down her cheeks. "He can barely bring himself to look at me." She reached for Sawyer's hand. "At us."

Lizbet's anger toward her sister vanished, and pity took its place. She most definitely would not want to be in Brooke's shoes. She glanced around for her father, and realized they were the only ones left in the room. He'd turned out most of the lights and disappeared into his bedroom without saying goodnight.

"We've all had a long day," Lizbet said. "Why don't we grab a couple of beers and go out on the porch."

"I'm beat," Sawyer said. "I should probably turn in and give the two of you a chance to talk."

"Please don't. I'd like to get to know you." Crossing the room to the kitchen, Lizbet removed three Corona Lights from the refrigerator and lined them up on the counter. She popped the tops with a bottle opener and held a beer out to Sawyer.

Sawyer appeared uncertain, but when Brooke nodded encouragement, she accepted the beer.

The storm had forced out much of the humidity from earlier in the day, leaving in its wake cooler temperatures and a light breeze. They sat for a while without talking, with their heads resting against the backs of the rockers, sipping their beers and enjoying the crickets and tree frogs singing their songs.

"Everything makes perfect sense to me now," Lizbet said finally. "I understand why you went to college in California and why you never come home to visit. What I don't understand is why you picked now to come out of the closet to Mom and Dad."

"I can't hide anymore, Lizzy. Sawyer and I are moving to Charleston." Brooke's eyes searched for her partner's. "Although I'm beginning to question the wisdom in making this decision."

Sawyer held Brooke's gaze. "Since when do you give up at the first sign of trouble?"

"Since I arrived on Wednesday," Brooke said. "I'd forgotten how difficult my mother can be."

"Give it some time," Sawyer said in a soft voice. "Charleston is a big city. We can lose ourselves here as well as we could anywhere else."

Lizbet held her tongue. While the population of Charleston was more than a hundred and twenty-five thousand, in many ways this city felt like a very small town. "What about your promotion?"

A guilty expression crossed Brooke's face. "I may have

left out an important detail about that. My new job here is the promotion I was referring to."

"Oh, I see. Is your new job in graphic design?" Lizbeth asked.

Brooke nodded. "With a smaller firm with more potential for growth."

"What about you?" Lizbet asked Sawyer. "Do you have a job here?"

Brooke answered for her partner. "Sawyer is in medical school. She finished her clinic rotations at Stanford in May and is starting the residency program at MUSC in the fall."

"I'm originally from Atlanta," Sawyer added. "While we like the West Coast, we're both ready to come back East, to be closer to our families."

"Sawyer's parents are more accepting of our relationship," Brooke explained.

Lizbet wondered why, if that were the case, they hadn't chosen Atlanta to relocate. But she didn't ask. "How long have the two of you been together?"

"Two years," Brooke said. "We didn't know each other at Stanford, even though we were in the same class. We met through some mutual friends a year after graduation. We've been together since then."

Brooke and Sawyer exchanged a look that left little doubt in Lizbet's mind how much they meant to one another. Her sister was in love with a young woman any parents would be proud to have as their daughter-in-law. This was all uncharted territory for Lizbet. Did parents call the women their gay daughters married daughters-in-law? Sawyer seemed to have it all—looks and brains and compassion. She wondered if they were planning to get married and have children, but decided not to ask. She approved of Sawyer and didn't want to scare her away by prying.

"You know Mom and Dad better than I do, Lizzy. Do you think they'll ever come around?"

Lizbet sipped her beer. "Mom and Dad haven't changed. You're the one who's changed. Surely you didn't think they would welcome Sawyer with open arms. No offense," she said to Sawyer who responded, "None taken."

"Mom is the issue, though, not Dad," Lizbet continued. "I see this thing playing out one of two ways. If you move here, which I would love by the way, Mom will be forced to accept your relationship. You and I both know you're her favorite. She's not going to kick you out of her life. If you stay out in California, or move somewhere else, you'll be out of her sight and therefore out of her mind. She'll pretend none of this happened, go back to fantasizing about you marrying a man, and you'll never able to come home for a visit again. At least not with Sawyer."

Brooke cut her eyes at Lizbet. "When did you get so smart, little sister?"

"Ha. There's a lot about me you don't know." Brooke's eyebrows shot up to her hairline and Lizbet burst out laughing. "I'm not gay if that's what you're thinking. Although I might consider it if I don't find a boyfriend soon. You and I don't know each other very well, Brooke, but I would like for that to change."

Brooke yanked on her ponytail. "There's nothing I want more." They sat for a moment in silence. "You should know that Sawyer and I are leaving first thing in the morning. I refuse to stay where we're not wanted."

"Where will you go?"

"We've booked a hotel room in Charleston. I haven't spent much of my adult life here. We want to explore downtown, to get to know the area and figure out the best places to live. We'll be around for a few more days in case..." Brooke inhaled an unsteady breath. "On the off chance Mom decides she wants to see me."

*

Lizbet fell into bed fully clothed and exhausted shortly after midnight, but the events of the day zooming around her head like race cars on a speedway prevented her from falling asleep. She asked herself if she approved of her sister's chosen lifestyle and was surprised her answer was yes. Lizbet had never met a couple more in sync. They communicated with a glance, a nod, a gentle squeeze of the hand. Instead of being furious at Brooke for bringing her here under false pretenses, Sawyer had taken it all in stride, supporting her partner even if she didn't totally understand her. Lizbet worried about the challenges they would face, but felt comforted by their obvious love for one another. A warm feeling settled over her at the idea of Brooke and Sawyer moving to Charleston. She would be gaining not one but two sisters. She envisioned the three of them going out to dinner, shopping together, and taking long walks along the Battery on weekends in the spring. For the first time since forever, she didn't feel so alone.

Her concern now was their mother's mind-set. If her behavior at the party was any indication, Lula's acceptance of Brooke's chosen lifestyle would be a long time coming. Ignoring her guests while they were in her own home was not their mother's style. "We must keep up appearances at all times" was Lula's motto. "Chin up, shoulders back. Always paint on a bright face no matter how much you're hurting inside." Sawyer was the type of person her mother would've handpicked to marry her daughter, if only that person was of the male persuasion.

Lizbet managed a few hours' sleep, but woke up at dawn to the sound of the screen door banging shut. Was Brooke leaving the house at daybreak to avoid a confrontation with her mother? She'd been too tired, and a little drunk after three beers, to get her overnight bag out of her car. But she needed to brush the cotton off her teeth before she could think clearly. She rolled out of bed and emerged from her room. Her sister's bedroom door was closed, as was her parents, but the backdoor stood wide open. Her bare feet padded across the room and out onto the porch. As she started down the steps to the driveway, she saw her mother, still dressed in her seersucker housecoat, lying face down on the sidewalk, her neck turned at an awkward angle with a puddle of blood pooling beneath her left cheek. Pooh sat whimpering beside her, licking her hand and sniffing her neck every now and then.

Lizbet rushed to her mother's side. "Oh my god, Mom! Are you all right?" She shook her gently but her mother didn't stir. She raced back up the steps and through the backdoor. "Dad! Brooke! Come quick! Mom fell down the stairs and she won't get up. Hurry!" Lizbet returned to her mother, trying once again to rouse her without success.

Her father—dressed in a T-shirt and boxers, with a full day's growth on his face and what little hair remained on his head sticking straight up in the back—was the first to arrive on the scene. Brooke was right behind him followed by Sawyer.

Sawyer knelt down next to Lula, searching her wrist and her neck for a pulse.

"She's a doctor," Lizbet said to her father when she noticed him watching Sawyer with his brow furrowed and eyes narrowed in suspicion.

"I'm in medical school, actually," Sawyer said, looking up at Phillip. "Are you comfortable with me checking her vitals?"

"By all means." He waved his hand at his wife's motionless body on the ground. "Do whatever you need to do."

Sawyer accessed the flashlight app on her iPhone and pried open Lula's right eyelid. "Has anyone called 911?"

"Not yet." Lizbet patted her pockets. "My phone's inside."

Brooke took Sawyer's phone from her. "I'm on it."

"Do you have a first aid kit?" Sawyer asked.

Her father thought for a minute. "There might be one under the kitchen sink. I'll go check." He said.

When the dispatcher came on the line, Brooke recited their address and requested an ambulance, explaining that her mother had fallen down a flight of brick steps, hit her head on the sidewalk, and was unconscious. She then repeated their mother's pulse and respiration rates as Sawyer called them out to her.

"Tell them her pupils are dilated and ask them to hurry," Sawyer added.

Her father returned with the first aid kit, and Sawyer held a gauze pad as close as she could get to the wound.

Much to everyone's surprise, despite their remote location, the rescue squad arrived within a few minutes and the ambulance shortly after that. One of the rescue workers, the crew chief as he introduced himself to them, asked a series of questions. "Has she been ill?" and "Has she been drinking alcohol or taking prescription medication?" and "When was the last time she had anything to eat?"

Her father answered, "No. No. And I'm not sure"

"Has she been under any stress?" the crew chief asked.

Lizbet saw Brooke and Sawyer exchange a look. Before they could confess to being the source of the drama, Lizbet said, "The normal stress that goes along with planning a Fourth of July party for ninety people."

After immobilizing her neck, the rescue crew transferred Lula's body to a stretcher, loaded her into the ambulance, and zoomed out of the driveway, sirens blasting, to MUSC in downtown Charleston as per her father's instructions.

"I need to get to the hospital." Her father's eyes shifted from his car to the house but remained planted in the same spot on the sidewalk.

"Mr. Horne." Sawyer placed her hand on his shoulder. "You'll need your insurance card at the hospital and your wife will want her purse. I'm hopeful this is nothing more serious than a cut on the head and a mild concussion, in which case she'll want a change of clothes to wear home when she's released." She squeezed his shoulder and nudged him toward the house.

At the top of the porch steps, he turned back to Sawyer. "Thank you for your kindness, young lady. I'm glad you were here. And please, call me Phillip."

Lizbet smiled at Sawyer and Brooke. "That's encouraging. He's never asked any of our friends to call him Phillip before."

"Nothing short of a minor miracle," Brooke muttered under her breath as they went back inside.

Phillip came out of the bedroom, still wearing his T-shirt

and boxers, with his wife's purse and a tote bag stuffed with clothes. "I'm ready to go. I just need to find my keys."

"Your keys are over here, Dad." Lizbet pointed at the ceramic dish on the table beside the backdoor where they always kept their keys. "But I think you'd better get dressed first. I'm not sure the staff at the hospital would appreciate seeing you in your boxer shorts."

He glanced down at his scantily clad body. "Oops." He set his things on the kitchen counter and returned to his room.

"He's spaced out," Lizbet said. "I should probably drive him to the hospital. Are the two of you coming?"

"I'm not sure Mom will want us at the hospital," Brooke said.

Lizbet's face fell. "You're gonna dump them on me. Dad's so distraught he forgot to put on his clothes. What if it's something serious?"

Brooke brushed a lock of hair off Lizbet's cheek. "Then you call us. We're not abandoning you, Lizzy. We're gonna pack up here and head to Charleston. We'll drop Pooh by the house and check into the hotel. If you need us, we'll be right there. But the last thing I want to do right now is add to Mom's stress."

CHAPTER TWENTY

LULA

WHEN LULA REGAINED consciousness, although she had no idea how she'd gotten there, she understood right away that she was riding in an ambulance.

"Welcome back." The EMT's kind smile and soft voice made up for his otherwise unattractive appearance. He reminded Lula of a gnome with his pointed bald head and his short gray beard covering only his cheeks and chin. "How do you feel?"

"Like a herd of elephants is tromping on my head."

He reached behind him for his clipboard. "That's understandable. You hit your head pretty hard. Do you remember falling?"

Despite the pain, she forced herself to think back. She had no recollection of falling. The last thing she remembered was meeting Brooke's girlfriend. *Sawyer and I have been together for two years now.* "What day is it?"

"Wednesday, the fifth of July," the EMT answered.

The fifth of July? She remembered nothing about the

party. Had she suffered some sort of stroke that was affecting her memory? "Where did I fall?"

"Down the porch steps at your beach house. You cracked your forehead open on the sidewalk." He removed a bloody wad of gauze from her forehead and replaced it with a fresh bandage, securing it with first aid tape. "Have you experienced any recent changes in health?"

Her thoughts were all jumbled, as if someone had cracked open her head, dumped her brains into a bowl, and scrambled them with a whisk. Who would that someone have been? Heidi the caterer or Brooke the troublemaker? Did he want to know about the crazy thoughts that kept popping into her head, and the strange things that flew out of her mouth unfiltered? She decided not to tell him.

"I've been tired lately, and a bit on edge, but I only have myself to blame. For some crazy reason, I decided to throw a last-minute Fourth of July party for ninety people. Oh... and I fainted a few weeks back. But that's because I got overheated. My air conditioning was out and I was cooking in the kitchen with the oven on high."

His pen flew across the clipboard as he jotted down notes. "What happened when you fainted? Were you out for very long?"

Lula thought back to that day, nearly a month ago. "I was sitting at the kitchen table. I'd just gotten off the phone with my daughter, who'd called to say she was coming home for a visit. I was excited. I haven't seen her in a long time. I stood up from the table too quickly and my knees went weak. I'm not sure how long I was out. My neighbors came to my rescue."

His beady eyes narrowed as he continued to write.

"Sounds like you've had a lot of excitement and stress in your life recently."

"I found out yesterday my daughter is gay. Twenty-six years old and she comes out of the closet by introducing me to her girlfriend of two years." Tears burned the back of Lula's throat. Why was she telling a total stranger about her family drama? "Needless to say, the news came as a bit of a shock."

He looked up from his clipboard. "I can understand how it would. It's not uncommon for our bodies to react to that kind of stress."

"Did I have a stroke?" Lula bit down on her lip to make it stop quivering.

He closed his clipboard and rested his hand on her arm. "We can't rule it out. The doctors will know more after they run some tests at the hospital. For now close your eyes and try to rest."

Lula dozed off or passed out again, she wasn't sure which. But the next thing she knew, the rescue workers were wheeling her into the emergency room. A team of nurses began working on her at once—starting Ivs, withdrawing blood, monitoring her vitals. They called her dear and sweetheart in honeyed voices as if speaking to a child. Or the elderly. Had she aged that much in a day? She certainly felt like it.

"Where's my family?" Lula asked the nurse who was inserting the IV.

"As far as I know, they haven't arrived yet. We'll send them back as soon as they do."

The doctor entered the cubicle and introduced himself as Dr. Hanson. His appearance—long face, dark mustache, and tall and lanky body—brought to mind Abraham Lincoln. He rolled a swivel stool to the side of her bed. "What's going on? Sounds like you took a little tumble."

"Toddlers tumble, Doctor. I fell down my porch steps and landed on the cobblestone sidewalk. I can't endure the pain in my head much longer. Will you get your prescription pad out and order up some relief?" She tugged at the brace around her neck. "And get this damn thing off of my neck."

"I'm sorry, but I can't take it off, not until after we do the CT scan."

"I didn't land on my neck, Doctor. I landed on my face, as evidence by this gash in my forehead." Lifting her fingers to her forehead, she felt the thick wad of gauze.

He ignored her and consulted his clipboard. "According to the report, you had a similar fall several weeks ago."

"That wasn't a fall. My air conditioner went out, and I got overheated. I fainted. It happens everyday in the summertime in the South. I take it you're a Yankee."

"Born and raised in Valdosta, Georgia." His eyes returned to the report. "But you can't deny you've been under stress lately."

"You're damn right I'm under stress," Lula said, her voice growing loud. "Didn't the gnome tell you? It should be on your clipboard. I just found out my daughter is a lesbian. My baby girl is a homosexual."

"Please, Mrs. Horne, keep your voice down. We have gay people on our staff, both doctors and nurses."

Lula pulled the blanket up over her chest. "That's your problem. But whatever you do, keep them away from me."

The doctor snapped his clipboard shut and signaled to the nurse. "Get this woman over to radiology."

*

The trip to radiology took thirty minutes, but by the time she returned to her cubicle, Phillip and Lizbet were waiting for her. Her husband hadn't bothered to shave or brush his hair and her daughter was still wearing her server clothes. *Must have been some party,* Lula thought. *Too bad I can't remember it.*

Lizbet approached the side of the bed and took hold of her hand. "You scared us to death, Mom. Are you okay?"

"Obviously not, Lizbet. I'm in the hospital." Lula pried her hand free from her daughter's death grip. "I must have gotten a touch of amnesia. I don't remember much about the party."

"That's because you stayed in your room the whole time."

Her green eyes, scared and confused, sought out her husband's. "I don't understand. Why did I stay in my room the whole time when we were hosting a party?"

Phillip moved to the side of the bed. "Because you were too upset to socialize." He paused. "Do you remember meeting Sawyer?"

"Sawyer is the reason I'm in the hospital. She made my daughter gay." Lula ignored Lizbet's eyeroll. "How did you explain my absence to our guests?"

"That you weren't feeling well," Phillip said. "Everyone understood."

"I'm sure they didn't blame me either, with Brooke flaunting her lesbian lover all over the place. Where is Brooke anyway? I hope she's boarding a plane back to California where she belongs. She's no longer welcome in my home."

Phillip cringed. He was already softening toward Brooke and her girlfriend. "Let's not concern ourselves with Brooke's situation right now," he said. "We can sort that all out later. The most important thing is to get you patched up so we can go home."

"And I'm just the man to do it." A doctor, with a baby face and a full head of yellow wavy hair, entered the cubicle. "I'm Trevor Pratt. I'm the plastic surgeon who will be taking care of your laceration."

He was just a boy, not much older than Lizbet. She felt old and tired. Time for her to step aside and let the youngsters take over the world. Theirs was not a world she understood, anyway.

Lizbet and Phillip stepped aside to make way for the doctor. Lula noticed Lizbet eyeing Trevor Pratt as he prepared to stitch up her wound. All was not lost. At least one of her daughters liked men.

Lula closed her eyes and listened to Phillip and Lizbet chat with the young doctor while he worked. Originally from Columbia, South Carolina, he told them he received his undergraduate degree from UVA and attended medical school at the University of Pennsylvania. He was in his third year of residency at MUSC. He loved Charleston and hoped to be hired full-time. When Phillip grew silent, Lizbet and Trevor struck up a conversation about the local social hangouts for their age group.

He had just tied off his last stitch when Dr. Hanson returned. The plastic surgeon wished Lula well and excused himself. She turned on Dr. Hanson. "Where on earth have you been? It's too early for lunch. I trust you have the results from my CT scan."

"Your wife doesn't like me very much," Hanson said as

he shook Phillip's hand. "Although I don't know why. I assure you I have the utmost concern for her health."

"Don't be offended, Doctor. She's not her best self today," Phillip said in a low voice, but Lula heard him anyway.

Hanson moved past Phillip to Lula's side. "I agree that it's too early for lunch, Mrs. Horne. But I'm guilty of sneaking a cup of coffee while I studied your scan results. I have good news and bad. The good news is, we can rule out a stroke and there is no evidence of trauma to your spinal cord."

Lula pointed at the neck brace. "Then, for the love of God, take this damn thing off my neck before you tell me the bad news."

Dr. Hanson called in a nurse, and together they removed the brace. He waited for the nurse to leave before delivering the bad news. "The CT scan shows a large mass on your brain, a tumor, which is most likely responsible for your falls and recent fatigue." He paused, giving them a chance to absorb this information.

A tumor? She had cancer growing in her brain? No wonder she'd been feeling so poorly lately. Her heart began to race and she broke out in a cold sweat. She felt dizzy, as though she might faint again or be sick to her stomach. She refused to look at her husband and daughter. How could she face their fears when she couldn't face her own?

"Okay." Lula sucked up her bottom lip as she inhaled a deep breath. "How do we get rid of this tumor?"

"I'm sorry to say that is beyond my level of expertise. I'm turning your case over to the Neurosurgeon on staff. He should be in to see you shortly."

"What is this neurologist's name?" Phillip asked. "We don't want a resident. We want someone with experience."

"Dr. Erica Walton. And yes, she's a resident. This is a teaching hospital, Mr. Horne. But don't worry, she's merely the gatekeeper. She'll refer you to the right neurologist to handle your case."

Lula gripped the bed railing. "I don't want any old neurologist, Doctor. I want you to get Lang Murdaugh on the phone."

CHAPTER TWENTY-ONE
LIZBET

LIZBET SLIPPED OUT of her mother's cubicle and scurried down the hall. She removed her cell phone from her pocket and texted her sister: "*Get over here now. The doctor says Mom has a brain tumor.*"

Brooke texted right back: "We're on the way."

She slumped against the nearest wall. How could her mother possibly have a brain tumor? There must be some mistake. She was only in her midfifties. She was too young to die. None of Lizbet's friends had lost their parents yet. With the exception of Dean Nelson and Meghan Reyes of course. But their mothers had both died from breast cancer. Lula didn't have cancer. Or did she? The doctor didn't say. Did he even know?

Lizbet wished she could take back all the horrible thoughts she'd had about her mother in recent weeks. Only moments ago, when Lula accused Sawyer of making Brooke gay, as if any person could make another person gay, Lizbet had thought of her mother as a small-minded bigot. Even though she hadn't called her mother that to her face, or to anyone else for that matter, she'd still thought it, and that weighed heavily on her conscience.

Last week her mother was planning a party and creating beautiful bouquets of flowers. And this week she was diagnosed with a brain tumor. What exactly would her treatment entail? Surgery and chemo if the tumor proved cancerous? Lizbet had taken for granted that her mother would always be there for her, that Lula would help her plan her wedding and babysit for her children. What if she never met her first grandchild? What if she didn't live to see next Christmas?

Lizbet was staring at her phone, at the photograph of Lula she'd taken on Mother's Day, when Trevor Pratt approached her. "I don't mean to pry but you look sad. Did you receive some bad news?" He patted his shoulder. "I have a strong one if you need to cry on it. Believe me, you won't be the first. Working in the emergency room is often gloomy business."

She smiled despite herself. The young doctor had an easy way about him. "I imagine it is." Averting his gaze, she stared down at the floor. "Dr. Hanson says my mother has a brain tumor."

Trevor leaned against the wall beside her. "Oh gosh. That really is bad news. If it's any consolation, the doctors in the Neurology Department are the best."

"Do you know Lang Murdaugh? He's our next-door neighbor. My sister and I call him Dr. Dog. We've known him all our lives. I don't know anything about his reputation except that, according to his wife, he works a lot."

"Dr. Dog," he said with a chuckle. "I'll have to remember that. And yes, I know him. He's one of the best. It always helps to have connections." He gestured at the phone in her hand. "Can I give you my number in case you need anything? I'm here all the time, if I can help you in any way."

She handed him her phone. "That'd be great."

He sent a text to himself and handed back her phone. "Now I have your number and you have mine. I'll check on you in a day or so to see how things are going. In the meantime do not hesitate to call me, even if only for directions to the cafeteria." His smile reached his slate-blue eyes.

She smiled back at him. "Thank you, Dr. Pratt."

"Please call me Trevor. I'm not much older than you."

She nodded. "Trevor it is, then."

She watched him walked down the hall, admiring the way his scrubs outlined his broad shoulders. She forced herself to look away. What was wrong with her? Her mother just received devastating news and she was lusting after her hot young doctor?

Down the hall in the opposite direction, she saw her father emerge from her mother's cubicle, and hurried toward him. "How is she?"

"Scared to death. Lang is finishing up with his rounds. He should be here soon."

"Dad, I better warn you that Brooke and Sawyer are on the way. I asked them to come. They have a right to be here."

Phillip took her by the elbow and led her out of earshot of Lula's cubicle. "Your mother won't like that very much. And truthfully, considering the tension between them, I'm not sure I want them here either."

Lizbet's phone vibrated in her hand. "Too bad. They're already here. I'm going to find them and bring them back. They can stay out in the hall if Mom doesn't want to see them."

By the time she returned from the waiting room with

Brooke and Sawyer, Dr. Dog had arrived and was speaking to her father in hushed tones near the nurse's desk.

"I didn't get a chance to say hello to you girls last night," Dr. Dog said when he noticed Brooke and Lizbet hovering with Sawyer nearby.

Brooke introduced Sawyer as her friend from California. "She's starting in the residency program here at MUSC in the fall."

"Good for you. And welcome to Charleston. I'm sorry we're meeting under such stressful circumstances." He swept his arm in the direction of an empty room across the hall. "Why don't we go in here where we can speak in private." He waited at the door while the rest of them filed into the room. "I haven't been in to see Lula yet," he said, closing the door behind him. "I wanted to speak candidly with you first." He sat down at the desk and accessed images of her mother's brain on a large computer screen. "If you'll gather around behind me, I'll explain what we're seeing here."

He used his pen to outline the large mass on Lula's brain. "I won't know until I do the biopsy, but I'm almost certain it's cancer. Normally I wouldn't say that to a family until I'm absolutely sure, but since we're friends… well, I would hope you'd do the same for me. And I'll be honest with you, I regret to say that because of the placement of the tumor, surgically removing it may not be possible."

For the next few minutes, he explained the various possible scenarios and addressed the what-ifs as they asked them. Most of which came from Sawyer. And most were too technical for Lizbet to understand. She was grateful to have Sawyer on the team Horne. Her training would come in handy as they faced whatever lay ahead.

Dr. Dog turned off the computer monitor and pushed back from the desk. "Let's take this one step at a time," he said, standing. "I've scheduled an MRI for this afternoon, and the biopsy for first thing in the morning. I'd like to admit Lula to the hospital for observation overnight. She can go home after the biopsy tomorrow if she's feeling okay." He moved toward the door. "I'd like to go in and see her now. You can tell her whatever you want, but I advise you to stick to the facts."

"I'll let you do the talking, Lang," Phillip said as he followed Dr. Dog out the door, leaving the Horne sisters and Sawyer staring at their backs.

Brooke leaned in close to Sawyer. "Translate that for me please, in a language I can understand. Give it to me straight. I need to know what we're dealing with."

Sawyer turned to Lizbet. "What about you, Lizbet? Do you want to know the truth?"

No! She wanted to scream. She wanted to run the few blocks to their house, to the home she'd grown up in, and crawl under the bed, hiding from the truth. She wanted to bury her face in her mother's apron like she'd done as a child when someone hurt her feelings or something scared her. But the tables had turned and she was now the adult forced to take care of the parent who had become the one in need. "Not really, but we need to be strong for Mom and Dad's sake. To do that we need to be realistic about her situation."

"This is hard, I know." Sawyer's lips parted in a sympathetic smile. No doubt she'd passed her bedside manner course with flying colors. "I think you should prepare for the worst and hope for the best. If the tumor proves inoperable, your mother's choices may be limited. You may be looking at palliative care, which means you remove the symptoms of the disease as much as you can to provide a better quality of life for whatever time she has left."

"You mean she might die?" Lizbet had already considered the possibility, but the words sounded foreign as they passed through her lips.

When Sawyer hesitated, Brooke nudged her. "We want the truth."

Sawyer hung her head. "Unfortunately, there's a very good chance she's going to die."

A wave of nausea overcame Lizbet and she fled the room. She raced down the hall to the bathroom where she emptied the meager contents from her belly into the toilet. This couldn't be happening. Surely there was some mistake. Her mother had worn herself out planning the party. And Brooke's drama had added to her stress. She just needed some rest. A night in the hospital would be good for her. In the morning, her brain would be clear and she could go home. Lizbet would take Sawyer's advice. She would hope for the best, but a gnawing feeling in her empty gut warned her that the worst was what she would get.

Sawyer and Brooke were waiting for her outside the bathroom. Brooke draped her arm around Lizbet's shoulders. "I'm sorry, Lizzy. Are you okay?"

Lizbet shrugged. "I have to be for Mom's sake."

Brooke squeezed her tight. "But you don't have to bear the burden alone. I'm here for you."

Sawyer tugged on Brooke's elbow. "I'm gonna take off now, and head back to the hotel. You need some time alone with your family."

"No!" Brooke and Lizbet said in unison.

"Don't go," Lizbet added. "We need you here." In a few short hours, she'd already begun to think of Sawyer as a sister.

"Actually, why don't I go with you." Brooke dropped her arm from Lizbet's shoulders. "There's no point in me hanging around here. Mom doesn't want to see me and I don't want to upset her."

"Gee thanks," Lizbet said. "So much for me not bearing the burden alone."

"No, listen. Here's what we'll do." Brooke looped her arm through Lizbet's and led her toward the waiting room. "Sawyer and I will drive out to the beach house and close the place up. Mom and Dad won't be going back anytime soon. We'll pack up their clothes and the leftovers from the party. I'll drive Dad's car back for him so he'll have it when he needs it. We'll feed Pooh and have supper waiting for the two of you when you get home."

"I guess that makes sense," Lizbet mumbled.

Brooke spun her around and hugged her full on. "I have a lot of making up to do to you for all the years I've been gone. I promise I won't abandon you again. You are not alone."

CHAPTER TWENTY-TWO
GEORGIA

HUNGOVER FROM THE Fourth of July festivities, locals and vacationers moved in slow motion in downtown Charleston on Wednesday. Of the few who found their way into Tasty Provisions, most were window shoppers stepping inside in search of relief from the heat.

The catering staff had the morning off, leaving Georgia alone in the shop. She packed away the red, white, and blue decorations, and then dusted, rearranged, and restocked the displays and shelves.

"I've been working at my computer all morning and I'm still not caught up," Heidi said when she came down from her upstairs office around noon. She surveyed Georgia's handiwork. "Wow! Would you look at this place. Georgia, you are a whiz at everything you do. Thank you again, by the way, for pitching in last night. We would never have made it without you." She handed her a wad of cash. "A bonus for your efforts."

Georgia pocketed the money. "Thank you. I was happy to help out."

Heidi went to the commercial refrigerator, jotted a list on the pad in her hand, and then took the list to Annie in the kitchen. "It's so quiet in here," she said when she returned. "I guess everyone is sleeping off the holiday. Now might be a good time for us to talk."

Georgia looked up from tallying the sales receipts. "Is something wrong?"

"On the contrary. Business is booming. The events we catered over the weekend resulted in a large number of requests for consultations. Everyone is planning ahead, which is a good thing. But we'll be slammed from September through the holidays."

"How wonderful for you!"

"You mean, how wonderful for us! You're a vital part of this team, Georgia. We have time to get organized, but we'll need to make some changes. Annie has been accepted at the culinary institute. She'll be leaving us in September."

Heidi's daughter emerged from the kitchen, her arms loaded with take-out casseroles. "Are you bragging about me again, Mom?"

Heidi and Georgia both laughed. "Bragging is a mother's privilege. I hear congratulations are in order." Georgia came from behind the counter and rewarded her with a hug. She felt the sharp angles of Annie's bones beneath her clothing. The girl worked hard and hardly ever ate. She found Annie intriguing. Wise beyond her years, she was the most creative seventeen-year-old she'd ever met. "I'm excited for your opportunity, but for all our sakes, I hope you're planning to come back."

Annie smiled. "If you'd asked me a month ago, I would've

told you I'm never coming back. But I've grown to love Charleston, and I want to be a part of Heidi's success."

"Of our success," Heidi said. "You're an important part of this business. In fact, the business didn't start taking off until you joined the staff."

"She gives me too much credit." Annie cast a loving glance at her mother. Georgia had heard rumors of a troubled past between the two, but they seemed in a good place now. "Seriously though, I'd like to work with a master chef for a few years, and gain some experience before coming back. But we'll see where I am when the program is over."

Heidi removed the casseroles from her daughter's arms and stacked them on the empty shelves in the cooler. "I'll support her whichever way she decides. Did you know Lizbet is thinking about applying to CIA? What will I do if they both leave me? I'll be losing my right- and my left-hand gals."

"But you'll still have Georgia," Annie said with a wink in her direction before disappearing through the kitchen door.

Heidi returned to the counter. "She's right, you know. I've grown attached to you. I hope you're happy here."

"I haven't been this happy in years."

"Good! Because as the business grows, so will your responsibilities and consequently your salary. After we go to market next week, I'd like to turn all the merchandising for the store over to you. You have great flair, Georgia. I know I can count on you to bring in unique items at affordable prices. You'll be your own boss. And you have my blessing if you want to go to markets other than Atlanta."

Georgia's mind buzzed with ideas for items she'd like to carry. "I'll have to investigate the best markets for our type of goods."

"Once Annie leaves, I'll need to be more hands-on in the kitchen. I'd like to pull you into the event-planning side of the business as well. The proposals and scheduling are becoming unwieldy. I simply don't have time to do it all. I may be getting ahead of myself, though. You might not be interested in going full-time."

Excitement stirred within Georgia for the first time in years. "I'm definitely interested, Heidi. And thanks for the vote of confidence. But I'm not sure I'm qualified. I know plenty about planning a party from the hostess side, but the catering side intimidates me."

"There's nothing to it. I'll teach you everything you need to know. Your experience as a hostess will serve us both well."

"In that case, count me in." Working longer hours would save her from the loneliness at home and distract her from the breakup of her marriage. "A new challenge is just what I need right now." Maybe she would sell the house and buy a waterfront condo.

"You'll no longer be working the floor except when we are short staffed. Will that be a problem for you? I know you enjoy the customers. Although you'll have plenty of interaction with our catering clients."

"I'm fine with it. Truly, I am." Georgia was more than fine with it. She was thrilled with the opportunity to take more of a leading role in the company. "By the way, Lisa, one of our part-time workers, is filling in for me next week when we go to Atlanta. I got the impression she'd like more hours. Should I see if she's interested in going full-time?"

"Which one is Lisa? I get them confused." Georgia had hired two part-time workers to fill in during their busiest hours on the weekends, one a college student and the other a middle-aged mother of two.

"She's the more mature of the two," Georgia said with a smile. "Her girls are in high school, which anchors her to home without requiring her to be there every waking hour."

"Then, by all means, let's see if she's interested. While you're at it, do you mind giving Lula a call? We've sold out of our bouquets. We'll need a fresh bunch before the weekend."

"Sure," Georgia said, although she had no intention of calling Lula. She had no intention of ever speaking to her again after she neglected to inform her of her husband's affair. But business was business. She would text her instead.

"After last night, I hope Lula's not ill."

As mad as she was at her friend, Georgia was curious about Lula's absence at the party. "I left right after dinner. Did she ever come out of her room?"

Shaking her head, Heidi said, "I saw her when we first got there, but I never laid eyes on her once the party started. I'm crazy about Lizbet, but I sensed strange vibes from the other daughter. What's her name? I never even met her."

"Brooke. By nature, she's the more reserved of the sisters. I never had the opportunity to speak to her last night either, but I got the impression she was upset about something." Georgia suspected that whatever was bothering Brooke was the reason for Lula's absence at the party. She reminded herself that whatever it was, it no longer concerned her. Not only was she losing her husband, she had lost her two best friends. The staff at Tasty had become her new family.

She'd confessed to her husband on the way home from the party that she was having a difficult time coming to terms with his adultery. "I need some time alone to sort things out. I think you should move out."

"Don't do this to us, Georgie," he'd begged. "I can't fight my addiction alone."

"I'm sorry, Langdon. But groping Sharon Parker's ass is not trying to fight it."

At least he'd had the decency to blush.

"Have you called any of the therapists on the list I made for you?"

"I haven't had time," he said. "Things have been crazy at work."

"That's what I thought. I want you out of the house, Langdon. Tomorrow." Once he was out of the house she planned to change the locks and never let him back in.

He'd pleaded with her to have a nightcap with him once they got home. "Can't we sit down and talk about whatever it is that's bothering you?"

She hated the way he turned everything on her, as though she was to blame for the problems in their marriage. "You need to sleep in the guest bedroom tonight. And I don't want you here when I get home from work tomorrow."

She'd been adamant he move out, which is why she was surprised and angry as hell to find Langdon's car parked in front of their house when she arrived home from work that evening. She marched inside ready to give him a piece of her mind. Searching the downstairs, she found him at the break-fast room table with a cup of coffee in front of him. "What're you doing here? I thought I made it clear. I want you out of the house."

He rose halfway out of his chair and motioned at the seat opposite him. "Georgie, please, sit down. We need to talk."

"We have talked, Langdon. There's nothing left to say." She went to the refrigerator, removed a bottle of Pinot Grigio, and poured herself a glass.

He sank back down to his chair. "This is serious, honey. And it has nothing to do with you and me. Lula has a brain tumor. Most likely an inoperable one, although we won't know for sure until we do the biopsy tomorrow."

She looked at him as though he'd lost his mind. "What're you talking about?" But even as the words left her lips, she knew he was telling the truth. Her mind flashed back a few weeks to their last tea time when she and Midge had found Lula passed out on her kitchen floor. All the times she'd seen her since then, Lula had seemed distracted, not quite herself. And she hadn't looked well—her complexion pasty, and dark circles under her eyes. What did any of it have to do with Brooke and the striking girl who'd never left her side during the party last night? Was it all just a coincidence? Brooke's sudden return home after three long years. The Fourth of July party Lula insisted on having, even though she hadn't hosted one in years. Did she expect it to be her last? "When did she find out?"

"This morning. She had a fall at the beach house. They brought her to MUSC in an ambulance. Your friend is a very ill woman, sweetheart. I've never been close to Phillip and Lula, but I don't envy them what they are facing now. And those poor daughters of theirs. I wouldn't wish this on my worst enemy."

Wine glass in hand, she dropped to the chair across from him. "She has options, doesn't she, if surgery isn't one of them?"

He shrugged. "We may try radiation to shrink the tumor

enough to surgically remove it. But that's a long shot." When he reached for Georgia's hand, she jerked it away. "I understand you're upset. I'll do anything I can for Lula and her family. But I'm skeptical as to a positive outcome."

Georgia stared across the table at her husband. She'd questioned everything she thought she knew about him in recent days, but never his profession. His skills as a surgeon, his reputation as being one of the top neurologists in the state, were indisputable. He performed miracles every single day. He fancied himself a god for saving all those lives. Why then, if he loved her as much as he claimed, wouldn't he save the one life that mattered the most? "This is Lula we're talking about. She's one of my oldest, dearest friends. I don't care what it takes. You have to find a way to save her life."

"I'll try." He hung his head, staring down into his coffee as though it held the answers. "But there's only so much I can do."

She left the table and took her glass of wine to the window. She saw Lizbet and Brooke next door moving about inside the Florida room. An hour ago she'd vowed never to speak to Lula again. But none of that mattered now. All that mattered was finding a way to save Lula's life.

She set her glass of wine on the counter and went to the back door.

"Where are you going?" Langdon asked without looking up.

"Next door. To a family who needs me."

CHAPTER TWENTY-THREE
MIDGE

MIDGE STRETCHED OUT beneath the sheets, basking in the warm glow from hours of lovemaking. She'd finally set aside her inhibitions about sex and let Bennett have his way with her. With a tenderness she didn't know he possessed, he'd made love to her in ways she didn't think possible. On Wednesday evening, the night after Lula's party, he'd taken her out on a sunset cruise in his parents' new boat. They sipped champagne and nibbled on brie and bread as they watched the orange ball disappear over the horizon. They talked again about her suspicions and he convinced her he wasn't all bad. He made love to her while they were out on the water, again when they docked at the marina, and all night long once they returned to her house—in the kitchen, the TV room, and her bed. She wanted to lounge in bed awhile longer, but she needed to get on with her day.

Careful not to disturb Bennett, she slipped out of bed and went downstairs. After retrieving the paper from the front porch, she brewed herself a cup of coffee while skimming the headlines. She then added cream and sweetener to hers, brewed a cup for Bennett, and took it upstairs to him.

He grabbed her by the wrist and pulled her down on the bed next to him. "What're you doing up? Come back to bed."

She pushed away from him. "I can't. I need to get in the shower. I'm meeting a new client at nine."

"It's probably just as well. I don't think I can perform right now anyway. You wore me out."

She blushed. "I'm the one who's worn out."

He fingered her cheek. "Look at you turning red. I can't believe that, after all we did last night, you're still shy about having sex with me."

"I'm getting there. I just need a little more time." She sensed a deeper bond developing between them. She only hoped that this Bennett, the one she'd initially fallen in love with, was here to stay.

He sat up in bed and reached for his coffee. "I'm going to cook dinner for you tonight. Something simple. I'm in the mood for seafood. Tuna steaks maybe. I'll pick up a bottle of that rosé you like so much and we'll sip wine, cook on the grill, and start making plans for our business. We can build our powerhouse, Midge. We'll be the cutting edge in real estate. Did I tell you my parents agreed to invest in the start-up of our boutique agency?" When a skeptical look crossed her face, he added, "And no, I didn't ask them. They offered."

"That's great news, honey." Being the sole investor in a firm with a man she didn't entirely trust had given her pause. But going in as equal equity partners, a far more attractive option, put her at ease about proceeding with their plans.

"I told you my mom believes in me. She always has.

I'm gonna make you believe in me too, just you wait." He touched the tip of his finger to the tip of her nose. "You're the real reason they're willing to invest. My parents love you. They want to throw a party for us at their house. Whatever we decide—a small wedding reception if you'll ever agree to marry me, or a business reception to announce the opening of our new agency. You'll have a whole new clientele once my parents introduce you to the owners of the prime downtown real estate."

"That's incredibly generous of them. Do they really like me?" Midge hadn't realized how important it was to her to have his parents' approval.

"They love you. What's not to love?" He took another sip of his coffee and sat it down on the table. "Now, what do you think about Calhoun Properties for the name of our firm? We just need to make it official. Say the word and we'll fly off to Jamaica for our destination wedding."

"I need a little more time, Bennett." She rose from the bed and walked across the room to her closet. "I don't want to rush into anything, either marriage or the business."

"I won't force you into anything you're not ready for. But if we want to see this thing happen during our lifetime, we need to start making plans. We're not getting any younger, you know. I'm thinking we'll only need one admin person to get started, but the location of our office is key. We want to pick the spot that sets the right tone. East Bay Street would be ideal, but I doubt we can afford the rent."

He was still talking when she went into the bathroom to shower, but was gone when she got out. He left a note beside his coffee mug on the bedside table. Take all the time you need. I'm not going anywhere. I love you. Bennett.

Midge dressed in a gray silk sleeveless blouse and a black pencil skirt that showed off a good portion of her shapely legs. She noticed her flushed cheeks as she was putting on her makeup. She had the appearance of a woman well loved. And she felt well loved. If only she could be guaranteed it would last.

Midge was hurrying out to her car when she saw Lizbet on the front porch next door. She stopped and waved. "The party was a success, despite the weather," she called to her. "I'm sorry I never got a chance to speak to your mother. I hope she's feeling all right." An expression crossed Lizbet's face, but she couldn't read it from the distance. She walked down the sidewalk toward her. "Is something wrong, honey?"

Lizbet left the porch and met her halfway. "Mom fell down the back steps yesterday morning at the beach and split her head open on the sidewalk. They did a CT scan at the hospital and discovered that she has a brain tumor. We won't know for sure until after the biopsy today but it looks like cancer."

Midge raised a trembling hand to her mouth. "But how can that be? She seemed fine—" The image of Lula lying unconscious on her kitchen floor prevented her from finishing her sentence. Surely that was unrelated. Anyone would have passed out considering how hot it had been in her house that day.

"I'm sorry I didn't call you," Lizbet said. "I assumed Georgia would tell you."

Georgia? After the party on Tuesday, Midge had sent Georgia a continuous stream of texts apologizing and asking for her forgiveness and begging for a chance to explain. She'd also left her a voice message—admitting that she made a very bad error in judgment in keeping Lang's affair from her and offering no excuses as to why, except to say she didn't want to see Georgia hurt. She hadn't heard back from Georgia. Hadn't really expected to. But, no matter how bad things were between them, wouldn't she have called to tell her their best friend had been diagnosed with a brain tumor?

"Georgia and I had a little falling out. Nothing for you to worry about." She studied Lizbet's face, noticing for the first time her swollen, red-rimmed eyes. "Bless your heart. You must be beside yourself."

Lizbet sucked on her quivering lip. "It helps to have my sister here. Her girlfriend is in medical school. She's been helpful in explaining the things we don't understand." She recognized Midge's confusion. "I guess you don't know if you haven't talked to Mom. We just found out Brooke is gay."

Midge nodded. "Georgia and I suspected something was up at the party. I don't imagine your mother took the news well."

"I'm not sure which has upset her more, finding out she has a brain tumor or discovering her daughter is gay."

Frown lines developed on Midge's forehead. "Poor Lula. She has an awful lot on her plate. What can I do to help your family? Can I make phone calls or run any errands for you? Do you need any food?"

"We're good for now. We have a lot of leftovers from the party, and Georgia is bringing dinner tonight from Tasty."

"Then count on me to bring dinner tomorrow night." She needed to help, if even in this small way. "You mentioned a biopsy. Will they have the results today?"

"I'm not sure. Dr. Murdaugh is her doctor, so I imagine he'll let us know as soon as he knows."

"Will you call me when you find out? Let me give you my number."

Lizbet removed her phone from her pocket. As Midge recited the number, she keyed it into her contacts.

"Call or text me anytime." She pinched the girl's chin. "Try to keep up your spirits. Your mama is one of the strongest women I know. She's gonna beat this. She has family and friends who love her and will see her through."

Lizbet nodded, her eyes filling with tears. "Thanks," she mumbled and turned to go.

Midge watched the girl walk barefoot across the grass to the front porch. She'd known both girls since birth. They'd become lovely young women. Good for Brooke for dating a medical student. It was hard to say, never having been a parent, what Midge would do in Lula's shoes. She wanted to believe she'd love her child just the same. Considering Lula's traditional values, accepting her daughter was gay would be harder for Lula than it would be for most mothers. She would need both her daughters in the days and months ahead. Midge said a silent prayer that Lula didn't turn them away.

CHAPTER TWENTY-FOUR
LIZBET

L IZBET WAITED WITH her father and sister in her mother's hospital room while the orderlies rolled Lula off to some remote part of the hospital for the biopsy. The threesome watched one morning show after another on TV, although they could barely hear it and none of them cared enough to turn the volume up. She noticed her father sneaking glances at his eldest daughter, as though trying to find something of the girl he remembered in the young woman she'd become.

Finally, around eleven, he spoke the first words he'd spoken all morning to Brooke. "I'm not sure how your mother's gonna feel about you being here." Lizbet had stayed with her parents at the hospital all afternoon yesterday. Lula had not mentioned her brain tumor, but she had carried on and on about Brooke and Sawyer. Her father had said very little in Brooke's defense.

"That's too bad, because I'm not leaving," Brooke said, her chin set in defiance.

"What're you doing here?" Lula said to Brooke when they wheeled her back into the room.

"Why do you think I'm here, Mom? I'm concerned about you."

Lula glared at Brooke. "You're not concerned about me. If you cared about me at all, you wouldn't have gotten yourself gay."

Brooke and Lizbet exchanged a look. "Gotten myself gay?" Brooke mouthed, an eyebrow arched in question.

"Is it normal for Mom to be acting out of character?" Brooke asked Dr. Dog when he entered the room a few minutes later.

"What do you know about my character?" Lula snapped. "You haven't been home in three years."

"Why don't we step out in the hall and let Lula get some rest," Dr. Dog said, motioning them to the door.

As they were filing out of the room, Lizbet heard her mother call out after them, "I know why you're going out in the hall. You don't want me to hear you talking about how much longer I have left to live."

Dr. Dog led them down the hall a ways. He leaned against the wall and the threesome gathered around him. "To answer your question, Brooke, it is very normal for someone with a brain tumor to experience a change in behavior." He crossed his legs and folded his arms over her mother's chart against his chest. "The diagnosis itself can cause emotional distress, and the hardship of treatment and uncertainty about the future can bring on depression. Your mother's tumor is located in the brain stem. In her case the location itself can bring on emotional and behavioral changes."

"In the interest of full disclosure," Brooke said, "you

should know that I came out to my parents on Tuesday. Obviously, I would have picked a better time to tell my mother I'm gay if I'd known about the brain tumor."

"Situations like these are always difficult for parents regardless of their health," the doctor said. "Some are more accepting than others."

Brooke stared down at her feet. "At this rate she'll never accept me. She's more concerned about me being a lesbian than she is about her medical condition."

Lizbet felt her father's body shudder beside her. Her sister had her work cut out for her for sure.

"That's understandable," Dr. Dog said. "It's easier for Lula to fixate on your problem than to face what lies ahead for her. All cancer patients are in denial at first."

Lizbet's skin broke out in goosebumps. "Do you know for certain it's cancer?"

"Not officially, no. But the indicators are there."

"When will you know for sure?" Lizbet asked.

"I'll put some pressure on the Pathology Department. I should have the results by the end of the day. If you'd like, I can stop in on my way home around six to go over them."

"I hate to ask you to go out of your way," Phillip said.

Dr. Dog clapped her father on the shoulder. "You live next door, Phillip. It's hardly out of my way. I'm happy to do it."

"I..." her father started and then looked at his daughters. "We're mighty grateful for the special attention. Does this mean Lula can go home now?"

Dr. Dog flipped open his chart. "I'd like to monitor her for a while, to make certain she's stable before I release her. We'll get her out of here sometime this afternoon." He checked his watch. "Now, if you'll excuse me, I need to go check on a patient."

The three Hornes stood staring at his back as he disappeared down the hall. "I should probably get to work," Lizbet said finally. Heidi had told her she could take the day off, but as much as she felt like she needed to stay at the hospital, she couldn't handle another afternoon of listening to her mother complain about her sister.

"You go." Brooke nudged her with her elbow. "I'll stay here with Mom and Dad."

Her father cleared his throat. "We don't need a babysitter. We'll be fine here alone. Anyway, Brooke, your presence seems to agitate your mother. She needs to rest."

"Fine. Then I'll go to the house and wait for you there. I can help you get her settled." Brooke turned her back on her father before he could argue, and headed down the hall.

"I'll see you at six." Lizbet planted a kiss on her father's cheek and took off after her sister. "You're being awfully pushy, don't you think?" she said when she caught up with her.

"Pushy is the only way I'm going to get my point across," Brooke said as she exited the building through the sliding doors.

"What exactly is your point?" She had to walk fast to keep up with her.

"I'm not going anywhere. No matter how much they'd like to get rid of me."

They arrived at Lula's minivan and Brooke rummaged through her bag for the keys. Lizbet had forgotten Brooke was driving their mother's car. Did her sister even own a car in California? Would she drive it across country when she moved?

"When are you starting your new job?" Lizbet asked.

Brooke located the key and unlocked the door. "The beginning of August. I was planning to turn in my notice on Monday. I'd like to work out my two weeks, but that all depends on what Dr. Dog tells us tonight. I can wrap things up from here if I need to. I have a legit reason. My boss will understand." She opened the door and slid into the driver's seat.

"Even if you're quitting to work for another firm?"

"I didn't find a new job because I'm unhappy with the one I have. I'm moving back home to be close to my family. Obviously, I would've transferred if they had an office here."

She started to close the door, but Lizbet held it open. "Have you started looking for an apartment?"

Brooke jammed the key in the ignition. "We're going to do that today since Mom doesn't want me around. Sawyer offered to move my things from California. Her brother is flying out to help her. He can drive my car back for me."

"I can't believe you. Have you picked out what dress you're going to wear to Mom's funeral?" Lizbet asked, her eyes brimming with tears.

"Oh, honey, don't cry. I'm just trying to be realistic about the situation. To be prepared." Brooke got back out of the car. "Everything will be all right." Brooke took her in her arms. "We'll take it as it comes. That's all we can do. You're not alone in this. I told you that. And I meant it."

Her sister's scent was both familiar and strange. Lizbet couldn't remember the last time their bodies had been so close. "Okay."

Brooke rubbed her back. "Run along to work now. It'll

help get your mind off things. I'll meet you back at the house at six."

Lizbet held her sister at arm's length. "Are you bringing Sawyer?"

Brooke's face registered surprise. "I haven't gotten that far. Do you think I should?"

"No and yes. Mom will freak, but Sawyer is good at asking the questions we don't know to ask. She might actually provide a calming influence."

Brooke let out a deep breath. "I'm not sure how calm it will be. But I'll let Sawyer decide whether or not she wants to come."

Lizbet dropped her sister's arms. "Georgia is bringing dinner from the store. Why don't I tell her to bring two casseroles and ask her and Dr. Dog to stay for dinner?"

"I don't know if that's such a good idea, Lizzy. I'm not sure any of us will be up for a dinner party."

"It won't be a party. Duh." The more Lizbet thought about it, the more her idea made sense. "We can keep it casual. We'll set the food out in the kitchen and everyone can eat wherever they want. I have a feeling the news won't be good. Having Sawyer and the Murdaughs in the house might soften the blow."

"Or start a nuclear war. But we'll give it a shot."

CHAPTER TWENTY-FIVE
LULA

AS HARD AS she tried, Lula could not grab hold of a single thought floating around her mind. Had they scrambled her brain when they drilled a hole in her skull and plunged a needle deep inside the tumor for their sample? Her husband rested in the chair beside her, rushing to her aid every time she shifted in the bed. He needed to stop fussing over her and start doing something to make their daughter not gay. What a wimp. *Namby pamby, pudding and pie.*

Go away! she screamed silently at the cancer voice inside her head. That's my husband you're talking about! The voice was growing bolder, determined to gain control of her mind. It wouldn't be long before it drove her insane, or snuffed out her light completely.

Struggling to sit up, she poked her finger at the nurse's call button.

"What're you doing?" Phillip shot up out of his chair. "I told you not to bother them. What do you need? Tell me and I'll get it for you."

Lula had buzzed the nurses' station half a dozen times in the past hour. She knew she was being a pest, but she didn't care.

When the nurse entered the room, she didn't bother to hide her irritation. "What is it now, Mrs. Horne?"

The young woman irritated Lula with her perky ponytail and dazzling white smile. She obviously didn't have a heinous disease growing in her pretty little head.

"I want you to take this thing out of my arm," Lula said, picking at the tape that held her IV in place. "I'm going home."

Nurse Kimberly approached the bed. "Don't do that." She brushed Lula's hand aside and smoothed the tape back in place. "I can't release you without the doctor's permission."

"Then call him on the phone," Lula demanded. "Tell him I have a long laundry list of things to do before I die and I need to get on it."

Kimberly's expression softened. "I understand, hon. I will page him, if you promise not to mess with your IV."

Lula snorted. "I am not your hon. Don't you know it's disrespectful to use a term of endearment when addressing a woman old enough to be your mother?"

The nurse's jaw tightened. "Yes ma'am. My apologies." She turned her back on Lula and scurried out of the room.

Phillip, who was rooted to his spot beside the bed, parted his lips in a tentative smile. "She'll be glad to get rid of you."

"If that's an attempt at humor, it's not funny. You'll all be rid of me soon enough."

He gripped the bed railing. "I know you're scared, Lula. We all are. But making everyone's life miserable isn't helping anything."

"Lucky for you, you won't have to put up with my unpleasantness much longer."

He stroked her leg beneath the blanket. "Aren't you getting ahead of yourself? You're already planning your funeral when we don't even know if the tumor is malignant."

She looked away from him, staring out the window at the pale cloudless sky. "I don't need a doctor to tell me what I already know, Phillip."

The nurse returned, her rubber-soled shoes squishing against the tile floor. "Looks like you're getting sprung. I'll just take this out." She removed the tape, and pressing a wad of gauze against the injection site, she slipped the needle out of Lula's arm. She attached a strip of tape to the gauze. "Do you need help getting dressed?"

Lula swung her legs over the side of the bed. "I think I can manage. I'm not dead yet."

Kimberly deposited the needle in the medical waste container. "In that case I'll go see about getting your release papers signed."

Lula went into the adjoining bathroom and changed into the clothes Phillip had brought to the hospital. She didn't recognize the woman staring back at her from the mirror. Her eyes were sunken and her skin was pale despite the weekend she'd spent lounging in the sun. She lowered herself to the closed toilet seat as she thought of Brooke and their time together on the beach, just the two of them catching up on the past three years. Why hadn't Brooke mentioned she was gay? She'd had plenty of opportunity. The answer was simple. She knew I wouldn't approve. If only she'd stayed in the closet a little while longer, I would have been able to rest in peace without knowing my daughter is a lesbian. But now I will spend eternity rolling over and over in my grave.

All the more reason to be cremated.

*

Brooke rushed out to the car to greet them as soon as they pulled into the driveway. She hurried around to the passenger side and held Lula's arm for support while she climbed out of the car. Lula shrugged her off as she started to the house. "I'm not an invalid, you know. At least not yet. I can manage on my own." But she stumbled and was grateful Brooke was by her side to keep her from falling. She caught a glimpse of her neglected garden on the way inside. Weeds had taken over the beds and her glorious blooms were wilting in the summer's heat. Chores needed tending—the laundry, the ironing, the dirty dishes Phillip had left in the sink—but she had only enough energy to climb the stairs to her bed. A week ago she'd tackled her housework with vigor. Now all she wanted to do was sleep.

It was six fifteen before she woke from her nap feeling less rested than she had beforehand. She tumbled out of bed and plodded across the room to the en suite bathroom. She needed a shower, but she felt too unsteady to risk it without help. How pathetic she couldn't manage something as simple as bathing alone. She combed her greasy hair away from her face and brushed blush across her cheeks. Using the handrail for support, she edged her way downstairs and then followed voices to the Florida room in the back of the house where her daughters were talking with Brooke's girlfriend. What was her name? She couldn't remember. She didn't remember her being so attractive either. "Who invited her?"

"I thought—" Brooke began.

"Actually, I'm the one who insisted Sawyer be here," Lizbet said. "She's a medical student. She can help us understand the biopsy results and make any decisions we need to make."

"I already have a doctor, Lizbet. He's been practicing medicine longer than she's been alive." Lula swept a hand in Sawyer's direction. "There is no us or we in this situation. There is only me. I will decide how I want to live out my remaining days."

"But, Mom!" Brooke hopped up off the sofa. "You—" A knock on the back door prevented her from continuing.

"That'll be Georgia with dinner," Lizbet said, and left the room to let her in.

Lula stared after her. "So we're having a party now? What're we celebrating, my untimely demise?"

"Mom, please," Brooke said. "No one appreciates the death humor. For your information, Georgia offered to bring dinner. Since Dr. Murdaugh was coming anyway to go over the biopsy results, we asked them to eat with us. We're keeping it casual. We're not setting the table or anything like that."

Lula's voice quavered when she said, "You should've asked. I'm not in the mood for company."

"Since when is Georgia company?" Brooke took Lula by the arm and led her to the chair next to Sawyer. "Sit down and rest while I get you some iced tea."

Before Lula could object, Brooke rushed out of the room, leaving Sawyer and Lula staring at one another.

Sawyer folded her hands in her lap. "I understand if you want me to leave, Mrs. Horne. I can't imagine how you must be feeling."

Sitting so close, Lula was able to scrutinize the girl. She was poised and confident, dressed in white jeans and a sleeveless navy blouse with her dark bob brushing her bare shoulders. Under normal circumstances Lula thought she might approve of this girl. If she was anyone other than her daughter's lover. Lula let out a deep sigh. "You might as well stay since you're already here."

Sawyer's warm smile cast a radiant glow across her face. "Thank you."

They sat in awkward silence until the others joined them a few minutes later. Based on their glum expressions, Lang had already broken the news. And the news wasn't good. Ding Dong! The witch is dead! Or would be soon.

Georgia introduced herself to Brooke's girlfriend. "I'm Georgia Murdaugh, next-door neighbor and friend. I don't think we've been formally introduced."

The girl stood to greet her. "It's nice to meet you. I'm Sawyer Glover."

Georgia turned to Lula. "I'm here for you, my friend. Whatever you need. We'll get through this together," she said, giving her a hug before sitting down in the chair opposite Lula.

Lula hated being the center of attention like this. She didn't want their pity. She wanted them all, including her husband and daughters, to leave her alone and let her die in peace. She waited until Phillip and Lang had settled into nearby chairs before she said, "Give it to me straight, Lang. How long do I have?"

He laughed nervously into his hand. "I can always count on you not to beat around the bush, Lula." He leaned back in his chair and crossed his long legs. "As we suspected, the tumor is malignant."

Although she'd been expecting it, hearing her death sentence recited out loud filled her with dread all the way down to her core. She bit her lip and forced herself not to cry as Lang talked on about the classification and grade of her tumor. His tone changed from serious to somber when he spoke of her options, or lack thereof, for treatment of her brain stem glioma. In essence, her brain was cheese with mold growing on it, mold that was widespread and deeply rooted. Because of the location of the mold, slicing it off with a knife could ruin the cheese. They could try to remove some of the mold, to extend the life of the cheese, but the mold would eventually grow back.

She waited for Lang to stop talking. "So why not simply throw away the cheese now and be done with it?" Five sets of eyes simultaneously settled on her.

Lizbet was the first to speak. "I don't understand, Mom. What cheese are you talking about?"

Lula lifted her fingers to the side of her head. "My brain is the cheese, and the cancer is the mold. What is the point in trying to save the cheese when it's already gone bad?"

"That's one way of looking at it," Lang said. "But there are other factors to consider. There are treatments that can give the cheese a better quality of life for whatever time it has left." He shook his head in response to the ridiculous statement he'd just made. "We're not talking about cheese here, Lula. This is your brain. Your options may be limited, but you still have choices."

"And what if I do nothing?"

"You will get very sick very quickly." He rose out of his chair. "You need to carefully consider your options before you make a decision of this magnitude. We have clinical trials you can explore if that's something that interests you. Talk to your family. Weigh your options. And call me anytime with questions. I'm right next door."

Georgia got up to go with him, but Lizbet, who was sitting on the sofa next to her chair, tugged on her tunic and pulled her back down. "Please stay for dinner. Thanks to you, we have plenty of food. I really need you here."

Lula stuck her finger in her ear to clear out the wax. Did Lizbet say she needed Georgia? Her youngest had never needed Lula for anything in her life. She'd never looked at her with such pleading eyes, like a toddler begging her mother for a chocolate chip cookie before dinner. Lizbet had always loved Georgia more than her. Now that Lula was leaving the picture, Georgia could adopt Lizbet as the daughter she'd never had.

Georgia and Lang exchanged a look. There was something Lula was supposed to remember about them... something important about their marriage. Oh well. Whatever it was, was lost in the bowels of her cancer.

"You go ahead." Georgia nodded Lang toward the door. "I'll stay and help them get supper."

CHAPTER TWENTY-SIX

GEORGIA

ALTHOUGH THE TENSION in the Horne household was high, Georgia was grateful for a reason to stay. She couldn't face being in the house alone with her husband, couldn't tolerate any more of his apologies and pleas to try and work their marriage out. Before they'd come over here, she'd asked him when he was planning to move out, and he'd responded with a curt, "Not anytime soon. Not with Lula in the state she's in."

At least he was now sleeping in the guest room.

She waited until she heard the backdoor shut before getting up. "Why don't I get dinner ready?"

"I'll help you," Lizbet said, and followed her into the kitchen. "I can't believe my mom is talking about her brain like it's a piece of cheese. She seems to have gone downhill so quickly."

"You heard Dr. Dog. If your mother refuses treatment, her condition will get rapidly worse."

Lizbet cut her eyes at Georgia. "You know about our nickname for him?"

Georgia smiled. "I may have heard you and Brooke whisper it a time or two."

Her young friend appeared horrified. "I'm sorry. We didn't mean—"

She gave Lizbet a half hug. "Of course you didn't. I've always thought it kind of sweet."

"Please tell me Dr. Murdaugh doesn't know we call him Dog behind his back."

Georgia opened Lula's towel drawer and removed two hot pads. "As far as I know he doesn't. I certainly never told him. The great Dr. Dog wouldn't think it so sweet."

Lizbet burst out laughing and Georgia joined in. She felt guilty carrying on in the kitchen when her best friend was struggling to come to terms with the worst news of her life in the next room. She put on a straight face and opened the oven to check on the casseroles. "These are ready." She gripped the casseroles with the hot pads and removed them from the oven. "Why don't we fix everyone a plate instead of setting up a buffet?"

"Good idea. We'll have less cleanup that way." Lizbet set out six plates while Georgia removed the mixed green salad from the refrigerator and drizzled on some champagne vinaigrette dressing. She spooned a helping of shrimp and grits onto each plate, added some salad and a chunk of homemade crusty bread. Lizbet delivered the plates to the Florida room while Georgia poured six glasses of tea.

Georgia had just sat down with her plate when Lula said, "I believe I'd like a glass of white wine. Will one of you be a dear and get it for me?"

No one made a move to get up, and Phillip said, "I'm not sure that wine is such a good idea."

Lula set her plate on the coffee table and slid to the edge of her chair. "Then I'll get it myself."

"I'll get it for you." Brooke was already on her feet. "As long as you promise to sip it." She went into the kitchen and was back in a flash with the glass of wine. She handed her mother the wine and returned to her seat beside Sawyer on the sofa. "Why don't we discuss your treatment options?"

"It's my decision, and I'm choosing not to undergo treatment. I'd like to make the most of my last days on Earth." Lula glared at them over the rim of her wine glass, daring them to argue with her. "I have much I need to tend to. Sorting out my bill from Tasty Provisions is at the top of my list. I trust you enjoyed yourself, Georgia. I wasn't able to join the party. I was shell-shocked after Brooke dropped her little bomb on me. I'm sure you've heard the news by now. I trust you've met my daughter's lesbian lover. What's your name again, dear?"

The room fell silent. Georgia snuck glances at the others. Lizbet was frozen in place, her fork suspended in midair. Brooke's face was a deep shade of crimson, and Phillip's eyes were darting about the room as if searching for an escape. The girl set her fork on her plate and dabbed at her lips with her napkin. "My name is Sawyer. Sawyer Glover."

Lizbet let her fork drop to her plate with a loud clatter. "You know her name, Mom. Stop being so difficult."

Georgia smiled at the pretty girl sitting wedged between the Horne sisters. "Sawyer, I understand from my husband that you'll be doing your residency at MUSC starting this fall."

"Yes ma'am," Sawyer said. "I have orientation tomorrow. I'm looking forward to meeting the other residents."

Phillip spoke for the first time all evening. "I didn't realize you were moving to Charleston."

Georgia noticed his face was pale and drawn from exhaustion. Like his wife, he was shell-shocked from the drama of the past two days.

Lula set her eyes on their oldest daughter. "Does that mean you're moving here with her?"

"Yes, Mom. I'm moving to Charleston with Sawyer," Brooke said. "We're in a relationship. That's what couples do. I was planning to tell you, but considering everything you've been going through, I thought it better to wait."

With trembling hands, Lula lifted the glass to her lips and took several big gulps of wine. "You can't leave California. You just got a promotion." She set her wine glass down, and Brooke snatched it away from her. "The promotion I was referring to is my new job here, in Charleston. The firm is smaller. I think I'm really gonna like it."

Georgia felt guilty for having started this awkward conversation. She hated being privy to their family business. But she couldn't very well get up and leave.

Lula eyed the empty glass of wine in Brooke's hand. "Where are you planning to live?"

"At home for now," Brooke said. "If that's okay with you. We signed a lease on an apartment today, but it won't be ready for a couple of weeks."

"And what if it's not okay with me?" Lula asked.

Georgia had to work hard to contain her surprise. This from the woman who, only a week ago, was jumping up and down in joy to have her daughter home again.

Brooke shrugged. "Then I'll find somewhere else to stay. It's not a big deal. I just thought you might like to have someone to help you out around the house, and to be here with you during the day while Dad's at work."

Lula directed her attention to Sawyer. "And what about you? Where will you live?"

"I'm going back to Atlanta after my orientation at MUSC," Sawyer said. "My brother and I are flying out to California next week. He's going to help me move our things."

"Sawyer has generously offered to pack up my stuff," Brooke said, rubbing her partner's knee. "She knows I'd rather be here with you right now."

Georgia was surprised at Brooke's brazen move when her mother was obviously not okay with the situation.

"I don't need a babysitter. I may be dying, but I'm not wearing diapers just yet." Lula forked up a shrimp and popped it into her mouth. "I hope this apartment you're leasing is in some nice gay community west of the Ashley. I'd rather not have you flaunting your relationship in front of my friends."

Georgia watched the color drain from Sawyer's face. "Lula, please," Georgia said. "You and I both know plenty of people who have gay children."

"Since when did you become so accepting of gays?" Lula asked.

"Lula!" Phillip said. "That's quite enough. What on earth has gotten into you tonight?"

Georgia felt her anger rising. "As a matter of fact, Lula, I helped organize Pride Week last summer."

"Oh, right. I remember you mentioning something about that. Sawyer,"—Lula flung her arm out at Georgia—"you're looking at a woman who has served on every nonprofit board in this city. I'm nowhere near as accomplished as Georgia. I'm not the wife of an important doctor. My husband is a boring old accountant. My obituary will be short and sweet. Lula McMillan Horne—wife and mother. All I've ever done is take care of my family. I wasn't even successful at raising children since one of my daughters turned out to be gay, and I doubt the other will ever get married based on her track record." Her eyes sought out her youngest daughter. "Now that I think about it, Lizbet, I've never known you to have a boyfriend. Maybe you're gay too. Are you gay, Lizbet?"

Lizbet's face beamed red.

"Lula," Phillip said, his voice even but stern, "I'm warning you to back off."

"Answer me, Lizbet!" Lula pounded her fist on the arm of the chair. "Are you gay?"

Lizbet dropped her eyes to the floor. "No, Mom, I'm not gay."

Georgia gripped the arms of the chair. She forced herself to remain calm by reminding herself that her friend had just been diagnosed with brain cancer. She'd known Lula to be unpleasant before, and it was no secret she was set in her ways, but she'd never known her to act this way to another human being. Least of all her children. Demanding, yes. Downright nasty, no. This was a woman who gave generously of her time to homeless shelters.

Georgia set her plate on the coffee table and shifted in her chair toward Lula. "I think you should feel blessed that Brooke has found such a lovely young woman like Sawyer to share her life. I'm sure the two of you will be great friends once you get to know one another." She winked at Lizbet. "And don't you worry about Lizzy. She hasn't found the right fella yet, but she will. She's one of the dearest people I know. And every bit as beautiful as her mother and sister. Now." She crossed her legs and folded her hands in her lap. "You mentioned a to-do list. Is there anything I can help you with?"

The change of topic seemed to settle Lula. "Well… " She paused, thinking. "My garden could sure use some TLC, but I plan to jump on that in the morning before it gets too hot. I hope to have some bouquets for you in a day or two. I'll bring them over when I have them ready."

"I can take them over for you," Brooke offered. "I've been driving your minivan. I'll rent a car tomorrow when I take Sawyer to the airport if you'd rather not share yours with me." She broke off a piece of bread and stuffed it into her mouth.

Phillip wadded up his napkin and dropped it on the empty plate in his lap. "According to Lang, your mother is not supposed to drive at all. He's worried she could cause an accident if she has a seizure."

Lula's head shot up. "A seizure? No one said anything to me about seizures!"

"Lang left several pamphlets on the table in the kitchen," Phillip said. "We'll go over the information tomorrow, when you're not so tired. There are a number of symptoms you may experience."

"That's just great!" Lula slammed her plate down on the coffee table, breaking the plate into two pieces. Shrimp went flying in the air as the grits formed a puddle on the carpet. "What am I supposed to do if I can't drive my own car? How am I supposed to get around?" She surveyed the room as though searching for answers, but the room remained silent. "I've had enough for one day. If you'll excuse me, I'm going to bed." She stood abruptly, and her knees buckled beneath her. Georgia dove for her, somehow managing to catch her before she fell. "Let go of me," Lula said, shrugging her off and staggering out of the room.

Georgia took in the long faces of the girls sitting on the sofa and Phillip in the chair across from them. This poor family needed some time alone. "I better get cleaned up." She gathered up the dirty plates, including the broken one, and took them into the kitchen. Eager to retreat to the solitude of her own bedroom, she quickly rinsed the plates and loaded the dishwasher. She was putting away the leftovers when she heard someone weeping. She listened more intently. Lula was calling for help from somewhere in the front part of the house. She hurried down the hall to the living room where she found Lula sitting on the bottom step, her face planted in her hands.

She tiptoed toward her, so as not to startle her. "Lula, are you all right?"

"No! I'm not all right," she cried. "I can't walk up the stairs."

"What do you mean you can't walk up the stairs?"

"I mean. I can't. Walk. Up. The. Stairs." Lula's voice escalated with each word. She wailed and moaned, nothing intelligible but sounds that broke Georgia's heart and brought her family running.

Lizbet was the first to arrive on the scene. Georgia leaned close to her. "Go next door and get Dr. Dog. Tell him to bring sedatives." She knew her husband kept a supply of Xanax on hand for emergencies like these.

Lizbet nodded, her gray eyes dark with fear, and dashed out the front door. She returned within minutes with Langford in tow. Lula continued to sob hysterically despite her husband's attempts to calm her down.

"What happened?" Langford asked, his voice close to Georgia's ear.

"I'm not really sure. She excused herself after dinner and headed up for bed. I heard her calling out for help ten minutes later. She told me she couldn't walk up the stairs, and then she just broke down."

"Okay, follow my lead." He nudged the others out of the way and knelt down in front of Lula. "Hey, sweetheart. I brought you something that will help you sleep. Are you ready to go to bed?"

Lula lifted her blotchy face to him. "I can't walk up the stairs."

"That's okay. We're going to help you." With surprising strength, Langford pulled Lula to her feet. Gripping her upper arm, Georgia supported Lula's right side, but Langford bore most of the weight on the left. When they reached the top of the stairs, he scooped her up, carried her to her room, and set her down gently on the bed. Georgia wondered how many women he'd carried to their beds, and then scolded herself for thinking ill of her husband when he was performing a good deed.

He removed a prescription bottle from his pocket. "See if there's a cup in the bathroom, Georgia, and bring her some water."

Georgia did as she was told. After handing him the water, she backed herself into the nearest corner, saddened by the sight of her distraught friend.

Langdon placed the pill on Lula's tongue and lifted the cup to her lips. "There now. It'll be a few minutes before it takes effect. I'm going to stay with you until it does." He lifted a greasy hank of her hair off her forehead. "Do you want to tell me what happened?"

Lula rolled her head to the side, away from him. "I don't know what happened. When I got to the stairs, my mind told my body to climb, but my feet wouldn't budge. Oh god, it's happening. I'm dying sooner than I expected." Fresh tears streamed down her cheeks. "I thought I had some time. How much time do I have, Lang? Be honest."

He blotted her tears with a tissue from the box beside the bed. "A lot depends on what course of treatment we choose."

"I already told you, I don't want treatment." She snatched the tissue away from him and blew her nose.

"I think you should wait and decide that in a day or so, after you've had a chance to digest everything that's happened. I'll prescribe some meds that will deal with all this emotional stuff and help you feel more like yourself."

"Pills won't make me change my mind." She grabbed hold of his wrist. "Tell me. I need to know. How long are we talking, months or weeks?"

He hesitated, and Georgia knew he was debating on how much to tell her. "With no treatment at all, you'll live only a couple of weeks."

"That's what I thought," she said, her eyelids already growing heavy. "I know you can't cure me, but can you keep the drugs coming?"

He smiled. "That I can manage."

Georgia watched their interaction, mesmerized. She was seeing a different side of her husband's professional life. There was so much more to his job than performing miracles.

Langford rubbed Lula's forehead until her breathing changed and she began snoring softly. Even then, he remained by her side. "It's harder when it's a loved one, but it's never easy to watch someone die," he said, his eyes still on Lula.

"What would you do, if it was me lying in that bed?" Georgia asked in a hoarse voice. "Would you insist I seek treatment?"

He turned to face her. "Probably not. The treatment itself could kill her, and it'll only buy her a few weeks, a month max. Either way, the quality of life won't be good. I can put her on a regimen of meds that will hopefully give her some good days. I'm afraid that's the best I can do for her."

CHAPTER TWENTY-SEVEN

MIDGE

MIDGE LEFT WORK sick after her appointment on Thursday morning. It wasn't a total lie. She was sick from worrying over Lula. She spent the afternoon pacing back and forth from window to window, keeping a close eye on the house next door. Aside from the mail and UPS men making deliveries, the house remained quiet. She missed seeing Lula's tattered sun hat flopping about her shoulders as she puttered in the yard—watering the annuals in her planters, weeding her flower beds, and clipping perennials in her garden. The Hornes' yard was by far the most well-tended yard on the block. Midge knew enough about gardening to understand the difference between annuals and perennials, but she'd stopped trying to keep up with Lula years ago. Instead, Midge paid a yard service to come every week to mow and blow, and once in the fall to seed. Aside from her patch of Bermuda grass, she lacked the green thumb to grow much else.

When she called Bennett in tears over Lula's diagnosis, he

rushed right over with takeout for her lunch—a grilled salmon salad from Amen Street, one of her favorite raw bars downtown. Hard as he tried, he was unable to pry her from the window. "I know you're worried, honey, but watching her driveway will not make Lula arrive home any sooner. Why don't you go for a run?"

"Are you crazy? I'd suffer a heat stroke running in the middle of the day."

"Then get on your treadmill. Or watch a movie. Do something to occupy your time while you wait for news." He planted a kiss on her neck. "I'll be back around six for dinner."

Taking his advice, she changed into running clothes and pounded her frustration out on the treadmill. After showering for the second time that day, she picked at her salad while she made out her menu for the dinner she would take to the Horne family the following evening—chicken divan, heirloom tomato salad with mozzarella and basil, and peach cobbler for dessert. Doing something for Lula gave her a sense of purpose. Menu in hand, she went shopping at the Harris Teeter for the ingredients. When she returned from the grocery store, Lula's minivan was parked in front of her house. She assumed it was Brooke as she'd seen her driving her mother's van the previous day. While the chicken boiled, she sat with her computer, returning e-mails to clients, at the kitchen island where she had a direct line of sight through her french door to Lula's driveway.

It was close to three o'clock when Phillip and Lula finally arrived home in his Ford sedan. Midge slid off her bar stool and moved to the french door. She watched Phillip hurry around to the passenger side to help Lula out of the car. He braced his wife's arm to steady her while Lula shuffled across the driveway, taking baby steps as though afraid she might fall. Midge thought back to Tuesday a week ago, the last time she'd seen Lula, when she'd gone over to talk to her about Lang's affair. She may have been a little off—distracted by the party and Brooke's upcoming visit—but she hadn't appeared ill. The woman she watched slowly mount the back steps had aged ten years since then.

Midge prayed out loud to the empty room, "Oh, God, please don't let it be cancer. Give her the strength to fight it whatever it is. And grant the doctors the expertise to make her well."

She retrieved her phone from the island beside her computer and keyed off a text to Lizbet asking for word from her mother's biopsy. Two hours passed before she received a response. "We are meeting with Dr. Murdaugh tonight at six. We should know more then."

Bennett arrived a few minutes after six with tuna steaks and two bottles of her favorite rosé. When he set his purchases down on the kitchen counter, she eyed the bottles. "Are you planning to get me drunk and have your way with me?"

His hands shot up. "Busted." He pulled her into his arms. "We have a lot to talk about. I wanted to make sure we didn't run out of wine."

She rested her head against his chest. "Better to have extra, in case I need to drown my sorrows over Lula's biopsy results."

He ran his finger along her bare shoulder. "I know how much you care about Lula, sweetheart. All you can do for now is keep the faith." He held her a minute longer before turning her loose to open a bottle of the wine.

They took their glasses out to her tiny brick terrace. She

was standing beside him at the grill watching him scrape the grate with a wire brush when they saw Georgia and Lang round the back of Lula's house and disappear inside. Midge and Bennett waved, but the Murdaughs either didn't see them or avoided them on purpose.

Midge blinked away her tears. "I've lost both of my best friends. One of them is going to die and the other is never going to forgive me for keeping her husband's affair a secret."

Bennett considered her empty glass. "I'm going to have to cut you off, if you're starting the pity party after only one glass."

She elbowed him. "Stop teasing me. I've had a bad day."

"And I'm here to make it better." He dragged a patio chair over near the grill. "Sit back and relax, milady, while I cook your dinner."

She raised an eyebrow at him. "You've been holding out on me. I didn't know you knew how to cook."

"There's a lot you don't know about me. But I aim to change that."

Much to her surprise, Bennett seared the tuna to perfection and laid it out on a bed of baby greens. He made a dressing out of wasabi paste, rice vinegar, and soy sauce and drizzled it over the salad. He poured another glass of wine apiece and they sat down at the table on the terrace to eat. Midge placed her phone next to her plate, so as not to miss it when the text or call came in from Lizbet. Bennett did most of the talking, but Midge listened with rapt attention while he laid out his plans for the new business.

"So you see, we can't move forward until we have a name," he said, taking his last bite of salad and pushing his plate away.

"Calhoun Properties is the perfect name. Marry me already, so we can make it official."

"Stop pressuring me, Bennett." She pointed her fork at him, a chunk of tuna stuck to the prongs. "I've only just discovered you can cook. I need to learn everything there is to know about you before I'll marry you."

"I'm not going to break bad again, if that's what you're worried about. I'm a new man."

He waited until she finished eating before scooping up their dirty plates and carrying them inside. As she watched him through the window, rinsing the plates and storing them in the dishwasher, she thought about how grateful she was to have him with her tonight of all nights as she waited for news from next door. He brought the bottle of wine and his iPad with him when he returned ten minutes later. He set the iPad in front of her. "I've bookmarked some properties we might want to check out."

For the next forty-five minutes, they sipped wine as they studied the commercial properties for lease and sale in the downtown area that might fit their needs. All of them offered a small reception area for walk-in traffic downstairs with ample office space upstairs. Bennett lobbied hard for a lovely building on East Bay Street, but Midge thought the two on Meeting and Broad would serve them just as well for less money. To his credit, he didn't mention marriage again.

He set her glass down and took her hands in his. "We can make this thing happen, Midge. I know we can. We'll have an attorney, someone outside of my family's firm, draw up the papers. We'll be equal partners and name the agency Calhoun Wilkins."

"Calhoun Wilkins," Midge repeated, letting the name roll off her tongue. "I like the sound of it."

"I do too, actually. This way, if you decide never to marry me, we'll move in together and live in sin." He dropped her hands and cupped her chin. "I'm serious, Midge. You're calling the shots. I just want to be with you on whatever terms you decide."

When she looked into his lovely blue eyes, she discovered compassion and sincerity. This time she listened to her heart and ignored the doubt gnawing at her gut. Smiling, she lifted her fingers to his lips. "You really are the darnedest person. One minute I want to strangle you, and the next I couldn't love you more." She pressed her lips to his. "I say we do it!"

"You won't regret it. Calhoun Wilkins will be a big success, just you wait and see."

Midge's mind began to spin. "Now is the prime time for me to make a move. The market will be dead for the rest of the summer. I can wrap up my last few listings, and begin planning for the fall."

He slid the iPad in front of him. "How about I schedule an appointment for tomorrow to look at our top four choices?"

The mention of tomorrow was the needle that popped a hole in her balloon. "Tomorrow is so soon. Can we wait until Monday, until I know more about Lula's condition?" She feared the worst with each passing moment she didn't hear from Lizbet. She felt guilty planning their future when's Lula's life was in the balance.

"Monday it is." He snapped shut the cover on his iPad. "Now. How about some dessert? I brought over some of that raspberry cheesecake gelato you love."

He started to get up, but she pushed him back down. "You cooked. The least I can do is get the ice cream."

She was returning from the kitchen, carrying two small bowls of gelato, when she heard the sobs. "Do you hear that?"

"You mean that noise?" he asked, taking one of the bowls from her. "It just started. It sounds like someone is crying."

"Someone is sobbing, Bennett. Hysterically. And it's coming from next door." They'd seen Lang leave earlier, but as far as she knew, Georgia was still inside. "This waiting is killing me."

Snatching up her phone, she left her gelato untouched and went back inside. She climbed the stairs to her guest bedroom where she could see both Lula's front and back doors. She would wait here all night for Georgia to come out if necessary. She wouldn't be able to sleep until she got an update.

She could still hear the sobbing from the distance through the window. Lula's front door suddenly flung open and Lizbet dashed out and across the postage stamp lawn to Georgia's house. She returned several minutes later with Lang in tow. They disappeared inside, and seconds later, the crying subsided.

"I'm sorry for ruining our evening," she said to Bennett when he came up to check on her. "This waiting is making me crazy. I saw Lizbet run over to Georgia's and bring Lang back with her, but that was thirty minutes ago. Something terrible is going on in that house."

When Bennett wrapped his arms around her from behind, she leaned back against him. She was grateful to him for not trying to make her feel better with empty words. There was nothing he could say.

"Why don't you go get in my bed? I'll be in in a minute."

She wanted to be alone, but she didn't want him to leave. He'd had too much wine to drive home anyway.

"Are you sure? I can take an Uber," he said as though reading her mind.

"No, it's fine." She turned her head and kissed his cheek. "I want you to stay."

"Okay, then. You know where I'll be if you want to talk."

Midge grew angrier by the minute waiting for some sign of life next door. She wasn't mad at Lizbet. Cancer or not, she was just a child who'd been dealt a horrible blow. But for Georgia to ignore Midge like this was downright cruel, no matter how ticked off she was about the Lang business. Lula was Midge's friend too. Georgia had an obligation to share the details of her illness. She could at least send her a simple text.

Midge was ready to give up and go to bed when Georgia and Lang emerged from the house. She shot off out of the room and down the stairs to the front stoop. As she marched down the sidewalk toward her, she called into the silent night, "Georgia, I need a word with you."

"Now is not a good time," Georgia said and kept walking.

Midge increased her pace. "She's my friend too, damn it," she said, grabbing Georgia by the arm when she caught up with her.

Seeing the concern on Midge's face, Georgia said, "Fine," and motioned for her husband to go ahead without her.

As they watched him go, Midge was tempted to ask if she and Lang were working out their problems, but she no longer had the right to ask about Georgia's personal life. She waited until he was out of earshot. "I've been sick with worry. Just tell me, is the tumor malignant?"

"I'm so angry at you, Midge, I can barely stand to look at

you. I no longer think of you as a friend. But Lula would want you to know, so I'm telling you that yes, it is cancer. A very bad kind of cancer."

Midge gasped. Tears filled her eyes and a sob caught at the back of her throat.

"It's all very complicated." Georgia glanced over at the Hornes' house as though worried they might overhear her. "I'm hesitant to say too much. You should talk to Phillip tomorrow. He can fill you in on the details."

When Georgia started to walk away, Midge grabbed her arm again. "You'll never know how sorry I am that I kept Lang's affair from you. I care about you so much, I didn't want to see you hurt. I was planning to tell you. I was just waiting for the right time to do so. I understand you're angry at me. I would be angry at me too. But the three of us have been friends for twenty-six years. We need each other now more than ever." She waited for Georgia to say something. But when she didn't, Midge turned to leave.

"Wait, Midge. Don't go."

Midge turned back around to face her.

"You're right. Lula will need both of us to help her through this." Georgia moved in closer to Midge and lowered her voice. "Surgery, chemo, and radiation are all options. But only for extending her life by a few weeks, not for sending the cancer into remission. Lula is refusing to have treatment. Hopefully, she'll change her mind tomorrow when she's had a chance to calm down. As you can imagine, this has been difficult on all of them. Lula is taking her fear and anger out on poor Brooke and her partner, Sawyer."

Midge shook her head. "I'm so sorry for them. What can

I do to help? I'm taking them dinner tomorrow night, but I feel so useless."

"There'll be plenty for us to do in the coming weeks. You probably don't know this, but Brooke and Sawyer are moving to Charleston. Brooke is planning to stay here at the house with her mother while Sawyer flies back to California to pack up their things. Poor Lula is already incapable of giving herself a bath, and things are only going to get worse. She'll need more help than Brooke can offer."

"I know a retired registered nurse who might have some free time," Midge said. "I sold her a house a few years back. She works part-time for sick folks. Should I give her a call?"

Georgia thought about it for a minute. "I don't want to overstep any boundaries, but poor Phillip is overwhelmed. I imagine he'd be grateful for the referral."

"I'll find out if she's available, and let Phillip take it from there. You know, I have another idea. Tell me what you think. Remember how upset Lula was when we stopped meeting for tea? Why don't we start that back up? At least for a few weeks, while she feels like it. Do you think you could manage the time off work?"

"I'm sure I can get someone to cover for me at the store. That's a nice idea, Midge. Thanks." Georgia's lips parted into a smile, a sign that she might one day forgive her.

CHAPTER TWENTY-EIGHT
LIZBET

LIZBET USED WORK as an excuse to avoid her parents for the next few days. She couldn't handle the hostile environment, listening to her mother lash out at Brooke, any more than she could face the realization that her mother might be dying. Even though she'd made the decision to stay away, she was concerned when no one from home called to give her an update. Had they made a decision about whether her mother would have treatment? Were the meds Dr. Dog prescribed helping any? Had her mother softened any toward Brooke?

On Sunday, while working at the yacht club, she observed the mother-of-the-bride say goodbye to her daughter at the wedding brunch, and was overcome with sadness knowing she might never share a similar moment with her own mother. She vowed to cherish whatever moments she had left, regardless of how cranky and irrational Lula behaved.

Lizbet boxed up several pieces of leftover wedding cake and drove the few blocks to her family's home. She found her father working in her mother's garden. "It's awfully hot out here, Daddy. Shouldn't you wait until later in the day when it cools down a little? Mom usually does her gardening in the morning."

Looking up from his edging, he wiped the sweat off his forehead with the back of his gloved hand. "Nah, I'm fine. But I appreciate you worrying about me. Brooke has done most of the work. I'm just finishing up a few remaining chores. The garden had gotten out of hand in a short amount of time. We didn't want your mother stressing about it."

Lizbet pinched a bloom off a butterfly bush. "It looks nice, Daddy. Mom will be pleased. How's she doing?"

"Not much has changed since you were last here." His expression grew solemn, and he sank the edging blade back into the dirt.

Lizbet cast an uncertain glance toward the house. "Where is everyone? Is it safe to go inside?"

He snickered. "I don't think anyone's going to bite your head off today. Except maybe Pooh. Poor boy hasn't been for his walk yet. Your mother is upstairs napping, and Brooke is camped out in the Florida room watching something on TV." He shooed her toward the door. "Go on in. I'll be there in a minute."

Lizbet let herself in the back door and set the box of wedding cake on the counter. She tiptoed into the Florida room. Brooke was stretched out on the sofa, her hands behind her head and Pooh curled up at her feet, watching a gruesome scene from a Game of Thrones episode showing on TV.

Brooke looked up when she saw her enter the room. "Hey, kiddo. What're you doing?"

"I just stopped by to check on things." She approached the edge of the sofa and rubbed Pooh's ears. "I'm sorry I haven't been around the past few days. What happened the other night freaked me out. I was scared to come back. How are you surviving? After all, you're the one she's mad at."

"I stay out of her way mostly. She seems a little better since she started taking the meds." Brooke pushed Pooh out of the way and moved her feet over to make room for Lizbet on the sofa. "By better, I mean not as angry. She's in some kind of trance, staring off into space. Only the Lord knows what she sees. She doesn't seem to hear anything anyone says, and she's barely spoken at all since the other night. If you can believe that knowing how much Mom likes to boss everyone around. Worst of all she absolutely refuses to discuss treatment."

Lizbet lowered herself to the sofa next to her sister. "What does Dad think about her not having treatment?"

Brooke hesitated. "I don't know, Lizzy. I've tried to talk to him. He's pretty much checked out. He seems content to let her have her way, even though he knows the cancer is affecting her ability to make an intelligent decision."

Fingering the fringe on one of the decorative pillows, she asked, "How long do you think she has, if she doesn't do the treatment?"

Brooke shook her head. "As far as I know, Dr. Dog hasn't said, and I'm afraid to ask. She's getting weaker by the day. I know that much."

Lizbet slipped off her shoes and, drawing her knees to her chest, placed the bottom of her feet against Brooke's. For the next few minutes, they giggled and squirmed as they struggled against one another in a game they'd called leg wars when they were little girls, back in the days when they were friends.

"I brought home some wedding cake," Lizbet said when they were both spent from their efforts. "Do you want a piece?"

"Yeh-ah," Brooke said, scrambling to a sitting position. "I never say no to cake of any kind."

They raced one another to the kitchen in their bare feet. Lizbet removed two of the cake slices from the takeout container and placed them on plates while Brooke poured them each a glass of milk. They sat down at the kitchen table opposite one another.

"Remember when we were little, and Mom used to bring us home a slice of cake from all the weddings she attended?" Brooke said.

Lizbet smiled. "I remember. She slid the slices under our pillows while we were asleep and asked us the next day if we'd dreamed of our future spouse."

"Ha. She never imagined my spouse would be a girl."

Lizbet studied her sister who was forking big chunks of cake into her mouth. She'd always envied her sister for being able to eat whatever she wanted while remaining so slim. Her super-short haircut accented her dainty features, but the overall appearance was one of a confident young woman. Her sister was clearly not struggling with her identity.

"Tell me something, Brooke." Lizbet set down her fork and wiped off her milk mustache. "You seem so sure of yourself, so put together. Why were you so afraid to tell Mom you are gay?"

Brooke's mouth dropped open and cake crumbs fell onto the table. "Seriously? You have to ask me that, knowing what a bigot she is?"

"I'm not sure I would necessarily call her a bigot." When Brooke stared at her like she'd sprouted a horn from her forehead, Lizbet laughed out loud. "Okay, fine. She is a bigot. But still, your relationship with Sawyer is obviously rock solid.

And you've known for years you're gay. Why not just come out and tell her?"

"Well…" Brooke sat back in her chair and crossed her legs. "When Sawyer and I decided to move to Charleston, I knew the time had come to tell Mom. I planned to break the news during our weekend at the beach, but we were enjoying ourselves so much, I didn't want to spoil it. I wanted to savor the last moments together before she turned on me." Brooke pointed her finger at Lizbet. "And that's exactly what happened when she found out. She's lost all respect for me. When she looks at me, it's like she's looking right through me, like I'm not even here. Now that I know she's dying, I'm sorry I even told her. I've made everything so much worse for her. For all of us."

"There was never going to be an easy time." Lizbet debated whether to ask her sister the one question she really wanted an answer for. Why not? Her sister appeared to have nothing to hide. "You've been with Sawyer for a while now. How did she not know that you hadn't come out to your family yet? She seemed to take it pretty well."

"Sawyer doesn't show her anger and she doesn't hold grudges." Brooke smiled, a dreamy look on her face. "I've met Sawyer's parents many times. They've flown out to California to see her, and we've been to Atlanta to visit them. Last year, they even took us on an Alaskan cruise. Her parents have accepted our relationship. I knew Sawyer wouldn't come to Charleston if she thought my parents wouldn't approve of me being gay. And I really wanted her here. I really wanted her to meet you, Lizzy. I wasn't the greatest sister to you growing up, and I'm sorry for that. But I'd like to try and make it up to you. I want us to have a relationship."

Lizbet dragged her finger through the icing on her plate

and licked it. "I want that too. If it's any consolation to you, I really like Sawyer. I don't think I would relate to her as much if she were a boy."

"That's definitely one way of looking at it." Brooke got up from the table and took their plates to the sink. She turned around and leaned against the counter. "That means a lot to me. More than you know. I can't tell you how much it hurts to think Mom might die while she's still mad at me."

"That's not going to happen," Lizbet said with more confidence than she felt. "She'll come around eventually. I'm sure she appreciates everything you're doing around here to help." Lizbet swept her hand at the spotless kitchen. "This house has never been so clean. And the garden looks wonderful."

"Being here is helping me more than it's helping her. I don't expect her to notice. She's too sick."

"Is she really that bad off?" Lizbet asked.

Her sister's eyes glistened with unshed tears. "It's scary how much difference a few days have made. She's so weak she can barely make it up and down the stairs. And scrambled eggs are the only thing I can get her to eat." Brooke shifted her gaze toward the ceiling. "You should go up and see her."

Lizbet followed Brooke's gaze. "Maybe I'll take her a slice of cake."

"I bet she'd like that."

Lizbet took the plate and left the kitchen. She trudged up the stairs, her family's sorrow weighing heavily on her mind. Somehow, she needed to find a way to heal her family. In order to do that, she needed to reach her mother—help her mother see what a wonderful person Brooke had become, and how happy she and Sawyer were together. Like any couple, they would have their challenges but they loved each other enough to work through them.

She entered her mother's room, noticing it was dark and filled with a funky odor that smelled like rotting fruit. She'd never known her mother to draw her bedroom drapes during the day, aside from that week in late September when Brooke first left for college and her mother, with an aching heart, retreated to her room.

Lizbet set the plate on the nightstand, lifted back the covers on her father's side of the bed, and crawled in facing her mother. For a long time, she watched the rise and fall of Lula's chest as she slept. It was some time before she finally stirred.

Lula opened her eyes and then closed them again when she saw her daughter beside her.

"How're you feeling?" Lizbet asked.

"I'm dying from brain cancer," Lula said with her eyes still closed. "How do you think I feel?"

"I don't pretend to understand how you're feeling, Mom, your pain or your fear. But I wish you'd understand this is happening to all of us, not just to you. We love you. We don't want you to die. Will you please consider going for treatment?"

"There's no point, Lizbet." Lula opened her eyes and rolled over on her back, staring up at the ceiling. "The treatments will only make me feel sicker than I already do."

She pulled the covers up over her mother's chest. "You won't know for sure until you try."

"I don't have the energy to try. There's no point in dragging this out. The sooner this is over, the better off you all will be. Now be a good girl and leave Mama alone to rest."

Lizbet sat up in bed, but she wasn't ready to go. "I'll go, but first I have a few things I need to say." She took a deep breath. "I know you're upset about Brooke, but can't you at least try to be happy for her? She's lucky to have found someone special to share her life."

She felt her mother flinch beneath the covers beside her. "Lizbet, please. I know what you're trying to do, and it won't work. I'll be dead soon and you can live your lives however you see fit. You won't need my approval."

"Brooke didn't become gay to upset you, Mom. That's just who she is. You should be proud of her. Just look at all she has going for her. She's smart. She has a great job. She's independent. She doesn't do drugs. She's caring," Lizbet said as she ticked off each point with her fingers. "I respect her for so many things, including her choice in partners. Sawyer is a good person. You'd like her too if you'd give her a chance. Look at it as though you're gaining another daughter."

"I'm dying, Lizbet. I don't have time to get to know her better."

"If you won't do it for Brooke, will you do it for me? I'm excited to be getting my sister back. I've missed her all those years she lived out in California. You can't deny that you have too."

Lula struggled to sit up. "Lizbet, I'm warning you, you are trying my patience. I have a massive headache as a result of the cancer growing inside my brain. Brooke has made her choices, but that doesn't mean I have to accept them. Even for you."

"Why am I not surprised? You've never done anything for me." Lizbet jumped to her feet. She managed to steady her voice despite the tears burning her throat. "I've tried to be a good daughter. I stayed in Charleston for you when Brooke went off to California and you begged me never to leave you.

I saw how much you missed her, and I tried to fill her shoes. For seven years I've done everything you asked. I've come running every time you needed help planning a party or taking out the trash. I was the one you called when you needed your computer fixed. But it was never enough. I was never good enough. Brooke was always your favorite."

"Shut up!" Lula screamed at the top of her lungs and then slumped back against the headboard, her hands pressed against her ears. "I'm begging you, leave me be and let me die in peace."

Lizbet stared, mouth agape, at her mother. Lula had never screamed at her before or told her to shut up. She'd asked for it. She'd provoked her mother on purpose, to show her how unreasonable she was behaving about Brooke. But her agenda no longer included her sister. The fury brewing inside Lizbet stemmed from years of feeling pent-up anger, frustration, and hurt toward her mother.

"Fine, I'll go if you don't want me here." Lizbet marched across the room to the door, and then stopped in the doorway and turned back around. "Why would I want to spend time with you anyway? You're selfish and mean and spoiled. You pout and throw temper tantrums when something doesn't go your way." The words spilled out of her mouth before she could stop them, and there was no taking them back. It wasn't fair to blame a dying woman for everything she'd done wrong as a parent. Mothers made mistakes. They were humans too. Even though the world held mothers to a higher standard than fathers. Mothers were meant to be perfect. And their children blamed them for everything wrong in their lives when they weren't. Just as Lizbet had done.

CHAPTER TWENTY-NINE
LULA

LULA DREW THE covers up to her chin as she listened to the sound of Lizbet's feet pounding the steps followed by raised voices in the kitchen. A minute later she heard the screech of her daughter's tires pulling away from the curb out front.

No matter how hard they tried to convince her, she would never approve of Brooke's relationship with Sawyer. Lula refused to be bullied into accepting something that compromised her principles.

Mean and selfish? Humph. She'd always tried to do right by her girls. She may have shown favoritism toward Brooke when they were little, but didn't all mothers have a special bond with their oldest child? She'd certainly never meant to hurt Lizbet. Her youngest daughter was precious to her. She understood now why Brooke had chosen Stanford for college. She'd wanted to get away from Lula so she could live in sin. Lizbet claimed to have stayed in Charleston for Lula's sake, but she was mistaken. Lula knew her daughter better than she knew herself. Lizbet had stayed because Charleston was her home. She was every bit the homebody Lula was.

What was so mean and selfish about wanting to be left alone to die? In her mind she was sparing her family the pain of having to watch her rot away. What a pity she couldn't choose where and when she died. Her eyes drifted to the bottle of sleeping pills on the nightstand. Or maybe she could. She was just so scared about dying, about what waited for her on the other side. Having Brooke living in her house served as a constant reminder of her failure as a parent. Having Brooke waiting on her hand and foot made her feel like an invalid. Brooke had taken over the chores of her house and her garden as though she was already dead. As if she could handle the responsibilities of her home better than Lula. Why didn't they just dump her in a nursing home to live out her last remaining days?

Lula reached for a sleeping pill and popped it into her mouth, gulping it down with saliva. Sleeping away the afternoon seemed like a pleasant alternative to coping with the living hell her life had become. She slipped into a peaceful sleep void of pain and bad dreams about her daughters. When she woke again, the day was gone and evening was upon them. She dragged her tongue over her parched lips. Her appetite had been MIA the past few days, but suddenly she craved a tall glass of sweet tea, poured over ice with a sliver of lemon and a sprig of mint. Her eyes focused on the silver handbell on the nightstand. Brooke had dug it out of a box of Christmas decorations. "When you need anything at all, you just ring this bell and I'll come running."

Ring the bell, hell. Maybe if she showed her family she could take care of herself, they would leave her alone. She tumbled out of bed, slipped on her housecoat, and shuffled down the hall. She stared at the flight of stairs, the first leg of the journey that would take her to that icy, lemony glass of sweet tea. She'd never carpeted the steps, because she admired the honey-colored oak treads, the same hardwood that would break her neck if she fell. Gripping the railing, she eased her body down to the top step, and then slid on her fanny step by step until she reached the bottom. She hauled herself up, brushed herself off, and plodded toward the back of the house where she discovered Brooke and Midge speaking in hushed voices with their heads pressed close together at the kitchen table. They stopped speaking when she entered the room.

"If you're planning my eulogy, don't bother. I want a private burial, with family only, at Magnolia Cemetery."

"Nobody's planning your funeral, Mom." Brooke hopped up and offered Lula her chair. "Come sit down. Midge stopped by for a visit. She brought us a shrimp and orzo salad for dinner. It smells really good, with feta cheese, dill, and a lemony dressing."

More than anything, Lula wanted to keep on walking out the backdoor to her garden where she could see Phillip working. She longed to see her beautiful flowers and feel the fresh air, no matter how humid, against her skin. But she was too wiped out from the trip to the kitchen to pass up the chance to sit. She avoided Midge's gaze as she situated herself in the chair. Her family's pity was enough to deal with without having her friends feeling sorry for her as well.

Brooke took a seat in Phillip's chair beside her. "Did you have a nice nap?"

"I've been asleep since ten o'clock this morning, Brooke.

I'd hardly call that a nap." She patted her daughter's hand. "Be a good girl, and fix me a glass of tea."

Brooke went to the refrigerator and removed a pitcher of tea. "Would you like some, Midge?"

Midge shook her head. "I can't stay but a minute. Bennett is waiting for me at home." She turned her attention to Lula. "I'm so sorry, Lula, about everything you're going through. It's the worst rotten luck. I don't really know what to say."

"Then do us both a favor, and don't say anything at all," Lula snapped.

Midge flinched, but recovered quickly. "Now, Lula, you know what a hard time I have keeping my big mouth shut. I have great news, by the way. Georgia has rearranged her work schedule so we can meet on Tuesday for tea just like old times. It's been so long, and we've all missed each other. We have a lot to catch up on."

Lula looked Midge in the eyes and said, "I'm busy that day," even though she had nothing on her calendar except sleeping. Who did Midge and Georgia think they were kidding? They wanted one last powwow before she croaked so they could attend her funeral with a clean conscience.

Brooke set a tall glass of tea with lemon and mint—the way her mother liked it—in front of Lula. "Not according to your calendar." She pointed toward the monthly At-A-Glance calendar hanging beneath the phone on the wall where Lula logged all of her appointments. "It'll do you good to visit with your friends."

"In that case I'll go. If I'm still alive," Lula said and took a sip of her tea.

Midge slid a slip of notepaper across the table to her. "A client of mine is a retired RN. She works part-time for people with needs similar to yours. I've spoken to her, and she's willing to help you out if you decide to hire someone."

Lula glanced down at the slip of paper and back up at Midge. "Thanks, but I don't plan to live long enough to hire a nurse."

"Mom! You are being so rude!" Brooke glared at her. "Midge cares about you. She's only trying to help."

Lula picked up the slip of paper and read the name out loud. "Gladys Guzman. What kind of name is that? Never mind, don't answer that. I don't really want to know." She held the note out to Midge. "Thank you for thinking of me. But Brooke and I are managing fine for now." She spread her arms wide. "She's a regular little Suzy Homemaker. Look around you. Everything is in tip-top shape, better than when I was in charge." She knew she was being mean, but she couldn't control herself. The only thing she cared about was going upstairs to her bed and falling into a drug-induced sleep.

"Aargh! You're impossible!" Brooke snatched her phone up off the table. "I'm going for a walk." She crossed the room in three strides and slammed the door behind her.

Lula peered over her glass at Midge. "I trust you can see yourself out. I don't have the energy to walk you to the door."

Midge folded her hands on the table in front of her. "I'm not going anywhere just yet. Not until I've had my say."

First Lizbet, now Midge. Why did everyone need to unburden themselves today? Lula felt the beginning of a headache that promised to be a humdinger. She wished Midge would stop yakking and go home. "Please, Midge. Spare a dying woman the lecture."

Midge stared her down. "I've known you for a long time, Lula Horne. You've stuck with me through a lot. You supported me in my efforts to conceive a child, and you helped me through the lonely years after my divorce. You are the strongest person I know. Not always the nicest. Nice isn't always warranted. But showing compassion for your family and friends is." She reached across the table and grabbed hold of Lula's hand, squeezing it tight. "I'm gonna talk tough love to you, because you need to hear it. The way you are behaving is downright shameful. You are scared. The girls are scared. Phillip is scared. This is a time to embrace your family, not push them away. What if you had a seizure right now and dropped dead on the kitchen floor? Do you want what just happened at this table to be Brooke's last memory of you?"

Wrenching her hand free from Midge's grasp, Lula lowered her head and stared into her lap. She felt like a teenager being scolded for breaking curfew. She'd behaved horribly, and she deserved to be punished. But why did the punishment have to be death?

"We can't begin to understand what you're going through. But we love you, and each of us is suffering in our own way. Yell at me if you want to get it off your chest. I'm tough. I can take it, much better than those precious daughters of yours." She pushed back from the table and stood up. "I'm right next door if you need me. I've always been here for you and always will be. You can count on that." Once again Midge reached for Lula's hand. She pressed the slip of paper with Gladys Guzman's contact information into her palm and folded her fingers around it. "Call her, Lula. Brooke shouldn't be the one nursing you and doing your laundry and cleaning your house. Lizbet left here earlier with tears streaming down her face. And poor Phillip's been out in the garden all day in the scorching heat, because he's too afraid to come inside."

Lula's head shot up. "That's absurd."

"That's the truth." Midge drew an imaginary X across her heart. "He told me so when I came in. Don't waste what time you have left. Talk to your daughters. Tell them things they don't already know about you. Give them advice on marriage and raising children. Show them how to set a Thanksgiving table, Lula-style. Be strong for them like you've always been strong for me. Don't let them think you're a shrew. Let them see your lovely soul."

*

Lula waited until Midge closed the door behind her before getting up from the table and moving to the window. She watched Midge and Phillip in the garden. Phillip listened attentively, his shoulders slumped and his brow furrowed, while Midge did all the talking, her lips flapping away as she recounted the tongue-lashing she'd given Lula. Her husband nodded his head from time to time in agreement with what she was saying.

Lula agreed with Midge as well. She'd hit a nerve on many counts. But her head hurt too much to think about how she wanted to spend her last remaining days on Earth. Lula sat back down at the table and buried her face in her hands.

Philip found her that way a few minutes later. "Are you feeling all right?"

"I have another headache. The tumor is beating against my skull like a drummer in a marching band."

He walked over to the lineup of prescription bottles beside the refrigerator. "When is Brooke coming home? She's the only one who knows what medicines you're supposed to take when."

"She should be home soon. She just went for a walk." Lula forced herself to smile despite the pain.

He noticed the slip of paper Midge had left lying on the table. "What's this? Who is Gladys Guzman?"

"Just some home-care nurse Midge recommended." She tried to grab the paper from him, but he stuffed it into his pocket. "I'll hold on to it in case we need it in the future."

Lula let him keep the paper. She was too tired to argue. "Are you hungry? Midge brought over some pasta salad with shrimp in it."

"Let me shower first." He bent over and kissed her cheek before leaving the room.

"I'll have it ready when you come back down," she called after him.

Lula sat at the table until she heard the shower turn on overhead. Shuffling over to the refrigerator, she removed the plastic container of shrimp and pasta, and then rummaged through the vegetable bin until she found a large ripe tomato. She scooped pasta and shrimp onto two plates, added a couple of slices of tomato, and sprinkled on some Jane's Krazy Mixed-Up Salt. When the pill bottles caught her eye, she opened the junk drawer for a pair of reading glasses. Although she didn't recognize the names of the medicines, she could read the instructions. Once a day for depression. One capsule at bedtime. To control seizures. As needed for pain. She popped the lid off the bottle of pain killers, shook out a pill, and swallowed it with water.

Phillip returned to the kitchen a few minutes later, smelling like Dove soap and wearing a fresh pair of khaki pants and a plaid button-down shirt. He saw the plates on the counter. "Shouldn't we wait for Brooke to eat?"

"Who knows when she'll be back. She probably ran into some friends."

They took their plates to the family room and turned on the TV to Sixty Minutes. Lula took a few bites of the pasta dish, but the pain in her head had curbed her appetite. Halfway through the show, she returned their plates to the kitchen and placed them in the dishwasher. She reached for the as-needed-for-pain bottle and popped another pill. The medicine had made her feel drowsy, but it had done little to relieve the pain. She glanced at the clock. Brooke had been gone for an hour and a half. She would be getting hungry soon. Lula took a bowl of vanilla ice cream and two spoons to the family room, but the cold food only increased the throbbing in her head.

Phillip expressed his concern for Brooke several times during the remainder of the show. He even tried to call her twice, but she didn't pick up. "Maybe she met some friends for dinner," Lula suggested. "Although I don't understand why she wouldn't call to let us know."

He nodded at the shoulder bag hanging from the back of a chair across the room. "Isn't that hers? I doubt she would go to dinner and not take her purse."

"True. Maybe she stopped in to see Lizbet."

Phillip nodded, his face relieved. "I bet that's it. Lizbet seemed upset when she left earlier. Brooke probably went over to check on her."

Lula felt a tinge of guilt knowing she was responsible for upsetting Lizbet. She dozed off at the beginning of the next program, and woke an hour later to the sound of Phillip's cell phone ringing on the table beside him. When he answered the call, she heard Lizbet's frantic voice from across the room. "Daddy, it's Lizbet. I just got a call from Roper Hospital.

Brooke was taken there by ambulance. I'm not sure what happened. The nurse said she was attacked, but she didn't have any information on her injuries."

"Attacked? Good lord." Phillip rubbed his balding head. "She went out for a walk hours ago. When she didn't come back, we thought she might be with you. How did the hospital know to contact you?"

"I was the last person she called from her cell phone. I'm on my way to the hospital now."

"I'll meet you there." He hung up and shoved the phone into his pocket. "That was Lizbet. Brooke has been in some sort of an accident."

"I heard." Lula winced at the pain in her head as she struggled to sit up.

"I need to get to the hospital," he said, standing. "Do you want me to have Midge or Georgia come sit with you?"

"Don't be silly. I can stay home alone by myself."

He appeared unconvinced. "Should I help you upstairs before I go?"

"I'll be fine. You need to get to the hospital." She walked him to the door and patted his shoulder when he kissed her cheek. "Please call me when you find out more about Brooke's condition."

She locked the door behind him, refilled Pooh's water bowl, and started toward the front of the house. She stopped at the sight of the pill bottles lined up on the counter. Desperate for relief from the pain that seemed to be getting worse instead of better, she shook two pain killers from the bottle and then dropped the bottle into the pocket of her housecoat. Crawling on her hands and knees, she made her way up the stairs, and collapsed in bed. But she couldn't sleep from worrying about Brooke. She blamed herself for the attack or the accident, whatever had happened to her daughter. Just as she'd done to Lizbet, she forced her to flee the house in anger. She was a mean woman, a pitiful excuse of a mother. She was a shrew. The more she worried, the more the pressure built up in her head. She wanted to saw off the top of her skull and let the brain matter erupt like a volcano. When she could stand the agony no longer, she groped for the bottle of sleeping pills beside her bed.

CHAPTER THIRTY

LIZBET

FLIPPING ON HER hazard lights, Lizbet sped to the hospital through the quiet downtown streets, running red lights and blowing past stop signs. She could make no sense of how this had happened to her sister. One minute they had been talking on the phone, discussing their mother's erratic behavior, and the next minute Brooke was mugged. What else could possibly happen to their family?

She was checking in with the receptionist when her father arrived at the emergency room.

"How is she?" he asked Lizbet.

"I don't know, Dad." Lizbet had been standing at the counter watching the young woman search her computer for five minutes. She glanced at the receptionist's name tag. "Diane can't seem to find Brooke's information in her computer."

"The name is Horne." Phillip jabbed the counter with his pointer finger. "Spelled H-O-R-N-E. First name is Brooke. If you can't find it, get someone who can."

Diane sat up straight in her chair, her brown eyes huge

behind the yellow round-eyeglass frames that made her look like an owl. "Yes sir." Her fingers moved faster over the keyboard. "Here she is." She reached for the telephone. "I'll let the nurses' station know you're here."

Phillip reached over the counter and snatched the receiver out of her hand. "I don't want to wait for someone to come and get me. I want to see my daughter now. Which means you need to take me to her."

Lizbet's jaw went slack as she stared at her father. She'd never known him to be so aggressive. He'd been through so much the past few days. The pressure was obviously getting to him.

With an exaggerated eye roll, Diane stood up and came around from behind the counter. "Follow me, please." She marched them through a set of double doors and down a hall to Brooke's treatment room.

Brooke was sitting up in bed holding an ice pack to the back of her head and speaking to a policeman while a nurse cleaned her bloody knees. Phillip rushed to her side. "Honey, are you all right?"

"I'll be fine, Dad."

"I'm Officer Diaz," the policeman said. "Your daughter is a lucky lady. She accidentally ventured into the wrong neighborhood. It happens all the time, but the outcome is usually a lot worse. She was just finishing with her report of the incident. If you'll give us a few more minutes—

Phillip's hands shot up. "Don't let us interrupt."

"As I was saying," Brooke continued, "a man stepped out from an alley, and approached me from behind. I caught only a glimpse of him. He was a white man with dreadlocks, about my height, in his late-twenties. He shouted at me to give him my money. When I told him I wasn't carrying a purse, he hit me over the head with a hard object—a piece of pipe or something—and shoved me to the ground."

Lizbet noticed for the first time that Brooke's hands were bandaged in gauze. She probably skinned them when she tried to break her fall.

"He must have knocked me out," Brooke said. "Because the next thing I knew, two EMTs were lifting me into an ambulance."

Officer Diaz finished making his notes and flipped the page back on his notepad. "Okay then, that should be all for now." He handed Brooke a business card. "If you think of anything else, please give me a call."

On his way out, he passed an attractive middle-aged doctor coming in—Dr. Peggy Walters, as she introduced herself. "Brooke experienced quite a blow to her head. She doesn't need stitches but she has a nice goose egg at the base of her skull. I've ordered a CT scan to make certain she doesn't have a fracture or any intracranial bleeding. They should be in to get her momentarily." The doctor asked to speak to the nurse who was tending Brooke's knees and they left the room together.

Lizbet approached the bed. "Where on earth were you? When you and I were talking on the phone, you told me you were over by the market. I guess that was only a few minutes before this happened."

Brooke shook her head. "Honestly, I'm not sure where I was. Way north of the market, I know that much. I wasn't ready to go home, so I decided to walk over to our new apartment. I got turned around, and the next thing I knew I was in a really bad neighborhood."

Her sister was indeed a lucky young lady. Didn't they

already have enough drama in their lives? "You have to be more careful, Brooke. Especially at night. There are many unsafe streets in downtown Charleston."

"I know." Brooke looked over at their father who was white-knuckling the bed railing. "I'm sorry, Dad. Worrying about me is the last thing you need. Speaking of Mom. Where is she? You didn't leave her home alone, did you?" No one had actually mentioned their mom, but she was very much on all of their minds. Lizbet was ridden with guilt for the things she'd said to her mother earlier.

The color drained from his face. "What else was I going to do? I was worried about you." He removed his cell phone from his pocket. "I should call her. She'll be worried." He clicked on a number and held the phone to his ear. After several long seconds, he lifted the phone away and stared at it. "Nothing's happening."

"Let me see it." Lizbet took the phone from him. "That's because you don't have service in here." She handed him back the phone. "Try walking down the hall a ways to see if you can get a connection."

Lizbet waited until her father left the room. "You realize you could've been killed, don't you?"

"I don't need a lecture, Lizzy."

"I'm not lecturing you. The thought of losing you when I just got you back in my life scares the hell out of me." Lizbet sat down on the edge of the bed. "You can't stay in that house, Brooke, not with Mom acting like a deranged lunatic. Why don't you move in with me? We can take turns going to the house and sitting with Mom. I'll talk to Heidi and see if she'll let me have some time off. You've been dealing with everything all by yourself. I want to do my share."

Brooke picked at the gauze on her hand. "I did a lot of thinking while I was out walking." She looked up and smiled. "Before I got mugged." She returned her attention to her bandage. "Mom is really scared and taking it out on us. And I get that. I've come to terms with her never accepting me as gay. I'm sad Sawyer will never have a chance to know her, the real Mom, the awesome things about her that we love. But there's nothing I can do to change that. I can handle her illness. I just need to be stronger. Suck it up. My boss has been understanding. She's agreed to let me wrap up my job from here while I take care of Mom. I need to do this, Lizzy, for Mom and for myself."

Lizbet studied Brooke's face, noticing for the first time the dark circles under her eyes. Who was this person, her sister? She was growing to admire her more and more every day. Whether she realized it or not, Brooke possessed their mother's strength, although her strength manifested itself in different ways. Hers was a quiet determined force whereas her mother came across as loud and sometimes obnoxious in her staunch beliefs. Despite all the sadness in her life, Lizbet once again felt a warm glow at the prospect of spending her future with her sister. She had much to learn not only from Brooke but also from Sawyer. She only hoped she didn't disappoint them.

"Then count me in," Lizbet said. "I'll pack my things and move back in the house. We'll see this thing through together—until the end." When she held up her hand for a high five, Brooke pressed her bandaged palm against hers.

"I'd like that very much."

They were still sitting there, studying one another with their palms pressed together, when Phillip returned to the room. "I need to get home. Your mom's not answering her phone."

*

The attendant wheeled Brooke off for her brain scan leaving Lizbet alone with her thoughts in the eerie silence. The things she'd said to her mother earlier filled her with remorse. She'd gone too far. If something happened to Lula, it would be Lizbet's fault.

When she grew tired of being alone with all her concerns, she wandered the halls in search of a cellular connection. Her father's phone rang several times before going into voicemail. "Dad, it's me. I'm still at the hospital with Brooke. She's getting her scan now. How is Mom? I'm worried. Please call me back when you get this message."

She stayed at the end of the hall in the service zone until she saw the orderly bring Brooke back to the room. Her doctor arrived a minute later. "Good news! There is no sign of a skull fracture or bleeding on the brain. Because you were knocked unconscious for a period of time, we have to treat you for a concussion." She handed Brooke a pamphlet on concussions. "Expect to feel drowsy for a few days. You most likely will experience headaches and sensitivity to light. Keeping the screen time to a minimum will help. Nausea, vomiting, dizziness are all normal. I'll have your release papers ready in a minute, and you can be on your way."

Brooke rolled her eyes. "Just what we need—another head case in the house. Will you put this in your bag?" She handed Lizbet the pamphlet. "Have you heard from Dad? I'm worried about Mom."

"That makes two of us. He didn't answer his phone. I left him a message but he hasn't called back."

They were walking to Lizbet's car in the parking lot when

his call came in. "Your mother was passed out cold when I got home. Several sleeping pills were scattered on the bedside table next to the empty bottle. I have no idea how many she took. I called the rescue squad. I'm following the ambulance to MUSC now."

Lizbet increased her pace. "Okay, Dad. I'll take Brooke home and meet you there."

"What happened?" Brooke asked as they climbed into the car.

"Looks like Mom may have overdosed on sleeping pills." Lizbet jammed the key into the ignition. "I'll take you home and come back."

"No you won't either. I'm going with you. Concussion or not, I'm worried about Mom, too. Besides, MUSC is right next door. It's ridiculous for you to go out of your way to take me home."

"Whatever you say." Lizbet was learning that arguing with her sister was like arguing with their mother. "Do you really think Mom would try to hurt herself?"

Brooke struggled to buckle her seatbelt with her bandaged hands. "Considering the way she's been acting and the things she's been saying, I think there's a very good chance she tried to hurt herself."

They arrived at MUSC as Lula's ambulance was pulling up to the emergency room. They joined their father and followed the stretcher into the building. Two EMTs whisked Lula's gurney into a cubicle and drew the curtains tight, shutting them out. A team of doctors and nurses in scrubs scurried in and out of the cubicle, ignoring their pleas for information. One Hispanic nurse that Lizbet recognized from their ER visit earlier in the week grew irritated with their questions and suggested they might be more comfortable in the waiting room. "It's going to be awhile. I promise we'll come get you as soon as we know anything."

Lizbet aimed her thumb at Brooke. "My sister was mugged earlier tonight. She was just released from the ER at Roper where they diagnosed her with a concussion. Is there anyway we can hang out back here?" Her gaze traveled to the empty cubicle across the hall. "It doesn't seem like you're very busy tonight."

The nurse gave Brooke the once-over, noticing her bandaged hands and knees. "Oh my goodness, you poor thing. Your family is having a rough go of it." She swept her arm in the direction of the empty cubicle. "By all means, make yourselves at home. But please, let us do our jobs. We will come to you once we have a better idea of what's going on."

Brooke stretched out in the patient lounge chair and closed her eyes. Lizbet could tell she was in pain, but she would never complain. Not when their mother might be dying from an overdose across the hall.

Lizbet and Phillip pulled up chairs next to Brooke. "I understand Mom is dealing with a lot right now, but committing suicide seems so drastic," Lizbet said. "And out of character. Her faith is so strong."

"Let's not jump to conclusions," Phillip said, his face etched in worry. "For all we know, this episode might be totally unrelated to the pills."

Lizbet fidgeted with her phone while Brooke dozed and Phillip sat with his elbows on his knees and his face planted in his hands, staring at the floor. It was nearly one o'clock in the morning before they were able to talk to the doctor—Dr.

Hanson, the same one from the other day. Didn't these people ever get time off?

Phillip stood to face him. "Your wife is awake, but she's still very groggy. I'm convinced she didn't mean to harm herself. I believe she took a combination of narcotics and sleeping pills to relieve the pain she's experiencing. She's coping with a lot at the moment. This is all very new to her, not only the diagnosis but the pain and physical challenges. I've spoken to Dr. Murdaugh. He's adjusting her medicine regimen. Sometimes it takes several tries before we find the right cocktail, if you will. I'm not going to admit her to the hospital, but I'd like to keep her here, in the ER, until morning for observation."

"Thank you, Doctor," Phillip said, offering his hand. "That's good news."

The doctor shook his hand and clapped his shoulder. "We're still working on her, but you can see her soon."

Phillip waited for him to leave. "It's gonna be a long night. Do you think anyone is still serving coffee around here?"

"I don't know, but I could use some too," Lizbet said. "I'll go see if I can find us some."

Brooke stood and stretched. "Why don't we all go? I would love some juice."

They walked the maze of halls to the waiting room, and then followed the signs to the cafeteria, which was still open despite the late hour.

"Dad, why don't I stay here with Mom and you take Brooke home?" Lizbet said while they waited to pay for their drinks—orange juice for Brooke and coffee for the other two.

"I appreciate your offer, sweetheart, but I'd rather stay here." He went to the condiment counter and dumped two regular sugars into his coffee. "We've all had a difficult evening. I know it's late, but I'd like to talk to you girls a minute before you go." With their choice of tables in the empty cafeteria, they chose one in the corner by the window.

Brooke unscrewed her juice and took a sip. "I'm sorry, Dad. Everything that happened tonight is my fault."

"You're the least to blame, sweetheart. And I mean that. You've been waiting on your mom hand and foot for days while I've been finding every excuse to stay out of the house."

Lizbet raised her hand. "I'm guilty too, Dad. I've been having a hard time dealing with everything, so I chose not to deal with it. And I said some things to Mom today that I'm not very proud of."

"But that she probably needed to hear," Phillip said with a sad smile. "We're learning as we go. Your mother needs someone with her at all times. We learned that much from what happened tonight. But we can't expect Brooke to be that someone. We need to work together and come up with a schedule. If we divide up the housework and take turns sitting with your mother, we'll still have time for our professional lives."

Her father worked hard as an accountant to support them, but her mother had always been the one in charge at home. Lizbet was relieved to see him taking control. "I agree, and I've decided to move back home for a while, for as long as you need me."

"That would be nice, Lizzy. Thank you. Thank both of you." His eyes settled on Brooke. "I know this has been especially hard on you."

Her sister turned away. "I let Mom get the best of me tonight. I promise to do better in the future."

"You're doing just fine." Phillip offered her hand a

squeeze. "We have a tough road ahead of us. The worst is yet to come. Part of working together means being there for one another. We've all come to terms with your mother's prognosis by now. Her dying will either tear us apart or bring us closer together. It's up to us to decide how it goes." He removed a slip of paper from his pocket. "There will come a time, probably sooner than later, when the three of us won't be able to handle your mother's care on our own. That's why, first thing tomorrow morning, I'm going to contact the nurse Midge recommended and request a consultation."

CHAPTER THIRTY-ONE
LULA

LULA KNEW SOMETHING had changed the minute she woke up. She felt better than she had in days. Definitely sluggish, but the intolerable throbbing in her head had lessened to a dull ache. She blinked open her eyes. The hospital. What on earth was she doing back here? Crawling up the stairs to bed was the last thing she remembered. And the pain. The god-awful pain. She noticed Phillip sitting in the chair beside her bed, slumped over and snoring softly. He would have a stiff neck when he woke up. Why wasn't he at the hospital with Brooke? Oh my god! Brooke! Lizbet had called to say she'd been attacked. What in the devil was going on?

His chair was too far away for her to nudge him awake. "Phillip, wake up," she said in a soft voice. When he didn't budge, she kept calling, her voice growing louder and louder, until he finally stirred.

"Where is Brooke? Is she okay? I don't understand why I'm back in the hospital. I'm so confused." She choked back tears.

He sat up in his chair, wiping the stream of drool from his mouth and rubbing his neck. "Calm down, honey. Brooke was mugged, but she is fine. She made a wrong turn and ended up in a bad neighborhood. She has a concussion and scraped-up knees and hands, but she's going to be fine. She's at home with Lizbet."

Lula grabbed a fistful of blanket. "Good lord. She's lucky she wasn't raped or killed. It was all my fault. I drove her out of the house with my nasty attitude." What had Midge called her? A shrew.

"I talked with the girls last night before they went home. We agreed to stop blaming ourselves, and start acting like a family again. Do you think you can do that?"

Could she? She honestly didn't know. But she needed to change her behavior unless she wanted her family and friends to remember her as a shrew after she was gone. She imagined her beloved Reverend Earnest Moore, who had presided over the congregation at the Episcopal church she'd attended all her life, conducting her graveside service. "Dearly beloved, we are gathered here today to lay Lula Horne, known to us as the shrew, in her final resting place."

Lula blotted her tears with the bed sheet. "I don't know, Phillip. But I'm willing to try. I feel a lot better. I know that much. Why am I in the hospital?"

He stood up and approached the bed. "You overdosed on pain killers and sleeping pills. Do you remember taking them?"

She thought of the pain killers on the kitchen counter and the sleeping pills beside her bed. "I didn't overdose on purpose, if that's what you're asking. I'm living in hell, no doubt about it, but I would never kill myself. Only the good Lord can decide when it's my time to go."

He lifted her hand and pressed it against his lips. "I'm glad to hear you say that."

"If I overdosed, I don't understand why I feel better today and not worse."

"Because the doctors adjusted your meds," he said, still gripping her hand. "According to Hanson, it can take several attempts before they get the cocktail just right."

She grunted. "Some cocktail. I'd rather have a vodka gimlet, but I'm in no position to complain." She looked up at her husband, her green eyes pleading. "I don't want to stay here. Please tell me they aren't admitting me."

"They're not planning to keep you. At least they weren't the last time I spoke to the doctor. Let me go see if I can find him." He set her hand down gently on the bed and went in search of the doctor.

It took thirty minutes to locate Hanson who, after a brief examination, declared Lula fit to go home, and signed her release papers.

"Let me call one of the girls to bring you some clothes," Phillip said.

"I don't want to wait that long." She was so relieved to be getting out of the hospital, she didn't think twice about parading through the waiting room in her housecoat.

*

"I don't want to upset you," Phillip said once they were on their way home, "but hear me out before you say anything. I called the retired nurse Midge recommended. She's stopping by the house in an hour. We don't have to hire her right away, but I see no reason not to at least talk to her."

She couldn't stop her body from breaking down on her. She would rather a professional help bathe her and tend to her bodily functions than her family. "I'm all for finding someone to help out, but can we agree to agree on who we hire?"

"That's fair. If we don't like this woman, we'll keep looking."

One meeting with Gladys Guzman and they knew they would look no further. Lula wondered about her age. While Gladys's hair was gray, her skin was relatively unlined. She wore nondescript clothes—navy slacks, a white knit tee, and a red cotton sweater despite the heat—but the tapestry valise slung over her shoulder was identical to one Lula's grandmother carried. Lula would come to know that valise as Gladys's bag of tricks—full of games and herbal remedies and lavender-scented oils.

Lula gave Phillip the nod and he hired her on the spot. "When can you start?"

"Today, if you'd like. I have three other patients I'm tending to at the moment. If it suits you, I'll come a couple of hours every day for now. We'll increase that time as needed." Gladys rubbed Lula's hand. "What say we have a bath? I bet you'd like to rinse off those hospital germs." Her pale blue eyes twinkled behind wire-rimmed glasses.

We? Was Gladys planning to bathe with her?

"That would be lovely. I must look a sight," Lula said, patting her matted greasy hair and running her hands down her soiled housecoat.

Gladys gripped Lula's arm with surprising strength as they climbed the stairs, tiptoeing to avoid waking the girls who were still sleeping after their late night in the hospital. They passed through the master bedroom to the en suite bath.

Gladys opened cabinets and drawers until she found everything she needed. "You had quite an ordeal last night. Do you have the strength for a shower or would you like to soak in a warm tub?"

"I haven't taken a tub bath in years," Lula said, lowering herself to the edge of the bathtub.

"Then you must have one today." Gladys rummaged through her valise and pulled out a brown glass vial with a medicine dropper. "Wait until you experience my homemade lavender oil."

The nurse left Lula soaking in the tub and went in search of a clean gown and robe for her to put on. When the water began to cool, she washed and rinsed Lula's hair with clean, warm water and wrapped a towel around her as she stepped from the tub. After she helped Lula into her gown, Gladys dragged in a chair from the bedroom and instructed Lula to sit down while she dried her hair. To Lula's delight, Gladys styled her hair with the curling brush better than any stylist she'd ever visited.

"What now?" Gladys asked when she was finished with Lula's hair. "Would you like to get in bed or go downstairs?"

Lula eyed the bed, noticing that Gladys had changed the sheets while she was in the tub. "I think I'll rest for a spell."

After tucking her in, Gladys retrieved the chair from the bathroom and pulled it up close to the bed. She dug in her valise and removed two hardback books. "What will it be, Nora Roberts or Dot Frank?"

Lula narrowed her eyes as she examined the covers. "Are those new releases?"

"Hot off the press."

"Hmm, this is a tough choice." Lula took the Frank book

from her and read the synopsis on the back. "Let's start with this one."

Gladys's soothing voice drew her into the story from the first sentence. Lula closed her eyes and listened as the plot began to unfold. When Phillip entered the room sometime later, she kept her eyes closed, pretending to be asleep as she eavesdropped on their conversation.

"She seems to like you," Phillip said. "My wife can be difficult at times."

"We're getting along just fine so far," Gladys said. "And don't you worry about a thing. I can handle difficult. In fact, I appreciate a spunky personality."

The book snapped shut and Gladys's tone grew serious. "At some point you'll need to address the second-floor bedroom situation. When the time comes, you might consider renting a hospital bed and outfitting one of the rooms downstairs. If you set her up in your Florida room, she could look out over her lovely garden."

"I've already thought of that," Phillip said. "I'll get right on it."

Lula was tempted to open her eyes, to stop them from talking about her impending death, but she was too intrigued by the discussion to interrupt.

"You'll want to call in hospice," Gladys said. "Might as well go ahead and put that piece of the puzzle in place. Even if they come only once a week right now, they'll be familiar with the patient and her surroundings, which will make the process more efficient when the time comes."

"How do I go about that?" Phillip asked. "Do I just Google 'Hospice'?"

Gladys snickered. "No, honey. Talk to your doctor. He

has to write the orders anyway. There are several programs in the area. He can tell you which one he recommends."

Lula heard a rustling sound which she assumed was Gladys gathering her things.

"We should probably let her get some rest. I need to get to my next patient anyway." Gladys's voice faded as she moved away from the bed. "You have my number. Feel free to call me anytime, night or day, if you need anything."

Lula rolled over on her side. So she was still dying after all. She'd hoped the lessening of pain meant an improvement in her health. A tear slid down her cheek, followed by a cascade of them. She planted her face in the pillow to muffle her sobs, and cried herself to sleep.

*

Lula sat bolt upright in bed at the sound of feet pounding the stairs and tromping down the hall. Lizbet and Brooke came to an abrupt halt in her doorway.

"You're awake!" Lizbet said when she saw Lula staring at them.

"How can anyone sleep with the two of you carrying on like a herd of buffalo on the Serengeti?" She flashed them a smile to make up for the irritation in her voice, and then moved to the middle of the bed so the girls could climb in with her. She ran her fingers through Brooke's cropped blonde hair. "How're you feeling, you poor girl?" She missed her long locks, but she had to admit the short style complimented her features. She looked more mature, and seemed more sure of herself than ever before. Was Sawyer responsible for her radiant glow? Lula had been so disturbed by the idea of her daughter being gay, she'd failed to see what a lovely young woman her daughter had become.

Brooke snuggled in closer. "I have a bad headache, which I know you can relate to, and my hands and knees sting a little. But I'm lucky. It could've been so much worse."

"My headache is better than it's been in days." She scratched Brooke's head with one hand and wrapped her opposite arm around her youngest. "What about you, Lizbet? How's your head?"

"My head is not my problem. My stomach is my problem." Lizbet placed her hand on her tummy. "It's growling. Can't you hear it? I'm starving."

"Speaking of food," Brooke began. Lula saw love in her hazel eyes when Brooke looked up at her. "You won't believe all the food Heidi sent over. Are you ready for lunch?"

Lula kicked back the covers. "I could eat a bite. Let's go downstairs. I'm tired of lying in this bed."

She descended the stairs slowly with one daughter on each side holding tight to her arms. Lula sat at the table while Lizbet and Brooke spooned an assortment of cold salads from plastic containers onto three plates.

"Why don't we watch a movie while we eat?" Lizbet suggested.

"That sounds like a fine idea to me," Lula said, already rising from her chair.

Once they were settled on the sofa, Lizbet scrolled through the movie thingamajig Lula could never learn how to use. She would have to try harder. Based on Phillip's conversation with Gladys, she would be spending a lot of time in this room, lying in the hospital bed he planned to rent for her.

They decided on Bridget Jones's Baby, and for the next

two hours they laughed until their bellies ached. They were so engrossed in the movie, they failed to notice the storm moving in.

"Looks like we're gonna have a storm," Lula said, pointing to the window where streaks of lightning flashed in the dark sky.

Lizbet leapt to her feet. "I'll make the popcorn!"

"And I'll get the ginger ale." Brooke gathered their lunch plates and they walked to the kitchen together.

As little girls, Lizbet and Brooke had been terrified of thunderstorms. Lula would draw the drapes in the house to block out the storm, and appease them with buttery popcorn and ginger ale while they watched reruns of The Andy Griffith Show.

The girls returned a few minutes later with their snack.

"I saw Georgia this morning at the store," Lizbet said as they dug into the popcorn. "She insists you come to her house for tea tomorrow at four. She said it'll be just like old times. Midge will be there too. I told her I'd talk to you and let her know." Lizbet held up her phone. "What should I tell her?"

"I already told them I'd go," Lula said. She didn't really feel up to it, but she knew she should go before her health declined even more. It might be their last opportunity to be together. She was sure Georgia and Midge were thinking the same thing, which would make it that much harder. "Tell her I'll be there. Provided, of course, I'm not feeling poorly."

Lizbet nodded as she thumbed the text.

They munched on popcorn and relived the stormy afternoons from their past—the power outages and downed trees, the time they'd witnessed a waterspout while out on their daysailer.

When they'd exhausted the subject of storms, Lula ventured, "While we have this time together, is there anything you girls would like to ask me, anything you'd like to know?"

"I want you to show me how to make piecrust from scratch," Lizbet said without hesitation.

"That's easy enough," Lula said. "There's not much to it, really. We have all the ingredients. Will you be around in the morning? I can show you then."

"Yes, I'm working a party tomorrow night, but I'll be here until three."

"Great! We have a pie-making date. Any ideas on what you'd like to put in your piecrust?"

Lizbet thought about it for a minute. "Peaches. I want to make a peach pie. I need to go to the store later. I'll pick up some peaches then."

She could tell Brooke wanted to ask her something, but she wasn't as forthcoming as her sister had been. Lula nudged her. "Come on. Don't be shy."

"I have a question for you."

Lula nodded for her to continue.

"How do you know for sure when you've met the right person?" Brooke said in a quiet voice, almost a whisper.

"When you can't imagine spending one second of forever without them. But keep in mind that forever is a big commitment. It takes more than love. Don't get me wrong—love is the main ingredient. But respect runs a close second. Your life will be easier if you find someone who is compassionate and supportive and lets you have your way most of the time." Lula smiled. "Do you think Sawyer might be the one?"

Gnawing on her lip, Brooke nodded.

"I'm not proud of the way I acted toward her. Do you

think she might give me another chance? I'd like to get to know her." In spite of the effort it took for her to say those words, Lula meant them, and Brooke rewarded her with a smile.

"She'll give you another chance. I promise you'll love her as much as I do. Just don't love her more than me."

Lizbet rolled her eyes. "As if that could happen. There's nobody Mom loves more than you."

"Except for you." Lula placed one hand on Brooke's thigh and one on Lizbet's. "I love both my girls the same."

CHAPTER THIRTY-TWO
MIDGE

BENNETT LINED UP appointments to look at the three properties they'd identified as potential candidates for their real estate office. All had unique features, but the one with the most potential was surprisingly the most affordable. As far as asking price was concerned, anyway. They'd have to sink more into renovating it than the other two, but the finished product would better suit their needs.

"Where are we going?" Midge asked when Bennett headed toward the waterfront instead of home.

"I have one more place I want to show you." He turned right onto East Bay and drove several blocks before taking a left and parking on the side street adjacent to a residential building.

"Isn't this near where the Lelands live?" she asked.

"Sort of. They're down that way a few blocks," he said, pointing south.

Midge felt a fluttering in her belly. Would she ever stop

anticipating the worst from him? "I don't understand. Why are we looking for commercial space in a residential building?"

He shifted in his seat to face her. "There's a condo for sale I really want to see."

"But—"

He held his hand up to silence her. "Just listen for a minute before you say anything. I've had my eye out for a waterfront condo for several years, and this one meets the criteria. I'm not pressuring you to marry me. That's not what this is about. I'm asking you to look at the place, and tell me if you would consider living there when you finally decide to marry me." He chucked her chin. "Because you'll eventually succumb to my charms and agree to marry me, and we'll need a place to live."

"My house on Tradd Street is my home, Bennett. I've lived there all of my adult life."

"That's the problem I have with it. It's a charming house, don't get me wrong. But it's your house. I feel like a guest when I'm there with you. I want a place that belongs to both of us." He opened his car door. "Let's go look at it. If I like it, I'm going to make an offer."

She had to jog to keep up with him as he entered the lobby. "How can you afford this? Are your parents lending you the money for a condo too?"

He pressed the elevator button. "I can buy it on my own. I'm getting ready to close a huge deal," he said with a sly grin.

When the elevator doors slid open, she grabbed his elbow holding him back. "Wait a minute. What deal?"

"That deal I told you about, the one I've been working on for a long time," he said, holding the elevator door open with his foot.

She eyed him suspiciously. "The deal that involves the redhead?"

"That's the one. I'm finally in a position to tell you about it. But you'll have to wait for the details. The realtor is expecting us. All you need to know for now is that I can afford the place." He took her by the hand and pulled her inside the elevator. He drew her to him and pressed his lips against hers. "Don't ask. I already know what you're thinking. I have enough money to buy the condo with plenty left over for the business. My parents agreed to loan me the money in the event my deal didn't go through before we made a down payment on an office building."

She pushed away from him. "Sounds like a shady deal if ever I heard one. You're about to make enough money to purchase a waterfront condo in downtown Charleston and put up equity in our partnership on a deal you've kept hidden from me. I wouldn't have even known about it if I hadn't seen you with the redhead. We're about to be business partners, Bennett. How can I commit to that relationship if you're going to keep secret deals from me?"

"Damn it, Midge." He ran his hand through his wiry crop of hair. "I promise you'll understand when I explain everything later. Can you please stop talking long enough to give me your opinion on this condo. Pretend like you're my realtor if that's what it takes."

She looked away from him, staring straight ahead at the crack in the elevator doors. "I guess I can do that, since I pride myself on being a professional." The elevator doors opened, and she forced his shady deal from her mind.

They were greeted by a too-thin woman about their age.

She held out a boney hand to them. "I'm Rebecca Schneider, listing agent with Waterfront Realty."

Bennett introduced himself. "And this is my realtor, Midge Wilkins, with Calhoun Wilkins Properties."

The lines in Rebecca's forehead deepened. "I've never heard of it."

"You will." Bennett beamed. "It's an up-and-coming boutique firm."

Midge crossed the threshold into the condo. Paneless wall-size windows offered expansive views of the harbor from all the primary rooms—living room, eat-in kitchen, and master bedroom. Even the spa tub had a breathtaking view in the en suite bath.

"Since we don't really need a guest bedroom, I figured we'd turn one into a study and one into a work-out studio," Bennett said of the three bedrooms.

His use of the word we irritated her, even more so because she could totally see the two of them being happy here, working in their new office space on Meeting Street during the day and coming home at night for candlelit dinners and lovemaking with the lights from the Cooper River Bridge twinkling in the background.

Don't get ahead of yourself, Midge. He has a lot of explaining to do.

"Could you give us a minute please, Rebecca?" Midge asked after they'd toured the condo.

"Of course. I'll just step into the kitchen and make a phone call. Let me know if you have any questions."

She left them standing by the window in the living room, the view made even more spectacular by the darkening cloud. "Just think what it'll look like when it snows."

Midge cut her eyes at him. "Because it snows in Charleston so often."

He touched her elbow. "Come on, babe. Don't be like this."

"You asked for my opinion as a realtor and that's what you're going to get. The views are stunning—I'll give you that—and the location can't be beat. The rooms are spacious, and the bathrooms and kitchen are up-to-date with top-of-the-line appliances and fixtures. I hope you're prepared to make a full-price offer, because that's what it's going to take to get it. These properties are hot commodities, but I don't need to tell you that. When did it go on the market?"

"This morning. Will you act as my realtor? I haven't done any residential work in a long time."

She sighed. "I'm happy to make the offer for you as long as you have the proper financing."

"I'm good for it, Midge. I promise. I have the earnest money in my bank account. I'll have the rest by the time I close."

"Give me a minute, then." She went into the kitchen to talk to Rebecca, realtor to realtor.

"My client seems genuinely interested in making an offer," Midge said, keeping her tone nonchalant. "I understand the property went on the market this morning. Have you had many showings?"

"Back to back, all day long. I'm expecting at least two contracts. Out of fairness to all interested parties, the owner will accept contracts until nine tonight. If your client is genuinely interested, I suggest he keep his offer clean. No contingencies, blah, blah. You know the drill."

"All too well," Midge said, accepting the business card the woman handed her.

They circled the condo once more before telling the realtor goodbye. Midge waited until they were on the way down in the elevator before she told Bennett she wasn't writing the contract until he convinced her he was good for the money.

"Let's get a drink first. I feel like celebrating."

Midge needed liquid courage to face whatever line of garbage he was going to feed her. She'd been stupid to trust him again. She'd listened to his mother blab on about her poor, sweet, misunderstood youngest son.

Bennett navigated the rush hour traffic as he weaved his way up East Bay to the Market Pavilion Hotel, the same hotel where she'd spotted him with the redhead. "I see we're returning to the scene of your crime. Do you bring all your women here?"

He parked on the curb in front of the hotel. "Yes. As a matter of fact, I bring lots of clients here for drinks. You can't beat the convenience. The rooftop bar is probably not a good idea today, since we're about to have a storm, but the lobby bar will do. Don't forget to bring your computer with you." They got out of the car and he handed his key to the valet attendant.

They found a table by the window in the lobby bar and ordered two Nitrotinis, a cucumber-infused lemonade for him and sweet tea for her. Vacationers came and went through the revolving door, returning from a day of touring the streets of Charleston. Midge envied them their leisure.

"Just think, Midge. If they accept my offer, we will grow old looking out at the water every morning, noon, and night."

Midge looked away from him and stared out the window

as the first drops of rain began to fall. "Forgive me if I don't share your enthusiasm."

The waiter delivered their Nitrotinis, and they waited for the vapor to dissipate before taking a sip.

Midge glared at him. "Start talking."

Bennett took another sip, smacking his lips together at the tartness. "My, you're bossy." He set down his glass. "For the past four years I've been quietly and discretely buying up properties in a run-down block on the north end of King Street. I scrimped and saved every dime I made, and every time a new building came on the market, I snatched it up. In my whole life I've never made a success of anything. I know people laugh at me behind my back. And I deserve that reputation after some of the stunts I've pulled. With the exception of my parents, I never told you or anyone else about my project, not only because I was terrified I'd fail and be the laughing stock of Charleston but also because I didn't want anyone infringing on my territory. I've accumulated all the buildings in this one block and two in the next block up. My ultimate goal was to create a downtown mall.

"The woman you saw me with works with a nationally recognized industrial developer from the DC area. I'm selling all the properties to the developer, Midge. I'm earning three times my investment, and Calhoun Wilkins will conduct all future transactions for the project. The developer hopes to eventually acquire all the buildings in the second block as well. The best part is, I get to stay on as a consultant." He moved to the edge of his seat, and Midge worried he might jump on the table and dance with excitement.

She sat back in her chair with her Nitrotini in hand. "Interesting."

His mouth fell open. "I just told you I made a fortune on my real estate deal, and all you've got for me is interesting?"

"Very interesting?" she teased.

"Everyone always assumes the worst of me. But this time I get the last laugh." He jabbed his thumb at his chest.

"And you're sure this company is the right company to develop it?"

Bennett appeared wounded. "Of course I'm sure. I did my homework. They didn't come looking for me. I reached out to them."

Midge was beginning to think his deal legit. "I'm not familiar with the downtown mall concept. How does it work exactly?"

"It's simple. You block off the street for pedestrian traffic only. The streets are cobblestone, worn smooth from use. You pretty up the area with new storefronts and landscaping, and then lease the buildings to restaurants, art dealers, and merchants. Neiman Marcus has already committed to opening a boutique-style store."

Midge's electric-blue eyes grew large. "Neiman Marcus is big time. Will the city let you do this? The downtown area is already so congested."

"Hell yes! This will be a gold mine for the city in terms of commerce. They've already given us preliminary approval."

"What about parking?"

"We're planning a parking deck in the next block."

"Sounds like you've thought of everything."

His enthusiasm was visibly dampened by her skepticism. "I've been working on this a long time."

They sat in silence as she absorbed everything he'd told her. Things began to make sense. How he never seemed to have any money despite the income she knew he must have from the properties he sold. Why he chose to live in a carriage house that was little more than a garage apartment. The way his parents were devoted to him despite his checkered past. The press his downtown mall project would bring to their new firm could launch Calhoun Wilkins into the next decade. She stared across the table at the little boy waiting eagerly for her approval. Her gut and her heart were finally in sync. She loved Bennett, and therefore would take a risk on him. On their relationship. On their future together as business partners. If he failed, they would fail together. Life happened. What did she have to lose?

She removed her computer from her bag and opened it on the table. "Ask the waiter for a menu," she said to Bennett. "Let's order some food. We have a lot of work to do."

CHAPTER THIRTY-THREE

LIZBET

L IZBET COULD HARDLY believe the change in her mother. The new mix of meds Dr. Dog had prescribed caused a drastic improvement overnight. Lizbet suspected the dosages Brooke doled out included an antidepressant and an antianxiety drug. Lula was more pleasant than she'd been in years. Maybe even more pleasant than she'd ever been.

Her father came home from the office with a new weekly At-A-Glance appointment book. The four of them gathered at the kitchen table and came up with a schedule for the coming week that included Gladys Guzman's two-hour shifts every morning. They'd all begun to accept Lula's prognosis and were committed to making her comfortable and to spending as much quality time together as possible. That included putting culinary school on hold for Lizbet, and a delayed start date for Brooke's new job.

Lula sat with the family during dinner, barely touching the crab casserole Georgia had delivered earlier in the day. She put on a brave smile, but the dark circles under her eyes told a different story. And when she thought no one was looking, she winced every now and then in pain.

After dinner Lizbet helped Lula upstairs while Brooke gave their father a hand with the dishes. "I'm tired of wearing my nightgown all the time," Lula said as they mounted the stairs. "Tomorrow I will put on some street clothes for tea time at Georgia's."

"That's a good idea," Lizbet said. "Wearing regular clothes should make you feel better. Do you have a particular outfit in mind? Is there anything we need to wash or iron for you?"

Lula waved her hand in a dismissive gesture. "No need to fuss. I'll just throw on a pair of khaki slacks and a blouse."

Lizbet straightened the bedcovers and plumped up the pillows while Lula brushed her teeth and washed her face. Her mother crawled into bed and Lizbet brought the blanket up to her chin and tucked it in tight around her body like a mother would do for a child. Their roles had reversed. She always knew it would happen one day. It was the natural progression of life. She just never expected it to happen so soon, when they were both still so young.

Lula patted the bed beside her. "Sit, let's talk for a minute."

Lizbet climbed onto the bed and tucked her feet beneath her. "Anything in particular you want to talk about?"

"We can talk about the weather for all I care. I'm just not ready to be left alone with my demons yet."

Lizbet dared to imagine what kind of demons a dying woman might face during the lonely hours of the night. "Well... let's see. We can talk about my cooking lesson. I never made it to the store this afternoon. I'll go first thing in the morning for the peaches."

"Is there anything else you'd like to learn to make?"

Lizbet experienced an ache in her chest. Better ask now while you still can. "Anything you feel like teaching me, Mom. Thanksgiving gravy and grandmother's cheese biscuits. Your rum cake and that unbelievable fudge you make. You're the best cook I know."

Lula wagged her finger at Lizbet. "You're telling me a fib, little Miss Priss. You work for the most sought-after caterer in the city."

Lizbet laughed. "That's not a fair comparison. Heidi's cuisine is modern but your cooking is old school."

"True. Many of my recipes have been handed down for generations."

"You mean, like your chicken pot pie?" Lizbet asked.

"Yes ma'am. That recipe dates back to the Civil War," Lula said with a mischievous twinkle in her eye. "I know. Why don't we make the chicken pot pie tomorrow instead of the peach pie? Both recipes call for the same crust. The peach pie is easy. You can handle that on your own. But there's a trick to getting the gravy right for the chicken pot pie."

Lula's pot pie recipe didn't call for vegetables, carrots and peas, like most. Her version consisted of lots of chicken, hardboiled eggs, and rich creamy gravy. It was different, and better, than any she'd ever tasted. "That sounds good to me. And we can have it for dinner tomorrow night." Lizbet rose from the bed and went to the window to draw the drapes. "You know, Mom, if you're feeling up to it, there are other things I'd like for you to show me. Brooke and I both want to learn how to garden."

"I would be happy to show you around my garden. I worked hard getting my perennial bed established. I'd hate to see it become neglected." Her mother was silent for a minute, a faraway look in her eyes. "We'll need to go through the silver in the sideboard as well. I inherited several heirloom pieces from both your grandmothers. You should learn the history."

Lizbet returned to the bed and sat back down. "You have boxes and boxes of Christmas decorations in the attic. I have no clue how to go about decorating this house for the holidays."

"Then we'll go through those as well. I always intended to organize that mess and label the boxes. I just never got around to it." Lula squeezed Lizbet's hand. "Let this be a lesson for you, sweetheart. It's true what they say. Make the most of every minute, and don't put off until tomorrow what you can do today."

Lizbet stood to go. "I'll remind you of that when I'm pestering you to teach me how to arrange flowers." She kissed her mother's forehead.

Lula slipped farther beneath the covers and closed her eyes." I just hope the good Lord grants me the time to teach you what you want to know," she said more to herself than Lizbet.

As Lizbet wandered down the hall toward her bedroom, she contemplated the unpredictability of life. In less than a week their family had been torn apart, first by Brooke's unexpected bombshell and then by Lula's brain tumor. But facing their mother's mortality was bringing them back together better and stronger than ever before. Now all they needed was a miracle.

Lizbet heard her sister's animated voice coming from inside her bedroom, and stopped just shy of the doorway to eavesdrop.

"I'm telling you, Sawyer," Brooke said. "Mom's done a complete about-face. She really wants to get to know you. Two days ago I would've said to get here as soon as you can, but she's much perkier now. Who knows how much time she has left, but I don't think you need to rush."

Lizbet listened for a few more minutes as Brooke and Sawyer discussed the logistics of the move and their new apartment and jobs. Listening to them talk like an old married couple brought a smile to her face. Brooke had often stayed up late in high school talking on the phone. But never to a boy. Come to think of it, the person on the other end of the line had always been a girl. Brooke had known who she was even back then. And she'd known how to go about getting what she needed to survive.

She went in her room and crawled beneath the covers fully dressed. Aside from the occasional Thanksgiving or Christmas holiday, the four of them had rarely slept under the same roof in seven years. The familiar sounds of her family involved in their nightly routines comforted her—her father watching the History channel on the TV in the Florida room and her sister talking on the phone in the room next to her.

Lizbet had no idea what her future held once her mother was gone. Her lease was coming up for renewal next month. Maybe she would move back home permanently. At least until she could save enough money for culinary school. Her father would appreciate the company. She wouldn't be around much anyway. She'd spoken to Heidi that morning, asking for flexibility in her schedule while her mother was ill.

"Take all the time you need. Things are slow now, but we will be slammed starting in September." Heidi seemed to already understand, probably from what Georgia had told her, that it wouldn't be long. "When Annie leaves for New York, I'll need you to pick up the slack, take on some of her responsibilities."

Lizbet sensed that, in two months' time, an increase in responsibilities at work might be a welcome diversion.

CHAPTER THIRTY-FOUR
MIDGE

MIDGE GROPED FOR her readers and cell phone on the bedside table. Scrolling through the e-mails in her inbox, she found the two she'd been waiting for. The answers to both were yes. She shook Bennett awake. "Both property owners accepted our contracts. We got our building and you got your new home."

Bennett sat straight up in bed. "Really?" he said, his little-boy face beaming with delight.

"Yes, really. Sixty days until closing on both."

He gathered her in his arms, lifted her off the bed, and twirled her around the room chanting, "We're starting our own business, and I'm buying a waterfront condo." He let her feet drop to the floor and they slow danced in a circle. "We're gonna have a beautiful life together, Midge baby. Our dreams are finally coming true."

She caught a glimpse of the house next door through her bedroom window and her heart sank. Lula had a beautiful life too—a lovely home, faithful husband, and two precious daughters. How unfair was it that Lula's life was coming to a premature end when Midge's was just beginning?

Bennett pushed her away. "I'm starving. Let's go fix some eggs."

In the kitchen, still dressed in their sleep clothes, Bennett brewed two cups of coffee while she removed a carton of eggs, a bowl of fresh fruits, and a package of turkey sausage from the refrigerator. As she cooked breakfast he sat at the island with a legal pad and pen making a list of all they needed to accomplish in order to launch their business.

After they left the Market Pavilion hotel the night before, he insisted on driving her past the site for his downtown mall on the way home. "Mark my words," he'd said, "this downtown mall will offer the most upscale shopping and dining experience in the state."

Midge believed him. Their beautiful life together would begin today.

She scooped scrambled eggs onto two plates and added a patty of sausage and a spoonful of fresh fruit. When she set his plate in front of him, she saw her diamond engagement ring on the counter across from him where she usually sat.

"What's this?" She stared at the ring as though it was a poisonous spider. Things were fine between them as long as she wasn't wearing his ring. "Bennett, I—"

"Just wear the damn thing, Midge. I'm not asking for a commitment. I just want the world to know you belong to me." He stood and rounded the bar to her side. He picked up the ring. "I loved my grandmother very much. Almost as much as I love you. Whether or not you and I ever get married, this ring symbolizes that love." He lifted her hand, preparing to slip the ring on her finger. "May I?"

No sane woman would ever say no to such a meaningful declaration of love. "Yes, you may," she said and kissed him on the lips. She was getting good at taking risks. With a little luck, her gambling would pay off.

They divvied up their to-do list while they ate breakfast. Bennett would interview potential contractors to discuss the renovations on their new building, and Midge would contact a lawyer friend of theirs, a mutual party, to draw up their partnership agreement. She would also hire a web expert, a friend from her yoga class who came highly recommended, to secure their domain name, set up their mail server, and begin designing their website.

Unable to contain her excitement, Midge drove straight to work and told the office manager she was leaving his company. Arnold was neither thrilled nor surprised to see her go. "With your talents and work ethic, I can't believe we were able to keep you as long as we did."

She cleaned out her desk and was home again by noon. Bennett was waiting for her with a trunk full of office supplies, including a three-in-one printer, he'd purchased from Staples. They dragged an old farm table out of the attic and set it up in the corner of the kitchen. With the printer positioned between them, they sat at opposite ends on opposite sides of the table.

They shared a salad for lunch and spent the first part of the afternoon tackling their to-do list and making phone calls to clients. When they were both on the phone, one of them had to leave the room. The setup, although not ideal, was only temporary and would work until they could move into their new building.

Midge went upstairs at three thirty to change from her work clothes into a pair of white jeans and a pale blue T-shirt. She'd always looked forward to sitting on Georgia's porch and chatting with her besties in the past, but today she dreaded seeing both her friends for very different reasons. Midge didn't blame Lula, poor thing. She was in pain and struggling to accept her prognosis. But her current state of mind made her difficult to be around. As for Georgia, Midge had exchanged several texts with her in the past few days to arrange the tea time and organize meals for the Hornes; but the tone of the texts, inasmuch as one can establish a tone in a text message, was all business. It troubled Midge to think her friendship with Georgia was lost forever, but there was little she could do to repair it. The most important thing was to put up a good front for Lula's benefit.

Yesterday's storm had preceded a cold front that had stalled out over the area, bringing cooler temperatures and a constant drizzle, a welcome relief from the scorching summer sun and sizzling heat. Midge had offered to stop in for Lula on the way to Georgia's, knowing the short walk was now a challenge for her sick friend. She grabbed an umbrella from the coat closet, exited the backdoor, and crossed the postage-size yard to Lula's house. How could she bear to look at the white frame house with the dark green shutters and yellow front door once Lula—the best homemaker she'd ever known—was no longer at home? She would have to move.

Midge walked the rest of the way up Lula's short gravel driveway, pausing for a minute to collect herself before knocking on the door. Lula surprised her, flinging the door open and dragging her in for a huge bear hug. This was not the same woman she'd encountered two days ago.

"I can't tell you how grateful I am to you for straightening me out the other day. I know it wasn't easy for you to say the things you said, but I desperately needed to hear them. Because of you I have a legacy to leave my girls."

CHAPTER THIRTY-FIVE

GEORGIA

GEORGIA PLACED THE cucumber sandwiches and cheese straws on the tray, swept them off, and arranged them once again. Why was she so nervous? Tea time, a tradition they'd shared for twenty-six years—thirteen hundred and fifty-some-odd Tuesdays according to her calculations—during which they'd whiled away the afternoon. Today would likely be their last. She'd taken their time together on Tuesdays for granted, but these gatherings had been the highlight of her week.

She carried the tea tray outside, set it down on the coffee table, and crossed to the other side of the porch to wait for Lula and Midge. As much as she'd missed being with them, she dreaded seeing Midge. She was still mad as hell at her for keeping Langdon's affair a secret. "I didn't want to see you hurt," Midge had said, a lame excuse if ever Georgia had heard one. Five weeks ago, on this very porch, Georgia had all but confessed to having trouble in her marriage. Midge should've known the news of Langdon's affair wouldn't come as a surprise. Midge wasn't afraid of seeing her hurt. She simply lacked the backbone to tell her.

Georgia heard Lula's voice, talking on about the chicken pot pie she'd made that morning, seconds before she came into view from the back of her house. With Midge cupping her elbow for support, Lula shuffled down the alley, careful to place one foot in front of the other. It broke her heart to see her friend become an old woman overnight. Lula, who once had more energy than the three of them put together, didn't deserve what was happening to her. She was ornery and set in her ways, but she had the kindest heart of them all. She gave her time freely without needing to be thanked. She volunteered in the community, not chairing boards like Georgia but down in the trenches serving meals to the homeless and taking care of youngsters at after school programs for the underprivileged.

Georgia waved and walked to the bottom of the steps to greet them. "You look much better than the last time I saw you," she said, taking hold of Lula's other arm and helping her up the steps.

"I'm moving mighty slowly, but my head is clearer than it's been in days, thanks to your husband's new cocktail of meds. Sadly, prescription pills are the only cocktail I'm allowed."

"I'm glad he was able to help." She was glad her husband was able to help someone, because he certainly hadn't helped Georgia. They got to the top of the steps and paused while Lula caught her breath. "If it's too damp out here, we can go sit inside."

"Not at all. The coolness is refreshing, like an early fall day." Lula broke free of their hold and made her way to the sofa.

It saddened Georgia to think Lula would never experience crisp fall days again or snow showers in the winter or the dogwoods blooming in the spring. "Can I get you a blanket?"

"I'm fine," Lula said. "No need to fuss over me. I'm getting plenty of that at home."

Georgia poured them all a glass of tea and sat down in the chair opposite Lula and Midge on the sofa. "Thank you, Midge, for making today happen." Georgia forced her voice to sound pleasant even though she couldn't bring herself to meet Midge's gaze. She eyed the deck of cards on the table. "Should we draw to see who goes first?"

"I'll pass," Lula said. "I think my news is obvious. But you two go ahead."

"Come now," Midge said, nudging Lula beside her. "Surely you have something to tell us we don't already know."

Lula's cheeks grew scarlet. "Maybe I do, but I insist on going last."

"We don't need the cards today." Midge held her hand out to Georgia. "You're the hostess. You go first."

The breakup of her marriage failed in comparison to brain cancer, but she wanted to keep things as normal as possible for Lula's sake. And didn't she want to smack the smug expression right off of Midge's face? "Langdon moved out this morning. Is that what you want to hear, Midge? I've already spoken to my attorney and the divorce is in the works. Feel free to spread that tidbit of gossip around town."

Midge stiffened. "You know me better than that. I'm not the least bit happy about your divorce. I didn't do this to you, Georgia. I'll admit I'm guilty for not telling you about his affair sooner. So shoot me for not wanting to see you hurt."

Georgia, surprised by Midge's angry tone, glared at her.

"For your information, I found out about my husband's little mistress on my own, way before Lula's party. Although it would've been nice to hear it first from a friend instead of seeing a text from my husband's trashy little tart appear on his phone."

"Stop it, please, both of you!" Lula placed her hands over her ears. "You're making my head hurt."

Midge rested a hand on Lula's shoulder. "You're right, Lula, and I'm sorry. This is between Georgia and me. She and I can discuss it later. Let's find something more pleasant to talk about."

Lula brushed Midge's hand away. "No, we need to clear the air now. But I think we can do it in a more productive manner than shouting at one another." She looked directly at Georgia. "I don't understand why you're mad at Midge and not me. I'm the one who convinced her to wait until after the party to tell you about Lang's affair. I'm the selfish one, Georgia. I was too preoccupied with Brooke's visit and planning the party to be distracted by your marital problems. It's hard to be mad at a dying woman, especially when you have Midge who is such an easy target. No offense, Midge." She patted Midge on the knee.

Georgia got up and moved to the railing, turning her back to them. Lula had hit a nerve. She'd been using Midge as target practice when the person she was most angry with was herself. Langdon had played her for a fool, and she'd let him. For years she'd suspected something amiss in their marriage. But she'd been too afraid her husband would leave her, too scared of being alone, to acknowledge it. She was the coward, not Midge.

She felt Lula beside her. "Come sit back down. We love

you. We're here to help." She let Lula guide her back to the sofa. "Talk to us. Tell us what happened."

Dabbing her eyes with her fingertips, Georgia told them about the night she discovered Langdon's affair. "He begged me to give our marriage another chance. I tried, honestly I did. And he did too. He brought me little treats and took me out for romantic dinners. We connected for the first time in years. But when I saw him fondle Sharon Parker's ass at your party, I knew our marriage was over. As the saying goes—once a cheater always a cheater. That night, on the way home from the party, I asked him to move out. But then everything happened with you, Lula, and he insisted on staying in the house to be near you. He's a good doctor. But a lousy husband." Suddenly parched she reached for her tea, gulping down half the glass at once.

"I can't imagine how hard this must be for you," Lula said, massaging her back.

How ironic that Lula is consoling me when she is losing so much more than a husband.

"I'm fine with it, honestly. Part of the reason for that is my new job. I'm going to Atlanta tomorrow on my first buying trip. Not only am I managing the store, I'm also helping Heidi work up proposals for her catering events. I don't know how long I'll continue to live here on Tradd Street. I feel like I need a fresh start. Every time I turn a corner in the house, I expect to see Langdon."

And once Lula's gone, she thought, I'll have little reason to stay.

"But enough about me." Georgia settled into the sofa cushions. "Midge, it's your turn to tell us what's new with you."

CHAPTER THIRTY-SIX

LULA

L ULA SUFFERED A pang of remorse for using her imminent death to guilt her friends into a reconciliation. But it didn't last long. She'd always aspired for peace on earth. Considering what little time she had left on the planet, peace amongst her neighbors would have to suffice.

"If you do decide to sell your house, Georgia, I hope you'll consider letting me handle the listing," Midge said, a mischievous smile tugging at her lips. "Bennett and I are going into business together as fifty-fifty partners. We've purchased a building on Meeting Street where our offices will be and we're having the paperwork for Calhoun Wilkins Properties drawn up as we speak."

Georgia scooted to the edge of the sofa and peered at Midge around Lula. "Are you crazy? Please tell me you're not going into business with that rotten rascal?"

Midge lifted her chin high. "Not only am I going into business with him, I'm going to marry him."

Lula noticed the engagement ring was back on Midge's

finger. "I didn't realize you were back together. I knew you were having some reservations. When did you decide to marry him?"

Placing her hands in her lap, Midge held her head high. "Just now. I haven't even told Bennett yet. The two of you are the first to know. But he'll be thrilled. He's been hounding me for weeks to say yes. And I've been listening to all the negative things everyone has to say about him instead of listening to my heart. I love him. And I'm going to marry him. And I would appreciate it, Georgia, if you wouldn't refer to my fiancé as a rotten rascal. He's not perfect and neither am I, but we make a good team."

"You know Bennett better than anyone else," Lula said. "I think it's wonderful, but if you want me to attend the wedding, you'd better set the date soon."

Midge gave Lula a squeeze. "I would love for you to be there, but we're taking the easy way out. Bennett wants to fly down to Jamaica for an informal destination wedding, just the two of us."

Georgia left the sofa and paced around in tight circles. "I can't believe you're going to marry him after all you know about him. He's been married three times already, for Pete's sake. You're making a terrible mistake, Midge. I feel it in my gut."

Midge shot up off the sofa to face Georgia. "It's not your gut feeling that matters. It's mine. I've seen a whole different side of Bennett in the past few weeks. Deep down he's a good person. Just very misunderstood. I'm confident we can make a success out of our business and our marriage, but if they fail, I'll at least have the satisfaction of knowing I tried.

"I've made safe choices all my life and look where those

choices have gotten me. I have no husband, no children, and no family other than my brother. I've wanted more out of my career for a long time, but I haven't known how to go about getting it. I've always been too scared to try anything new. The time has come for me to stop being a coward. But I know it won't be easy, and I could really use the support of my friends."

Georgia surprised Lula by lifting her hand to Midge's cheek. "You are so right, Midge. Who am I to criticize you? I've known for a long time that my marriage was in trouble, but I was too much of a coward to face a future on my own. Let's make a pledge to one another. From now on, if we can't be strong alone, we'll reach out to one another and be strong together."

Lula's eyes glistened with unshed tears. "Will wonders never cease? I can go to heaven now knowing the two of you are friends again, and have each other to support one another in my absence."

Georgia let her hand drop from Midge's cheek. "Great goodness, Lula. Do you have to be so morbid?"

"Indeed I do." Lula swiped at her eyes with the back of her hand, and inhaled a deep breath to steady herself. She turned toward Midge. "A very good friend helped me see that, while I can't control my destiny, I can do something about the legacy I leave behind for my family. And that's where I need your help." She patted the cushion on either side of her, signaling Midge and Georgia to sit back down. She waited for them to get settled before she continued. "I'm not happy about dying, but I've accepted that it's going to happen, probably sooner rather than later. I want to use whatever good days I have left to create something special for my girls. I have a lifetime of things I want to show and tell them, but I don't know how to go about doing it."

"What kinds of things?" Midge asked.

"Things like making homemade piecrusts. I showed Lizbet this morning, but I'd like to document it for future reference—and for Brooke in case she ever wants to learn. I have words of wisdom I'd like to share with them, things I want to tell them on their wedding day and when they give birth to their first child." My grandchildren that I'll never get to meet, Lula thought to herself. "I hope that will happen for Brooke. Gay people are getting married and having children all the time." She noticed Georgia and Midge exchange a look of utter astonishment. "I know what you're thinking. Blame it on the cancer. It's eating away the stubborn and selfish part of my brain that makes me act like a shrew. I may never understand it, or approve of it, but I'm trying to accept that my daughter is gay. I've invited her girlfriend, her partner, to visit this weekend. I owe it to Brooke to at least get to know Sawyer. Everyone else in the family adores her."

"Good for you, Lula!" Georgia held her tea glass up for a toast. "I'm proud of you."

Lula clinked her glass. "Baby steps."

"Whatever it takes," Georgia said. "Have you thought about creating videos to leave the girls?"

"You mean filming myself?" Lula patted her unkempt hair. "I'd shatter the camera lens into pieces, looking the way I do."

"Stop! You look beautiful." Midge leaned into her. "I think creating videos to leave your girls is meaningful and personable. People do it all the time."

A bewildered expression crossed Lula's face. "But I

wouldn't know where to begin. You know what a dunce I am when it comes to electronics."

"I can help you," Georgia said, and paused for a minute to think. "My Canon shoots video. We can use it for the longer segments, and our iPhones for the more informal moments. We can either combine them into one long iMovie or create a library of the short segments earmarked for certain occasions—however you want to structure it."

Midge clapped her hands. "Count me in! This will be fun. I'm a great project manager. I've never used iMovie before, but I'm eager to learn."

"Hold that thought." Georgia hopped up and went inside, returning a minute later with a tripod tucked under her arm, a camera strap slung over her shoulder, and a legal pad and pen in hand. "Here." She handed the pad and pen to Midge. "You start making a list of the videos Lula wants to shoot while I set up the camera."

"The list is long," Lula warned Midge.

Midge held up the pen. "Start talking."

For the next few minutes, Georgia fussed with her camera while Lula reeled off a list of the things she wanted to show her daughters, like how to make boxwood wreaths at Christmas and use oasis to create flower arrangements, and the things she wanted to tell them on special occasions. Not just when they got married or when their children were born but for when times got hard and they needed a shoulder to cry on.

Once they had a rough draft of the list, Georgia turned on the camera and returned to the sofa.

"Are you filming us now?" Lula asked.

Georgia nodded, a wide grin across her face. "I think it's

appropriate for us to start the video series with a segment on Tea Time at Georgia's. We can each talk a little about what our friendship has meant to us over the years."

Lula placed an arm around each of her friends. "And how rare true friendship is. And how we sometimes have to work to make our relationships work, just like we do for marriage, but the love we share is undying and can conquer all."

CHAPTER THIRTY-SEVEN
LIZBET

L IZBET HAD MUCH to do to get her mother's perennial garden ready for the service the following day. Family, plus Midge and Georgia, were gathering to celebrate Lula's life and spread her ashes over the garden. Heidi was providing the cheese biscuits and Georgia insisted on bringing the sweet tea. In some ways the nine months since her mother's death had flown by. In other ways time had crept by like the slug she spotted creeping along the tender new foliage of the daylilies poking their heads through the earth.

Lizbet donned her garden gloves and slipped her feet into the green Crocs she'd purchased in her mother's honor. She pulled Lula's floppy sun hat over her head. Wearing it somehow made her feel less like an amateur. She went out into the garden, stopping to admire the new bronze statue in the corner. Her father had commissioned a local artist to fabricate the statue, a depiction that looked so much like her mother it brought tears to Lizbet's eyes. The hat, apron, and garden clogs were spot-on, as were the freckles that dotted the statue's face.

Lizbet dropped to her knees on the grass and began ripping weeds out of the ground. She'd learned a lot from watching her mother's videos, but she still had a lot to learn. During the reception at the house following Lula's memorial service, Midge and Georgia had pulled Brooke and Lizbet aside and given each of them a portable hard drive that contained Lula's Life Lessons—a library of show and tell videos their mother had created for them. The gift had not surprised them. For weeks Midge and Georgia had been following Lula around the house with a camera. Even during her last days, they took turns sitting by her hospital bed in case she thought of something else she wanted to say.

Lizbet's emotions were too raw to view the videos at first, even the ones labeled Coping with My Death and Taking Care of Your Father After I'm Gone. The day after the funeral, Brooke had moved out of the house and into her new apartment with Sawyer, leaving Lizbet and Phillip alone with their ghosts. The house had felt like a cavernous tomb with Brooke and her mother gone. She even missed Gladys Guzman. She'd grown to love the old woman during the weeks she'd nursed her mother. All throughout the fall, numb to the pain, Lizbet had gone through the motions of living. Eating, without allowing herself the pleasure of taste. Sleeping, without ever feeling rested. And working, as much to occupy her mind as to keep her away from the empty house. Heidi had become Charleston's preferred caterer. Most weeks she was booked six out of the seven nights. And, as promised, when Annie left for culinary school, Heidi had looked to Lizbet to fill her shoes.

Lizbet wore herself out, and on Thanksgiving Eve she

came down with the flu. To avoid her germs, Brooke and Sawyer invited their father over to their place for Thanksgiving dinner. It was the weekend that followed, while she was recovering from the flu, when she finally got up the nerve to venture into her mother's video library.

The hard drive was organized into sections with each section housing several folders. She started with the section marked Christmas. She spent one whole day watching videos, and the next two weeks following her mother's instructions for creating a Horne Family Christmas. She made boxwood wreaths for the doors, displayed fresh evergreens on the mantels, and arranged Lula's collection of angels and Christmas trees about the house to her mother's specifications. She prepared the same dishes, plus a few of her own, for their family dinner on Christmas Eve. Under Heidi's tutelage, and with the skills she'd learned from the videos, Lizbet was gaining confidence in the kitchen.

Phillip surprised them all on Christmas Eve by announcing he was moving into an apartment and turning the house over to Brooke and Sawyer, just as his mother in-law had done for Lula and him all those years ago. Brooke and Sawyer were thrilled, as their apartment had turned out to be a disaster. The roof leaked, the furnace was always broken, and there was never enough hot water in the tank for more than one shower.

"What about your lease?" Lizbet had asked.

"We'll threaten to sue if our landlord gives us a hard time," Brooke answered.

"Considering the number of things that have gone wrong with our apartment, I'm sure we would win," Sawyer added.

Later that night Brooke had sought Lizbet out in her room. "I hope you don't mind us moving back in here. If it's a problem for you, we'll only stay until we can find something new."

"Are you kidding me? I'm twenty-two years old and single. I don't want the responsibility of a house. Besides, I hope I'll be going to New York next fall. If you're sure I won't be in your way, I'd like to stay here until then."

"Stay as long as you'd like," Brooke said. "The door is always open, even when you come back from New York."

"You mean if I come back from New York." Lizbet had never wanted to leave Charleston when her mother was alive. Now she couldn't wait to get away. While she loved being near her sister, she was ready for an adventure. Annie's Snapchats and Instagram posts showed just how much fun she was having in the big city.

Sawyer spent most of her time at the hospital, but on the rare occasion the three of them found themselves at home, they cooked elaborate dinners and stayed up late talking and drinking wine on the porch. As much as she enjoyed being with Brooke and Sawyer, Lizbet often felt as though she was in the way, like she was keeping them from being a real couple. She'd already sent her application to culinary school. She expected to hear any day whether she'd been accepted. The time had come for them all to move on with their lives.

Dr. Trevor Pratt, the plastic surgeon who'd sewn up her mother's forehead after her fall at the beach, had been a devoted friend to her throughout her mother's brief illness and in the months since her death. Now he wanted more than friendship, and part of Lizbet wanted that as well. But she was hesitant to make a commitment until she was certain of her future.

Lizbet was so lost in thought as she pulled out the weeds,

she didn't hear Brooke calling her name until she was standing in front of her. Lizbet stood up and shook the numbness from her legs. Placing her hand over her eyes to shield them from the sun, she spotted her new neighbor cutting the grass in Georgia's old house next door. The landscape had changed on Tradd Street in the nine months since her mother died. Balls and bicycles and skateboards, the toys of middle-school boys, were strewn all over Georgia's lawn while toys of toddlers and strollers dotted Midge's yard.

At the end of September Georgia had been the first to move from the neighborhood, and Midge had followed her in November. Lizbet saw Georgia most days at work, but she missed Midge's quiet presence. Her mother's two best friends had been fixtures in the Horne home during Lula's final weeks. They fed the family when they were hungry and comforted them when they were sad. Georgia had a new boyfriend—her rebound relationship she claimed, nothing too serious—while Midge, in a state of marital bliss, was setting the downtown residential market on fire. Most of the for sale signs bore the Calhoun Wilkins logo. Despite their busy lives, Lizbet suspected Midge and Georgia saw the same sadness on their faces that she did when she looked in the mirror.

"Let's take a break." Brooke waved a gloved hand at the house. "I don't know about you, but I'm parched."

Lizbet brushed the dirt off her knees and followed her sister into the kitchen. Brooke removed two orange Gatorades from the refrigerator and tossed one to Lizbet. "How's the weeding coming?"

Lizbet made the so-so motion with her hand. "For every weed I pull, it seems like two grow back in its place."

"Dad should be here soon with the mulch. Hopefully,

that will suffocate the little suckers." Brooke gulped down her Gatorade. "I finished pruning the roses. But the buds have all these tiny green bugs on them." She spotted Lizbet's laptop on the kitchen table. "My computer is upstairs. Can I use yours? I want to check if Mom left a video on insect control."

"I don't remember seeing anything about bugs, but help yourself."

Brooke sat down at the table and opened the computer. Her fingers slid over the mouse as she accessed Lula's library. "Yep. Here it is. Problem Insects." She clicked on the file.

Lizbet peered over her sister's shoulder as they watched Lula point out the different kinds of insects in her garden. "Those are the ones!" Brooke pointed at the screen. They listened on as their mother instructed them on how to get rid of the aphids. Lizbet felt a lump in her throat at the sound of her mother's voice. "Add a few tablespoons of Dawn dishwashing liquid to a bucket of warm water. You'll find my spray bottle under the sink in the kitchen. Fill the spray bottles with the soapy water and spray the plants wherever you see the bugs."

"Sounds easy enough." Brooke exited out of the video program. "Wait a minute." Her eyes narrowed as she read through the list of videos in her library folder. "You got one of these too." She pointed at a file labeled For Your Eyes Only. "Obviously, yours is different than mine. What did she say to you?"

Lizbet shrugged. "I don't know. I haven't watched it yet."

Brooke's head shot up. "Why not? That's the first one I watched."

Lizbet rolled her eyes. "Only you would watch the last video first."

"Let's watch it!" her sister said, clapping her hands

together like a little girl. When Lizbet hesitated, Brooke nudged her. "If not now, then when? We're here together. We're spreading her ashes tomorrow. The timing is perfect."

Lizbet couldn't explain why she hadn't watched the video yet. Other than that she was afraid to look at it alone. She sighed. "Okay. I guess now is as good a time as any." She accessed the video file and clicked play. Their mother's face appeared on the screen, her freckles faded and her skin as white as the pillow she lay on in her hospital bed in the Florida room during her final days.

Lula began to speak, her voice no more than a whisper. "Lizbet, my love. The time has come for me to say goodbye."

Lizbet clicked pause. "I can't watch this."

Brooked squeezed her hand. "Yes, you can. I'm here with you." She clicked play again.

Lula continued, "If you remember nothing else about me, remember that I loved you with my whole heart. Not half my heart as you may have believed. I didn't share my love for you with your sister. I never loved one of you more than the other. I loved you each in your own way. Brooke is more high strung and volatile, like me, and you are level headed and gentle like your father."

Lizbet snuck a peek at her sister who was nodding her head in agreement and smiling.

"You were my rock, Lizzy," her mother went on. "I always felt grateful, and a little guilty as well, that you stayed in Charleston for college. Having you nearby meant the world to me. Although I never told you, I appreciated it every time you ran to my rescue." Lula lifted a trembling cup of water to her lips and took several sips before setting the cup back down on the bed table. "Your talents lie in the kitchen. Your special intuition enables you to recognize which spices compliment which foods and which ingredients go best together. Go to New York and become the gourmet cook you were meant to be. Fly free, my dear girl." Her mother smiled. "Although something tells me you will end up back in Charleston. You are a homebody at heart. Just like your mama."

Lula closed her eyes and several moments passed before she opened them again. "I owe you an apology, Lizbet. The episode of your thirteenth birthday has weighed on my heart now for years. Brooke came to me six months after the fact and confessed that she was the one who had snuck out that night. Or rather snuck back in. She was the one who'd been drinking, not you. I knew the truth deep down, but my stubborn pride refused to let me admit what a terrible mistake I'd made. Just as my stubborn pride has refused to acknowledge that mistake all these years. I make no excuses for what I did. I had no reason to suspect you when Brooke was the obvious offender. She was four years older than you, after all, a senior in high school at the time.

"The ordeal brought you and Georgia closer together, and I am grateful for that now. You will have her to lean on in the months after I'm gone. But for the longest time, I was jealous of your relationship with her. I never understood why you found it easier to talk to her than me. In retrospect I realize that I haven't always been the easiest person to get along with. I hope you'll find it in your heart to forgive me for that."

Lula breathed an unsteady breath. "And now it is time for me to say goodbye." She pressed her hand over her heart and pursed her lips into a kiss. "Be brave, my sweet girl. Until we meet again."

Brooke closed the laptop shut and reached for the basket

of napkins, handing a wad of them to Lizbet. They wiped the tears from their cheeks and blew their noses.

"Whoa!" Lizbet fell back in her chair. "Did Mom say the same thing to you in your For Your Eyes Only video?"

"Mine was an apology of a different sort. She told me how sorry she was for being rude when she first met Sawyer and for not being more understanding to me about being gay. And she told me her diamond engagement ring was mine if I ever wanted to give it to Sawyer." This brought on a fresh round of tears for both of them.

"Are you going to give it to her?"

Brooke shrugged. "Probably one day. Now is not the right time, though. We're both so busy with our careers."

"I don't get it, Brooke. Was that a deathbed repentance? Because I never saw that side of Mom."

"She was a good person, Lizbet. She just let her stubborn pride get in the way of showing it. She believed certain things should be a certain way, and when they weren't she was too pigheaded to admit she was wrong about them." Brooke scooted her chair closer to Lizbet's and lay her head on her shoulder. "That's a big lesson for us both."

Lizbet kissed Brooke's hair. "I'm so glad I've got you back in my life."

"You better believe it, kiddo. Because I'm not going anywhere. I'll always be right here on Tradd Street waiting for you whenever you need me."

Acknowledgments

I'D LIKE TO thank the gracious people of Charleston for making my recent extended stay so pleasant. To the basket weavers in the market who greeted me every morning with a smile when I went out for my walks, the staff at the Belmond Charleston Place for their Southern hospitality, the nurses at MUSC for answering my many questions, and for the fabulous restaurants for providing amazing meals and satisfying my insatiable craving for seafood, both cooked and raw. My favorites from this trip included 167 Raw, Hank's Seafood, Hominy Grill, and Five Loaves Café, but my list has grown in anticipation of my next visit.

I'm grateful for the many wonderful things I learned from my mother. She shared with me her love for gardening which I drew on in this novel.

I am blessed to have supportive people in my life my friends and family who offer the encouragement I need to continue the pursuit of my writing career. I am forever indebted to my beta readers—Mamie Farley, Alison Fauls, and Cheryl Fockler—for the valuable constructive feedback, helping me with cover design, and promoting my work. And for my Advanced Review Team for their enthusiasm of and commitment to my work.

I wouldn't survive a day in the world of publishing without my trusted editor, Patricia Peters, who challenges me to dig deeper and helps me make my work stronger without changing my voice.

A special thanks to Damon Freeman and his crew at Damonza.com for their creativity in designing stunning covers and interiors.

A great big thank you to my family—my husband, Ted, and my amazing children, Cameron and Ned, who inspired me every single day.

A Note to Readers

I AM HUMBLED by your continued support. You brighten my days with your emails , Facebook posts, and continuous stream of tweets. Your appreciation of my work inspires me to work harder to improve my writing skills and create intriguing characters and plots you can relate to.

While I love Richmond, Virginia, my home for the past twenty years, I miss the easy-going way of the folks who reside in the Lowcountry. Writing about these quirky characters and their unique way of life is the next best thing to experiencing them on a daily basis. I love the beauty of the area—the marshlands and moss-draped trees—and the southern accents and local cuisine.

I love hearing from you. Feel free to shoot me an email at ashleyhfarley@gmail.com or stop by my website at ashleyfarley.net for more information about my characters and upcoming releases. Don't forget to sign up for my newsletter. Your subscription will grant you exclusive content, sneak previews, and special giveaways.

ASHLEY FARLEY IS the author of the bestselling Sweeney Sisters Series. Ashley writes books about women for women. Her characters are mothers, daughters, sisters, and wives facing real-life issues. Her goal is to keep you turning the pages until the wee hours of the morning. If her story stays with you long after you've read the last word, then she's done her job.

After her brother died in 1999 of an accidental overdose, she turned to writing as a way of releasing her pent-up emotions. She wrote SAVING BEN in honor of Neal, the boy she worshipped, the man she could not save.

Ashley is a wife and mother of two young adult children. She grew up in the salty marshes of South Carolina, but now lives in Richmond, Virginia, a city she loves for its history and traditions.

Ashley loves to hear from her readers. Feel free to visit her website at ashleyfarley.net.

Made in the USA
Middletown, DE
25 August 2019